Midlife Murder

A Texas Trailer Park Mystery

Amy Eastlake

BooksForABuck.com
2008

Midlife Murder

A Texas Trailer Park Mystery

By Amy Eastlake

Published by BooksForABuck.com

ISBN: 978-1-60215-081-2

Special thanks to Karen Leabo and Rebecca Russell who gave extensive comments on earlier versions of this work. Unfortunately, the author cannot blame them for any remaining problems

Amy Eastlake

Chapter 1

"The newly elected chairwoman of the North Texas Republican Women's League is…" Secretary Debbie Smith took a long pause, fumbling with the envelope as if there were any suspense at all.

She widened her eyes. "Oh my gosh, the winner is Kayla Switzer. Congratulations, Kayla."

I'd heaved myself halfway out of my seat to acknowledge what should have been a routine confirmation vote when the name penetrated—it was the wrong name. It was supposed to be Heather Montag. *Kayla Switzer?* That woman was barely in her thirties and had joined the League only two years before. No way could she have beaten me.

I reminded myself to be a good sport and pasted on my brave face, pretending I'd stood to congratulate the woman who'd *stolen* the post I'd held for the previous five years—years during which time I'd increased fund-raising by over a thousand percent, tripled membership, and seen the League become a major force in Texas politics.

If the membership wanted Kayla, I could deal with that. I'd just invite Kayla to the afternoon tea I'd ordered catered at my nearby home and show her the kind of graciousness so important for any woman, especially a woman in a leadership position.

Right about then, Kayla blew me off to accept congratulations from her cronies and from the women I had counted as friends was worse.

Carrying an extra fifty or so pounds left me perennially short of breath, but it did mean I could bull through a crowd. I pushed my way through the fawning masses and tapped Kayla on her shoulder. "Congratulations, Kayla."

"Oh, Heather," Kayla cooed. "I just know I can count on you as we move forward. I'm hoping you'll take an important role in my cabinet."

I relaxed just a little. They hadn't forgotten me, didn't want to dispense with all of the talent and energy I brought to the League. "Well, I think I'd be a good fundraising Chair."

Kayla pushed her silicone-enhanced breasts forward like twin rockets and giggled. Unlike most of the other members, she worked full time, but she managed to steal away from her law firm to make just about every meeting. Her deep suntan and slender figure hinted she might also slip away for workouts at the gym—something I never seemed to have time for myself.

"I'm so sorry, Heather, 'cause I promised that spot to Lisa. I was thinking you'd be great for refreshments. You always seem to know the right food and drink."

Refreshments? That wasn't a cabinet post—it was the job given to newbies who needed to prove they would stick with the organization.

"I'll check my schedule."

"Do that," Kayla said, her gaze slowly traversing my bulk. "And let me know as soon as you can. I know you're good with food."

Sandy Rachel, who'd been second in command in the League for years, laughed at the new chairwoman's slam as I stumbled back, swallowing hard to hold back my tears. When I'd joined the League a decade before, we'd had consisted of five women and an aging poodle. I'd thrown myself into the League, served every position, including refreshments chair, and turned it into a fund-raising force. Until five minutes earlier, I'd considered every single member among my closest friends.

Leslie James, one of the new members tugged on my sleeve. "I'm so sorry," she whispered. I noticed, though, that she didn't meet my eyes, as if being caught talking to me would contaminate her. Still, she gave me hope. I could come back, regain my friends.

Maybe I'd sacrificed too much for the League. Although my father's money had funded my husband Martin's startup years before, Montag Industries was Martin's baby and he made sure I knew it. I arranged the annual Christmas party and helped introduce new executive's wives to Dallas society, but that was about it. Since that didn't take much of my time, I'd made the League my deal and I'd lived for it.

If I did say so, I'd done good for the organization. I'd personally recruited just about every member. I'd hit Martin up for contributions, and I'd built a network of donors that made North Texas a required stop on the political circuit. Even if they had wanted a chance, I found it even harder to believe that anyone in the organization would blow me off.

Even if they didn't understand the way donor networks work, they knew Martin and the other executives at Montag Industries contributed millions to NTWRL every year. There was no way these women would throw that kind of money away. Yet they didn't seem worried that I'd suggest that Martin shift his political contributions to another branch of the party.

What did they know that I didn't?

I pasted back on my smile, mingled with the others in the country club banquet room, and thanked everyone who'd meet my gaze for their support— even though I knew many of them had stabbed me in the back.

I couldn't help jotting down a few names in my iPhone. So-called friends had promised me their support, then they'd turned around and given their votes to Kayla. A good third of those women had husbands who worked for Montag Industries. I wouldn't tell Martin how to run his company, but I could let him know that some of his executives' wives couldn't be trusted.

For once, I wasn't the last to leave the meeting—but my pride insisted I not be the first, either.

Janice Blump, called *Blimp* when she wasn't there approached me. "I'm so sorry, Heather. When they told me you were out, I didn't know what to do."

Heaven forbid that she let me know. I opened my mouth to say something sarcastic, but realized she was the only semi-friendly voice I'd heard. "Things change."

"Yeah. But that much?"

I had to agree this was a surprise. What was even more depressing was that only Janice and I seemed to notice.

The Country Club meeting room was only a couple hundred feet from our eighteenth-hole home, in Texas, in September, it might as well be a thousand miles. Of course I drove, cranking up the air conditioner in my Escalade as I covered the short distance from parking garage to parking garage.

To my annoyance, my garage door opener didn't work. Richard, our handyman, must have neglected to change the batteries.

When my key didn't fit the front door, though, and Maria, our housekeeper, didn't open the door when I rang the bell, I pinched myself, hard. Had I slipped into one of those nightmares where everything went wrong?

Pinching didn't help.

I got back in the car, turned up the air, and called Martin's ever-efficient secretary.

"Hi Betty, it's Heather. Would you put me through to Martin?"

"I'm sorry, Mrs. Montag. Mr. Montag is in a meeting."

"I'm locked out of the house, Betty. I need him." And since when had she called me Mrs. Montag? Betty and I gone first-name years before.

A dead silence told me I'd been put on hold. Betty was probably off getting things done. Martin's admin was a lot like me in that respect—always has more irons in the fire than just about anyone else. After a moment, the phone clicked. "Someone will be at the home shortly, Mrs. Montag. Please wait there."

"Thanks, Betty."

"Will there be anything else, Mrs. Montag? Things are quite hectic here."

"That'll do it, Betty."

Her hang-up sounded loud.

She'd always had time to chat with me before and Martin hadn't said anything about major acquisitions or executive deals, but then, he wouldn't. And come to think of it, he had been even less talkative than usual during the previous couple of weeks.

My instincts warned me that something was wrong. Could the League meeting only been the beginning?

* * * *

Betty hadn't been lying. Not exactly.

Three minutes after our conversation, a navy blue Hummer pulled up and Gary French, Martin's Corporate Security Manager, got out looking very professional in his navy pinstripe suit.

"Hey, Gary. You didn't have to come all the way out here yourself."

"Not a problem, Mrs. Montag."

"Anyway, I'm really embarrassed about this but my key doesn't seem to work."

"Let me take a look, Mrs. Montag."

"What's with all the formality? I've been Heather to you ever since we met." Gary had been in college with Nick, our eldest son, and Martin had hired him directly after graduation, at the same time he'd hired Nick.

I stepped out of my car and pulled the house key off the ring. Gary plucked it from my hand and handed me a large manila folder.

"What's this?"

"It is my duty to serve you with these papers, Mrs. Montag. I'm very sorry."

I shrugged. "If this is corporate stuff, why don't you open the door to the house and I'll get you a margarita. You can wait while I sign them."

I'd been Corporate Secretary until a few months earlier when Martin had decided it was taking too much of my time. I'd ended up signing about a hundred documents every night, everything from high-powered SEC filings to changes in toilet paper acquisition. It had been a silly formality, really, but my father had insisted on it back when he'd given Martin the money he'd needed to start the company. I could just as well have given Martin a rubber stamp with my signature on it, but he said there were government regulations and that kind of stuff.

"These aren't corporate papers, Mrs. Montag."

"Oh. Well, come on in anyway and visit. I've hardly seen you for the past couple of months."

"I'm sorry."

That answer didn't make sense. "Huh?"

"Read the papers, Mrs. Montag. Then you'll understand." He practically ran back to the Montag Industries Hummer and took off.

"But the door…" I stopped because I was talking to nobody. I wasn't a kid, but I wasn't old enough to stand on the side of the road and babble to myself without raising some eyebrows. I got back in my car and opened the envelope.

I stared at the top sheet for a good two minutes before my brain processed what was happening.

Divorce?

Martin was divorcing me?

My humiliation at the NTRWL made sense now—everyone else must have known. We'd just see about whether Martin could get away with that.

* * * *

"Ma'am, you can't go in there." A couple of guards got between the conference room door and me.

Gary hired mostly ex-college football players as guards. Like him, none of them had been good enough to make it in the pros, but they'd spent their college years chasing that golden ring rather than hitting the books so they weren't prepared for business, either.

They tended toward broad shoulders and looked like they spent more time lifting weights than doing anything practical. I had a good head of steam up and just kept walking toward them.

They bounced back and glared at each other. But what were they going to do? Shoot their CEO's wife?

I slammed open the door to the Montag Board Room and stomped in, throwing the divorce papers on the table in front of him. "What the hell do you think you're trying to pull, Martin. You can't divorce me. We're a team."

Martin stood as I entered. He'd always been one for proper manners. I couldn't help notice how elegant he looked with his still-black hair, his lean-muscled body, and his perfectly tailored clothes—clothes that I'd carefully selected to maximize his business impact.

"We've grown apart, Heather. It's time to move on with our lives."

"But—"

One of the women in the meeting, a trim little blonde I vaguely recognized as one of the lawyers in Kayla's law firm, got between Martin and me.

"The recommended property settlement is extremely fair considering your minimal, and/or negative, contributions to the family's financial status," she explained. "If you have problems, I suggest having your attorneys contact us. I'm sure you noticed that your divorce package includes a restraining order forbidding you from coming within five hundred feet of Mr. Montag. You are already in violation of that order and I'm afraid that will count against you if you decide to contest the proposed settlement. You'll definitely want to talk to council before further jeopardizing your case."

My mouth was open, but no noises were coming out. At the back of my mind, I'd hoped this divorce thing was one of Martin's practical jokes.

"When you trespassed here, I took the liberty of notifying the police of your presence," Howard Bale, Martin's best friend and the company's Chief Financial Officer, said. Bale was tall, completely bald, and had bushy eyebrows that jutted straight out from his head like porcupine quills.

"While Frisco's jail is first-class by criminal standards, it is hardly the type of luxury that you're used to," the blond lawyer put in.

"Jail?" I finally found my voice. "You're threatening me with jail because I came here to talk to my husband?"

"Soon to be ex—"

I'd been having a rough day and I lost it. "Shut up, you anorectic poodle. Martin, if you had any balls at all, you would have come to me with whatever's bothering you and we could have talked about it. Well, I'm not going to take it. I'm not just going to fight you, I'm going to wipe you out. So, don't say you haven't been warned."

I was just getting warmed up. So, when the little slut stuck her perky little body between me and my husband, I gave her the smallest little shove.

She smacked into the wall with a satisfying thump. Who says there aren't advantages to carrying around a few extra pounds?

I grasped Martin by the lapels of the bespoke gray wool suit I'd had made for him to celebrate our thirtieth anniversary.

"You let Kayla and the others at the League know this was coming, didn't you?"

He wilted under my attack as he always did, but I was still working up a good mad. The League might not be the most important thing in the universe, but it mattered to me. Letting them know when he'd been playing me along kicked my sense of betrayal into high gear. "That's why I didn't win the election, isn't it? Because everyone knew that you were dumping me. Everybody but me. They were laughing at me behind my back and I didn't even know it. And you had the keys changed at our house, which is why I couldn't get in. I knew you weren't much on morals, but I had no idea I was sleeping with a snake."

I knew I'd made a mistake when I said those words.

Martin's eyes darted to the pretty lawyer, then back to me. "As if we've slept together for the past ten years."

I was pretty sure it was a lot less than ten years since we'd had sex. And the only reason I'd kicked him out of my bedroom was he wouldn't do anything about the snoring that kept me from getting any sleep. I hadn't ever said he couldn't stop by for conjugal rights. And he did, once in a while.

"Don't blame me for your own failures, Martin. Because—"

Somebody grabbed me from behind, cutting me off before I gave Martin the second barrel.

I yanked away from one grip, and swung my fist at the man who held my other shoulder.

Abruptly, the room was full of cops. Cops with drawn guns. Cops who looked like they'd love to shoot me.

* * * *

The court assigned me an attorney. Thanks to the paperwork Martin had gotten me to sign over the past couple of months, I didn't have any money at all. Although our family had millions, much of it contributed by my late father, Martin's lawyers claimed that I had signed away any claims on it.

As Martin had gleefully explained to me while the police twisted my arms behind my back and led me away, I'd get a support allowance soon and spousal support once the divorce went through, but if I fought the divorce or tried to get more, I wouldn't get anything at all until after the lawyers did their work— and got their cut.

He also told me the amount of spousal support—a lousy twenty thousand a month. That might seem like a lot to some people, but it wouldn't even make the car payment on Martin's Lamborghini. Considering that Martin had been listed in the *Forbes* 500 Richest a few years earlier, he'd worked overtime to try to shaft me.

"These are serious charges," Barry Levitz, my court-appointed attorney, explained. He had to be younger than my son Nick, and his aw-shucks manner looked authentic rather than an affectation. As if he'd stepped directly from the farm to the courtroom.

"Assault on two civilians." Barry ticked off the charges. "Resisting arrest. Violating a court restraining order. It'll help that you have no criminal record, but still, you're looking at doing jail time."

* * * *

It didn't come to jail time, of course. Judge B. T. Libtor had enjoyed plenty of support from the NTRWL and the assistant D.A. assigned to the case had political ambitions of his own. Unlike just about everyone else I'd been dealing with lately, those two hadn't forgotten that they owed me.

The three lawyers sat me down in a comfortable meeting room, got me a decent cup of coffee, and explained my options.

Following Barry's advice, I agreed to a deal, pleading guilty to trespassing in exchange for the other charges being dropped.

That's when they explained community service to me.

I'd assumed they would count my volunteering at the church or with the Republican Party as my community service. Apparently, though, they won't let you just do what you were going to do anyway. I got assigned a program working with girls at risk—way on the other side of the tracks in Dallas. I mean, sure, Martin and I would sometimes take the corporate limo to go down to the Morton Meyerson Symphony Center or to meet with old-time Republican leaders, but Dallas had recently become Democratic. And South Dallas, where B.T. sent me, was practically a foreign country.

Still, as Barry reminded me, even a foreign country was better than prison. And I figured girls from the wrong side of the tracks could really use some help from a woman with experience and old-fashioned conservative values.

"Can I drive you anywhere?" Barry asked when we left the county courthouse in McKinney.

It hadn't really hit me until then, but abruptly, I felt like someone was sitting on my chest.

I had nowhere to go.

I struggled for breath, and tears rolled down my cheeks cutting channels through my foundation and turning my mascara into raccoon-eyes.

"It's all right, Mrs. Montag." Barry patted me on the hand. "Divorce is always tough. But you seem like a survivor to me."

I'd thought of myself that way, too. But I'd assumed I would be surviving *with* my husband and my family.

Not wanting to drip tears and re-liquefied makeup all over Barry, especially since I suspected his pay was low enough that the extra dry cleaning bill would cause problems, I pulled myself together.

"I left my car at Montag," I said. "Maybe you could drop me there."

"Not a good idea. You've been ordered to stay clear of corporate property. Besides…"

The way his voice trailed off had to be bad news. "What?"

"Well, it turns out that it isn't really your car at all. The Escalade is a corporate property. It was assigned to you while you were corporate secretary and the company claims it never got around to collecting it after you resigned from that position. But it's theirs now."

"B-but… I can't believe he's doing this to me." I took a deep breath. "In that case, I might as well just go home and try to get on with my life."

"What home is that?"

I gave him my address and he just looked at me shaking his head.

"Texas is a community property state," I reminded him. "I'm not a lawyer, but Martin can't just kick me out of my house."

Barry kept shaking his head so I ended on a weak note. "Or can he?"

"The corporation also owns that home."

Again I wanted to pinch myself, but there wasn't any waking up from this nightmare. "When did that happen?"

"Ownership was transferred six months ago."

"All my stuff is there. My clothes. My jewelry."

"You'll have to list your personal property and make sure the court is aware of it. Of course, the value of those items will be included in the community property."

"I? What about you?"

"The court appointed me to help you with your assault charges, not your divorce. Courts generally don't appoint attorneys for civil cases."

"But Martin is robbing me blind. That's got to be a crime."

"I'm sorry, Mrs. Montag. You can probably find a lawyer who'd take your divorce on contingency fees. As you say, Texas is a community property state. Mr. Montag certainly has extensive assets and his proposed settlement leaves you with far less than half of those."

"Contingency?" Contingency was practically a curse-word in my circles. Everyone knew that trial lawyers manipulated the system, told sob stories to run-away juries and liberal judges, and then contributed their thirty pieces of silver to the Democrats. I'd never be able to hold up my head with the League if I used a contingency lawyer.

"I don't know how else you're going to pay for an attorney, and you'll need a good one. Mr. Montag seems to have turned just about everything over to the corporation and he's got half the lawyers in Denton County on retainer."

"Turning property to the corporation is the same as turning it over to himself. He runs the company."

"He may *run* it, but Montag Industries is a publicly traded company. It'll be tough to get a judgment against it."

I sighed. My son Nick worked for Montag and lived in a corporate-provided apartment so I supposed I wasn't allowed to go there, either. Which left my daughter, Leah. The only problem with that was, Leah hadn't gotten around to officially letting us know she was living with her boyfriend. Visiting them would give her choice tacit approval—and I didn't want to approve of him.

I swallowed hard. I'd have to eat crow.

"It's a bit of a drive but if you wouldn't mind." I gave Barry Leah's Richardson address and then tried to call her.

My phone was out of service.

I was way past tears now. I was mad. "Let me guess. The corporation owns the phones, too."

Barry handed me his own phone—a base-model Nokia that would have gotten him laughed out of NTRWL circles—and I punched in Leah's numbers.

The only consolation I had was that I'd hit bottom. Things couldn't possibly get any worse.

That's what I told myself, anyhow.

Chapter 2

Leah and Richard weren't home, but they kept a spare key hidden under a rock near their door. She always left her car keys in the car, so I had wheels.

Maybe I had hit bottom and was bouncing back.

Fitting my body into the Honda was a bit of a struggle since the steering wheel didn't adjust and the car had been designed for somebody small like Leah rather than a full-figured woman, but once I squeezed in, I had fun.

I hadn't driven a stick shift since college days, and I jerked and grinded the gears a fair amount before I got my groove back, but then I drove around funky neighborhoods that reminded me of where Martin and I had lived when we'd first been married and only had the money my parents had given us to start Montag Industries. Driving was fun, and driving a little car down close to the road helped me understand why Martin enjoyed his Lamborghini so much. I reset Leah's radio to Rush Limbaugh and listened to his comforting voice as I drove around Leah's Richardson neighborhood.

An hour later, I felt well enough to head to the grocery store. I bought enough staples to stock up Leah's empty larder and refrigerator, blowing almost all of my ready cash, and headed back to her place. I might not have been invited, but I intended to be a good guest.

I'd bought the basics for a salad but Leah and Richard still weren't home when dinnertime rolled around. I decided I just couldn't face rabbit food and so I whipped up one of my famous red velvet cakes. Martin was always complaining that I didn't cook enough, leaving too much for Maria to do. I was turning over a new leaf.

Leah and Richard hadn't come home by the time I finished cooking and frosting the cake. So I sat down in front of their TV, and watched *A Long Day's Journey into Night*, and ate cake.

After my third slice, I called my son, Nick. With his upbeat philosophy and his caring about people, Nick always made me feel better.

He cut me off before I could explain what Martin was doing to me and quoted me something from the Bible about being an obedient wife. As if I'd ever been anything but.

"What?" Had someone kidnapped my son and replaced him with this clone?

"You've been too caught up in your things and haven't paid enough attention to Dad. If you'd been obedient—"

"My problem isn't obedience," I told him. "My problem is, he doesn't want me as his wife. He probably wants someone younger."

"He probably wants someone thinner."

I gasped. There are some things people just don't talk about. I'd never been one of those stick-figure women, even when I'd been in high school, but being big-boned wasn't a crime. Not that I knew of, anyway.

"Okay, I admit I never lost all of the weight I put on when I had Leah, but…"

"But nothing, Mother. You've got to be a hundred pounds overweight."

"There are lots of men who find curvaceous women to be attractive."

"Oh, Mom. You know I love you, but it's time you faced reality. You're not curvy, you're fat. It's bad for your health, if nothing else."

I'd been wrong when I'd thought I'd hit bottom. This had to be the worst. "Well, at least your father never minded."

"He minded all right. He once told me that he'd never have to be a bigamist because there was enough of you to make two women."

Tears welled in my eyes. "Uh-un. He *never* said that."

Martin and I hadn't fought often, but when we had argued, we'd made sure any disagreement stayed between the two of us. When I was pregnant with Nick, we'd agreed that we'd always present a unified face to the children. Learning that he'd betrayed that basic agreement seemed even worse than all of the other disappointments.

"He said it, all right. In fact, he always adds a joke or two about it at the corporate sales meetings."

I hadn't thought my humiliation could get more complete. "In front of four hundred salesmen? I swear, I'll eviscerate him. This is so wrong."

Nick's sigh was a little exaggerated—so I'd be sure to get it, I guessed.

"Look, Mom. If there's anything you need, let me know. But remember what you've always told me—it takes two to make a relationship go bad. Dad's been under a lot of pressure lately, but you really weren't there for him and he defended himself as best he could."

"Defended himself by attacking me?"

"Mom, I've got to go. If you need anything, let me know, but don't expect me to take sides on this."

I stared at Leah's phone for a good minute trying to think of anyone I could call. At first, I was trying to think of someone who would make me feel better. Then I just tried to think of anyone who would just be friendly. But my friends and family had turned on me.

I'd stayed busy with politics and with entertaining for Martin, but my upcoming divorce cut me off from both of those circles. The election at NTRWL had showed that my friendships there had been about my ability to raise money from Martin, rather than being hardworking and liked. And my so-called friends from business associations would gravitate toward Martin, of course.

So I put down the phone and finished the cake instead. The sugar overload helped. But not enough. With every bite, I still heard Nick repeat those hateful words from Martin, the man I'd thought I'd loved.

* * * *

Bam, bam, bam.

"Get the door, Maria," I shouted.

I squinted my eyes tighter and pulled the covers over my ears, but the hammering sound continued.

What was Maria's problem?

Despite my best efforts, the pounding noise made a return to sleep impossible. With awakening came both a sugar-hangover and the memory of the previous day.

Maria wasn't getting the door because I wasn't at home. In fact, I didn't have a home.

I assumed whoever was banging on the door wanted Leah. Since they weren't going away, I yanked the sheet off of the guest room bed I'd been using, wrapped it around myself, then headed downstairs.

"Who is it?"

"Police. Open up."

Why would the police want Leah?

I peered out the peephole to make sure it really was the police, then made sure the security chain was in place before opening the door a crack. "What is it, officers?"

One of them kicked the door, ripping the chain right out of its holder and the doorknob out of my hand. Two seconds later, I was surrounded by gun-pointing cops.

Again.

"Against the wall. Hands behind your back. Now. Move, move, move."

I tried, but clearly I didn't comply quickly enough because two of the cops grabbed me and shoved me against the drywall hard enough to dent it.

The pain got worse when they twisted my arms behind me.

This whole fiasco had to be some sort of mistake. The only thing I could think of was a screw-up about what I was supposed to be doing down in Dallas.

"I didn't think I was supposed to start my community service until tomorrow." Could I really have slept through an entire day and not noticed? I wondered if the cops always came out like this when convicts missed their community service dates. I'd always heard that they coddle criminals.

"Don't struggle. Hands behind your back. Now."

A female officer patted me down quickly and impersonally, but I still resented the intrusion, not to mention the way she dug into my body, as if I'd conceal a weapon between folds of fat.

In my hurry, I evidently hadn't tied the sheet tightly enough and I felt the knot loosen and the sheet begin to slide down.

I wore my slip under it—none of Leah's nightgowns fit me and I hadn't thought of that while I'd shopped—but I didn't want all of these cops looking at me in my underwear.

No man but Martin had ever seen me naked. My husband's words about me being as big as two women came back to me then like an ugly stray dog that wouldn't go away.

"She's unarmed," the girl-cop reported.

I reached for the edges of my sheet and started to turn around, but a couple of the burly cops shoved me back into the wall. This time my sheet really did fall off and the drywall crumbled, leaving me looking at two-by-four studs in the wall.

"What's this about?" I demanded. Just yesterday I'd been laughing along with Rush Limbaugh as he'd done his riff on people whining about police brutality. The humor escaped me at that moment.

"Where were you between midnight and two in the morning?"

My community service was during the day—I was almost positive. What was this about?

"You mean last night?"

"No, twenty years ago."

"Huh?"

He sighed. "Of course last night."

The cop asking me the questions wore a rumpled navy suit that was too small for him. His gut hung over his weapon belt and his *café au lait*-colored skin might have been a dark suntan, or from any number of racial mixes. Not that I was prejudiced, I just liked to know who I was talking to.

"I was here. In bed."

He glared at me. "By yourself."

"Of course by myself."

"Can anyone verify your location?"

"I beg your pardon?"

"We have multiple witnesses to the fact that you threatened Mr. Martin Montag's life yesterday."

"That's ridiculous."

"According to witnesses at a meeting you disrupted at Montag Industries, you promised to kill Mr. Montag. Your son tells us that you repeated that claim last night at approximately nine thirty in the evening."

"I don't think I used those words."

"Don't get smart, lady."

"Of course I was angry but this whole conversation is completely out of line. Did Martin tell you I was threatening him? He's playing hardball on this divorce thing, doing his best to make sure I get nothing. He's already alienated my son and managed to get a protective order against me. Which is the stupidest thing I've ever heard of. A protective order for Martin? What a joke."

"Is it?" The detective frowned at me. "Then how do you explain the fact that Mr. Montag was killed within twenty-four hours of when you first made those threats?"

There's a lot of sick humor about fat people sweating. All of a sudden, it wasn't funny. Beads of perspiration popped out all over my body.

"Martin? Dead?"

"Do you own a handgun, Mrs. Montag?"

My brain was running around in small circles trying to come to terms with what I'd just heard. Sure I was mad at Martin. Mad that he'd dumped me after more than thirty years of marriage. Mad that he'd played financial games in doing so. And beyond angry that he'd humiliated me with the NTRWL and insulted me to our son and to all those hundreds of salesmen.

But really, I'd assumed we would somehow work things out. Martin and I had too much shared history, not to mention shared children, to remain angry at one another forever. Martin was an old pro at negotiations. He'd led with the stick, but a part of me had been waiting for the carrot. Now, if I could believe this cop, my husband was dead. Whatever game he'd been running on me would remain forever unfinished.

"I'll have to arrange the funeral, of course," I said. "Are you police holding his body, or has it been sent to a funeral home?" Pulling myself together for the funeral would give me a chance to show the world that I wasn't going to just roll over.

"I asked if you owned a handgun?"

"A handgun? Why are you asking me this?"

"It's a simple question, Mrs. Montag. Do you, or do you not own a handgun?"

"I suppose so." When Texas passed the concealed weapons laws, I'd taken the class along with most of the other League women. "Martin bought me a cute little Glock ages ago."

The cop looked at me as if I were in the slow reading group. "You *suppose* you have a weapon?"

I started to shrug, then remembered that I was just wearing my slip. "Look, I told you that it was ages ago when Martin gave me the weapon. I carried it in my handbag for a couple of months, but it weighed so much my doctor said it was giving me tendonitis in my shoulder. So I stopped carrying it."

I heard a couple of snickers but I didn't care. So what if these guys thought I was a weenie for finding a gun too heavy to carry. One reason we'd moved to Frisco in the first place was so we could get away from city crime, so we wouldn't have to carry guns.

"Do you know what happened to your weapon after you stopped carrying it? Or did you just leave it around somewhere?"

"No I didn't just leave it around. And I don't understand why you're asking me these questions. Under the Second Amendment people have the right to bear arms, don't they?"

The cop ignored my question. One of the other officers, this one a scrawny kid with copper-red hair who looked young enough to be filing stories with his high school newspaper, reported that they'd found no weapons in their search of Leah's condo.

I thought about demanding a warrant, but I wondered if warrants were still required under our current war on terrorism, or what Rush Limbaugh would say about someone who used technicalities to get in the way of solving crime. Still, what did *I* have to do with crime?

"If you no longer carry your weapon, where is it?" my cop repeated.

I thought about it, finally remembering that Martin had suggested leaving it in my glove compartment.

Which I explained to the cop. "I don't normally drive into bad neighborhoods," I concluded, "but Martin thought I should have it handy if I ever did."

The cop scribbled something down on his notepad.

My brain finally kicked in about this time, after it was way too late.

Admittedly, the dots were painfully easy to connect, but I hadn't had my morning cup of tea yet, had been awakened early and shoved into, almost through, a wall by muscle-bound cops, and was now standing practically naked in front of them.

"Ohmigod. You think I did it, don't you? You seriously believe I shot my own husband."

He narrowed his eyes. "Nobody said anything about *shooting*."

"Spare me. I saw that Columbo episode before you were born. You said Martin was killed. And then you asked me about a handgun. I may have majored in Art History, but I'm not a complete dunce. Of course he was shot."

* * * *

As if I hadn't gotten enough from the cops, Barry gave me a long lecture when I called him.

"Never talk to the cops without a lawyer," he concluded.

"But I'm innocent. When I asked if I needed a lawyer, they told me I shouldn't need one if I was innocent."

"Sure you *shouldn't*. You also shouldn't need to lock your car doors when you park. But you do it anyway because what *should be* isn't always what *is*."

"At least they didn't arrest me," I said.

"You say that like it means anything."

"Of course it means something. If they thought I'd done it, they would have arrested me."

"Heather, you aren't thinking this through. From the way you describe it, they absolutely believe you did it. They don't figure you for a flight risk, so they aren't going to bother with the hassle of arresting you until they get more evidence. But they're going to keep looking. Sooner or later, they'll decide they have all they're going to find and then they'll arrest you."

I tried to spin it. "Since I didn't kill him, they can look as much as they like."

Even over the phone, I could hear Barry shaking his head. "You threatened to kill him in front of multiple witnesses. Because he died before the divorce was completed, you'll inherit millions of dollars, as you're still, legally, his wife. That gives you a heck of a motive. Your weapon is missing from where it was supposed to be and the caliber matches the gunshot used to kill Martin. That gives you a means. You are trained with that handgun and you scored perfectly on the range when you took your test. That, and the fact that you have no alibi for the entire period during which the murder took place gives you the opportunity.

"That's plenty to take a case to trial. And Texas juries, especially from the rich suburbs, love to convict."

"But—"

"Believe me, the cops are good at filling in the details. They'll find evidence that makes you look guilty even if you aren't. They've already got enough to arrest you any time they want, but they know once they arrest you, you'll be able to start fighting them. That's why you're still walking free."

"I can—"

Barry plowed right over me. "With today's law-and-order mood, you're going to have to hope for a sympathetic jury filled with recently divorced women."

I paused. Arguing with Barry wasn't getting me anywhere. I didn't need to convince him, I needed to know what to do next. "You're right. I should have asked for a lawyer. I'm sorry."

It pained me to apologize, but Barry was right. I shouldn't have let my reflexive sympathies for law and order get in the way of my own safety.

"I'm not browbeating you for fun or because you hurt my feelings, you know."

"I understand. But I can't undo the mistakes I made. What am I supposed to do now?"

"Hire some private investigators, maybe. If *you* didn't kill Mr. Montag, *someone else* did. If you find the real killer, that would take the heat off of you."

I tried to look at the bright side. "At least I have some money, now. Right?"

"I don't know what you mean."

"The divorce wasn't final. With Martin dead, I should have access to the checkbook again, and the credit cards. Even if the house still belongs to the company."

"Oh, no. You can't use *Martin's* money. Not until his will has been probated and not until the courts are assured that they wouldn't be turning over the proceeds to his killer."

"Then how am I supposed to hire detectives? Can a court-appointed attorney get money to do that?"

"What court-appointed attorney? If you'd demanded a lawyer, you would have been assigned an attorney. That hypothetical attorney could request funding for investigators. But since you're not under arrest, you don't have access to a court-appointed, and the court and police don't have to give you anything. Catch-22."

"But what about—"

"I was working with you on the assault charges. I have no standing."

"I don't suppose you'd want to work for free."

He paused long enough to give me hope. "It won't help. I still can't get any funding for investigators unless you've been charged."

I was so screwed. "But—"

"Don't forget your community service starting tomorrow, Heather. If you blow that off, things will get even worse for you."

* * * *

I'd just hung up the phone when Leah and Richard arrived home.

I didn't want to ask where they'd been or what they'd been doing, but I suspected they hadn't spent the night at the library boning up for their exams.

Richard looked dapper in an unstructured linen suit I'd seen on our American Express bill—at three thousand dollars. Leah's face was drawn, her blue eyes glistening with unshed tears. Unlike Richard, who was dressed to the 9's, Leah wore a pair of jeans and a t-shirt advertising some sort of bicycling event. She'd tried to get me into that sport but I couldn't imagine anything sillier than an adult woman of a certain size riding around on a children's toy.

"What are you doing here, Mother?" She pushed a long hank of blond hair back from her face.

"Sit down, Leah. I've got bad news."

"If this is about you killing Dad, Nick called and gave me the details. Why, Mother?"

"Of course I didn't kill your father."

"Nick said you promised to eviscerate him."

"That was a figure—"

"Listen." Richard got in my face. As always, he'd picked up Leah's mood and was egging her on. "Losing her father has been tough on Leah. Whatever issues you had with him have nothing to do with us."

Lots of people had been getting in my face lately. Compared to the cops I'd just spent two hours dealing with, Richard was something of a nothing.

I poked him in his skinny but still soft belly. "Back off, frat-boy. Why don't you go play your videogames and let my daughter and me talk?"

"Mother," Leah gasped in outrage. "I can't believe you said that to Richard. We're going to get married so you might as well start treating him with a little respect."

That rocked me, but not for long. "Oh, really. And when did this marvelous engagement occur? As soon as Richard learned your father was dead and that you'd probably be coming into an inheritance, right? I'd say Richard was a gigolo, but I'm afraid he would give the profession a bad name."

"That's it, Mother. Get out."

Obviously I'd hit too close to home with my guess about when he'd asked her to marry him. Leah didn't like her nose being rubbed in her mistakes any more than I did.

"Come on, Leah. This isn't about Richard. I want to—"

"You're right, Mom. This isn't about Richard. This is about you. Look at the mess you made out of my condo. There are dirty pans in the sink and it looks like you fell into my wall and halfway knocked it down. Unlike you, I have to get by with someone coming in twice a week rather than a full time maid, but I suppose you never thought of that. I want you out of here, now. Before you destroy anything else, like the rest of my life."

"But Leah. I thought we—"

"You thought you'd come to me with your sob story about how Dad was leaving you and I'd rally around you like you were some abused spouse. Well, guess again. If anyone was abused in that relationship, it was Dad, not you."

"That's just not—"

She covered her ears with her hands and shook her head. "I don't want to hear it. I don't want to hear you any more."

I didn't need that kind of abuse from my own daughter and started to get on my high horse, but when I was halfway to her front door I realized I had nowhere to go and no way to get there.

I grabbed Leah's arm and pulled her hand away from her ear.

"I don't have a car. I don't have a house. You can't kick me out."

"Watch us," Richard chimed in.

"Shut up, Dickless."

"*Mother.*"

Okay, that had been over the top. "Sorry, Leah."

I didn't mind apologizing to my daughter. I didn't have to apologize to Richard.

"Why is this my problem? Go bother Nick. His apartment is twice as big as my condo and he has maid service."

"Nick doesn't want me."

"Like I do?"

"Besides, there's a restraining order keeping me away from Montag Industries properties. You know the company owns that apartment complex."

"Stay in a hotel."

"My credit cards don't work." My eyes teared up and my throat got tight as the hopelessness of my situation weighed down on me. "Your father cut me off before somebody killed him."

"Considering how often you threatened to cut Leah off, I'd say that's poetic justice," Richard said.

"Shut up, Richard," Leah told him.

"And I'm supposed to start community service tomorrow. It's something called the StrongGirl program and I have to go to Dallas. Not just Dallas, but Oak Cliff. You know I'm prejudiced, but it's all people, well, you know."

My boo-hoos had started in earnest now. I realized I wasn't just crying because of my own situation, although it was pathetic. I was mourning the loss of a marriage I'd poured all of my hopes into, mourning the death of a husband who had been, despite what I'd recently learned of his meanness, a great provider, a supportive father, and even an adequate lover—especially considering what I now knew about his feelings on my plus-sized figure.

"Mother, I hate it when you cry."

"Sorry." But the tears kept coming.

My knees wobbled and I collapsed to the floor like an overcooked soufflé, shaking and sobbing like a bowl of Jell-o—a big lardy bowl of it.

"She's coming between us again," Richard whined. "Why don't you just kick her out? She'll land on her feet. Like a weasel."

Leah shook her head slowly. "Back off, Richard. She is my mother."

She wrinkled her forehead for a moment and I managed to refrain from reminding her about wrinkles. I could see she'd been pushed too far already.

"I have a rental," she said. "It's in Oak Cliff so it would be convenient for your community service. Since I'm between renters, you could stay there for a while."

"Now that's an excellent idea." Richard perked up. "That's far enough that she won't be back often. Don't be late with the rent or I might have to break your kneecap."

"You are such a little twerp," I said, pulling myself together and sitting up. I swiped at my eyes with my cuff. "Thanks for the offer, but really. I *can't* live in Oak Cliff. What would my friends say?"

Leah put her hands on her hips. "If your friends are so concerned, let one of *them* to put you up."

I let myself imagine calling one of a League member and letting her know I was homeless, the lead suspect in a murder case, and on community service. And, oh, by the way, could I move in with you indefinitely? Not going to happen.

"Where, exactly, is this rental?"

"I'll print out directions."

"And I'll drive you to the DART station," Richard offered. "No charge for the mileage."

Chapter 3

Leah's rental was in a *trailer park*.

I'd imagined a cute bungalow in Kessler Park, which was a decent neighborhood even if it was south of the Trinity River. Instead, Leah's father had given her a horrible little trailer for her income property. It was parked in a low-lying area where the river floods all the time.

Leah had printed me off the directions to get there by rail and bus. I felt wild and courageous taking public transportation for the first time since I'd been in college, and was surprised to find an ethnic and professional mix on the rail. I must have assumed it would be all minorities and people with tattoos.

So I was feeling better before I got off the bus and walked the entire half-mile to the trailer park.

By the time I arrived, I was dripping with sweat, my heart was racing so fast I thought it had gone into overdrive, and I was so not ready to see a bunch of decrepit trailers with a flock of chickens between them, scratching for bugs or seeds or something even more disgusting.

Maybe seventy-five mobile homes and trailers squatted in a field a mile or so from the river. I had a moment's hopefulness when I noticed some of them were nice—there was even a Winnebago that would have looked at home in the circular driveway of one of the estates in my own Frisco neighborhood. Of course, in Frisco, nobody would actually *live* in a Winnebago. They were for traveling and exploring the country without having to leave the comforts of home.

It was possible that someone was exploring the country and had decided to stop in the Shady Rest Mobile Park. I didn't think so.

Unfortunately, Leah's rental wasn't one of the nicer ones. It was what, I later learned, was referred to as a "single-wide."

The front door felt barely sturdy enough to stand up to a two-year-old's kick. Heat rushed out when I opened the door, along with the foul odors of sweat, rotting trash, and mildew.

Dirty dishes sat in the sink, the bed was unmade and rumpled, and condom wrappers littered the floor.

I gritted my teeth. My politics were all about people pulling themselves up by their own bootstraps. I could do it myself. I could survive even a pit like this.

I tried to pump some of the heat out of the place by opening and closing the front door repeatedly. It didn't help much, and when I got bored of that, I explored.

Exploring my new home didn't take long.

The trailer contained two tiny bedrooms, a single living area with a kitchen in the corner, and a bathroom I practically needed a microscope to see. I'd have to decide in advance whether to go into the bathroom frontward or back, because I wouldn't be able to turn around inside.

In the kitchen, a pair of cockroaches appeared to be having consensual sex on what I supposed was my new dining room table.

I had to clean up. First, though, I had to get the temperature down to something a human could stand.

It took me a few minutes before I realized my new home didn't have central air. I'd never lived in a home without central air and had a hard time imagining surviving a Texas summer without it. Fortunately, there was a window unit. I plugged it in and turned cranked it up to maximum.

It made a huge amount of noise, especially considering how little cool air the thing pumped out.

I pointed the blowers toward the kitchen, stripped dirty sheets off the bed and tossed them outside, and then got to work scouring dishes.

This was an adventure, I told myself. At our next League meeting, I'd be able to tell the others that I'd lived with the poor people, experienced their life and shared their difficulties. I'd be like an explorer bringing back news from the other side of the world.

Don't panic. Those immortal words had been planted in my brain during a misspent period of my youth. They seemed like good advice how. If I could manage three hundred League women and host parties for hundreds of employees, customers, and suppliers of Montag Industries, I could scour some pots and pans—since the trailer didn't even have a dishwasher.

I'd made good progress on the dishes and was halfway toward convincing myself that I could survive these primitive conditions when the doorbell chimed.

Given my experience earlier that morning, I halfway expected jackbooted stormtroopers. I was surprised to see a skinny woman with long brown hair and a pair of oval glasses. Her clothes were about what I'd expect in a trailer park, jeans with rips in the knees and who knew where else, a too-tight t-shirt that showed off what figure she had, and she even had a tattoo on her upper arm— one of those barbed wire designs that would permanently exclude her from any my sorority, or any League function.

But what really caught my notice was the chicken roosting on her shoulder, looking perfectly content.

"Yeah?" I confess I shouted through the door rather than open it.

"I'm Tina Anderson."

Like that was supposed to mean something to me? "What do you want, Ms. Anderson? If you're worried about the sheets I threw outside the door, I'll take care of those later."

"I'm the trailer park manager. Just checking to see that everything's okay."

The manager? What was I in trouble for this time?

I opened the door. "My daughter told me she owned this unit. Is there a problem?"

"No problem. Some units, the park owns. Other units, the park just rents out the slabs and hookups. Your daughter's is one of those."

I tried to pay attention, but the woman had a chicken on her shoulder. She kept talking to me like there was nothing odd going on at all, until she finally noticed that my gaze was glued on the thing.

"Oh, I'd forgotten about Charlaine. Don't worry, she won't bother you."

"I'm sure she's a fantastic pet. I once had a pair of lovebirds." I was trying to find common ground here, something I was normally good at.

"Right. Anyway, I wanted to welcome you to the neighborhood, let you know that I'm here if you need anything, and offer to show you around if you want."

I realized I wasn't being a very good hostess and invited her inside.

Tina poked her head in. "Need any help with picking up?"

Where had she been two hours earlier? "I think I've got it under control."

"Well come-on out of there, then. Until your AC cranks up, it's hotter inside than it is out. I've got a picnic table and a cooler full of beer out under the trees. Finish the cleanup when it gets cooler. In the meantime, we can get acquainted."

It was about two in the afternoon—way before my usual time to have a drink. And when I did drink I generally had a nice glass of merlot or a margarita. Beer was something else I hadn't done since my days in the sorority at SMU.

Still, I'd been moaning about having nobody to talk to and pretty clearly this Tina Anderson wanted to talk.

The woman's name, though, got me thinking. "I know some Andersons. You're not any relation to…" I stopped once I realized how silly I was being. I mean, there were probably fifty thousand people named Anderson in Dallas. There was no way a trailer-trash woman could be related to *The* Andersons.

"Andy Anderson of Anderson Software? He's my ex-husband."

I almost dropped my jaw. Anderson Software was huge. Even bigger than Montag Industries. I'd met Andy Anderson at social events. Although he definitely *wasn't* a supporter of the Republican Party, his mother was. Seeing his ex-wife reduced to managing a trailer park really brought home the danger I was in. Even if the cops didn't put me in jail, this might be me. At least she was still young, and pretty enough if you liked the trashy type.

"So, are you re-married?"

She shook her head, managing to restrain herself from laughing at my stupid question. Of course she wasn't remarried. Otherwise why would she still be an Anderson? "I haven't had much luck with boyfriends."

In my experience, men liked trashy-type women. If *she* had problems dating, I hated to think what *my* life would be like.

Of course, it was possible that Tina needed some help dealing with men—help I could provide. Women in the trailer park community probably didn't understand how to manage relationships. I might not have much of a future myself, but I had attended hundreds of seminars on traditional-values approaches to creating and maintaining strong relationships. From looking at Tina and noticing things like she wasn't wearing a bra under that t-shirt, I could tell she needed the kind of assistance I could offer.

I decided to hold off on the advice, though, until I got to know her better.

It's amazing how often people refuse to listen to good advice if it isn't couched just right.

* * * *

Tina helped me carry the sheets, blankets, and mattress cover to a Laundromat a couple of blocks away. We stuffed the bedding into a couple of washing machines, I fished in my purse for quarters to feed the coin collectors.

I was worn out by the time we headed back to Tina's promised picnic bench.

Charlaine, the chicken, hopped off Tina's shoulder when we reached the edge of the park, and then hopped back on when we returned.

I'd spent a lot of time outdoors when the kids had been involved in youth soccer, but it had been years since I'd walked so far. I took the bottle of beer Tina handed me and rolled it across my sweaty forehead.

"That chicken…is like a real pet?" I hoped Tina wouldn't notice I'd had to catch my breath in the middle of the sentence.

"This chicken and I have been through a lot together." Tina popped the tops off two bottles and shoved one toward me. We sat down at a picnic table under some tall oaks.

Although *sat* might be an overstatement. I practically flopped, leaning my head against the table's cool concrete.

We didn't have a lot of tall trees in Frisco. Because Frisco is a relatively new community, the trees were all about the same height and didn't provide much shade.

Although I had fond memories of lying under live-oak trees listening to Martin recite poetry to me during my college days at SMU, I had forgotten exactly how much cooling they could generate.

Sitting under their shade was almost like being in one of those Gothic cathedrals we'd visited the year Nick had graduated from High School. We'd all taken a month off and gone to Europe to celebrate. No matter how hot it was outside, you'd walk into one of those cathedrals and it would be cool and quiet, with soft light filtered through the stained glass windows.

The picnic table under the trees was like that. In fact, the biggest difference was that the trees filtered the bright Texas sunshine through green leafs rather than through multicolored glass. That and not smelling like incense.

Cicadas sang their mating calls, a soft rumble came from nearby Interstate 30, and blue jays squawked and scolded each other. Somehow, though, the overall effect was peaceful.

I took a sip of the beer. It wasn't a premium brand, but I was so hot from the walk and the work that it tasted wonderful to me.

Tina didn't seem to be in a hurry to start a conversation, so I decided to give it a try. From my years in the League, I had plenty of experience meeting with new people. "So, how did an Anderson of Anderson Software, end up in a trailer park in Oak Cliff?"

She grinned at me. "It took a lot of work, but I managed."

"Huh?" I'd been expecting to hear some sort of hard-luck story.

"Take a good look at me, Heather. Do I look like the type who's comfortable playing golf or attending tea parties?" She shook her head firmly. "No way. Andy and I were nerds together in high school. Computer programming was our idea of a fun time. Andy took his computer skills and turned them into a business. For him, that was a natural progression. But hiring a bunch of people and getting so big I wasn't even working with the code any more wasn't me. After a while, it wasn't just the business that came between us. Things got complicated. So, we split up."

"But you could have gotten a lot of money from him." I knew from my own experience that building a successful business takes more than one person. Just as Martin couldn't have built Montag Industries without me, I suspected Andy couldn't have built Anderson Software without Tina. Especially not if she'd been involved in creating their initial software projects.

"I make my own way," she said.

Naturally I approved, at least at some level. Self-reliance was the kind of attitude that Rush Limbaugh advocates and that, according to Rush, too few of the poorer population hold. So I told her that.

She looked at me like I had just announced I had an infectious disease. "I didn't know anyone really listened to that right wing propaganda."

I took a deep breath before I let myself get defensive. Still, any notions I'd had that the two of us could be friends vanished. Which shouldn't have been a big surprise. I must have been insanely desperate to think friendship was possible across such vast social and educational barriers.

"So, that's my story," Tina continued, exactly as if she hadn't just insulted everything I believed in. "For me, it was trailer trash to trailer trash all in one generation."

I bit my tongue to stop from giving her instructions on maintaining a positive attitude and told her my story: the disgrace of not being re-elected despite the promises of my so-called friends; the horror of having my house locked against me; the embarrassment of being rejected by Martin in front of his lawyers; my children turning on me and accusing me of murder; the disaster of the cops—not once, but twice.

"Yeah, the police can be troublesome."

I supposed that, living where she did, Tina had her hands full of criminals and police. "The lawyer who helped me when I was arrested for assault says I should hire private detectives, but I don't have the money to do that. Not unless they arrest me first," I concluded. "When I told him I was innocent, he just laughed and said the juries tend to buy whatever the cops want to sell them, not the truth."

"Good luck on getting any money out of the system. I think you're going to be on your own."

Since I'd led protests against spending government money to mollycoddle criminals, I felt a little hypocritical obsessing about not having any money to hire help for myself. Rather than deal with those feelings, I decided to change the subject. I asked Tina if she'd heard of the StrongGirl program I was supposed to assist as my community service.

She took a deep drink from her beer, tossed the bottle into a wire-web trashcan next to the table, and let out a dainty burp. "You're going to be working with them? Cool. StrongGirls started right here in the Cliff. It's all about helping at-risk girls stay in school."

That sounded right up my ally. I had heard the lectures and suspected I could recite them from memory. "Great. Abstinence and Say No to Drugs, right? I've heard all sorts of programs on that with the League so I should be able to fit right in."

Tina looked at me, her mouth working as if she had something she had to say right away but couldn't get the words straight in her head.

Instead, she busied herself pulling another couple of beers out of the cooler.

"I'm still working on mine," I said picking the bottle up to show her. To my surprise, it was almost empty so I accepted the second from her. I didn't think I'd ever drunk beer straight from a bottle, so this was a new experience for me. One I didn't think I'd be repeating.

"Anyway, what StrongGirls is about is *not* a bunch of lectures on behaving like someone out of the fifties. But they'll go through that in your orientation."

"Well. If you ask me, this country could use a good dose of the values from earlier decades. I don't just preach, I live—"

She held up a hand to stop me from venting. "Sorry, no insult was intended. I used to put my foot in my mouth like that all the time in the days when Andy dragged me along to business meetings. I just don't fit into your world, Heather. I don't understand people who like it there. But you've got to understand that *these* girls don't come from *your* background, either. The rules that worked for you don't work for them. If lectures could solve their problems, they would already be solved. What they need are practical skills, not people who just tell them to stop doing the things that everyone they know is doing."

That rocked me back on my heels. I was intelligent and had gotten all A's in college. I could tutor them in English, History, or even Math. But what *practical* skills could I teach a bunch of teenage girls? My skills were organizing women to work together, shopping for the right clothing to make a statement, and managing catering staff to help with Martin's business affairs. I didn't think girls from the wrong side of the river would find those skills useful. For that matter, if any of my skills had any practical financial value, I wouldn't be in the situation I was in, living on a handout from my own teenage daughter.

A pretty blond woman rubbed her eyes as she came out from one of the nicer looking trailers. Although it was after four in the afternoon, she looked as if she'd just gotten up.

When she saw us, she headed for the picnic table, nodded at Tina, and grabbed a beer from the cooler.

That in hand, she sagged down on the picnic table bench next to me, and stuck out her hand.

"I'm Angie. You must be new here."

"Heather Montag," I said.

"Hey, you're the chick who killed her husband when he tried to dump her, right? I heard about it on the news. Way to go. I hate a guy who tries to weasel out of his debts."

"Of course I didn't kill him."

Angie flipped a couple of long strands of beautiful blond hair behind her back and lowered her voice to a sexy whisper. "Save that line for the cops. You don't have to lie to us. What did he do? Sleep with another woman?"

Had Martin slept with another woman? If someone had asked me that question forty-eight hours earlier, I would have denied the possibility with all my strength. Now, I wasn't so certain. He was away from home as many nights as he was there—traveling for business, he always said. But how hard would it have been to travel with one of the pretty secretaries or saleswomen who filled the cubicles at Montag Industries headquarters? Our sex life had slowly faded away, a product of middle age, I'd thought. But maybe it had only been *my* sex life that had died. Maybe Martin had found new outlets.

Instead of being hurt by the possibilities, I wondered whether Martin's potential unfaithfulness could someone else a motive for murder. Unfortunately, I couldn't see it. By divorcing me, he was setting himself up as the goose who lays the golden egg for anyone who'd been willing to accept standby status. Killing him would have killed their chances of stepping onto the gravy train. A gold-digging woman would wait.

"Looks like your brain-gears need more lubricant," Angie said. "Have another beer."

In the summer heat, I'd finished my second beer in record time. This was so not me. While certain of the members of the NTRWL indulge in an afternoon drink or five, no one from *that* group was ever invited to run for the important officer positions.

Being suspected, even briefly, of killing my husband guaranteed I'd never be elected to anything again. I took the beer Angie offered me, tried to unscrew the cap—and promptly snapped off one of my sculpted fingernails.

"Maybe my life wasn't so perfect," I admitted, more to myself than to the two women.

"Yeah," Angie said. "Well, you're in paradise now."

I looked at the mostly-dilapidated trailers, the beat-up pickup trucks, and the chickens. The funny thing was, Angie almost seemed to believe it. This was so wrong.

Chapter 4

The glare of the morning sun, peeking through cheap vinyl blinds, practically blinded me.

I recognized the combination of a queasy stomach and a throbbing head from my sorority days. This was why I always limited myself to one drink.

I struggled from the bed toward the bathroom. Every step took conscious effort and my brain slopped around inside my skull as if it had shrunk a size or two. A heavy weight of pizza pressed down on my stomach.

I'd gone thirty years between beers before the previous day. I decided to wait another thirty before my next. Still, the time spent with Tina and Angie had been cathartic. The two were so different from me I found it hard to imagine being friends with them, but they still rallied around me, gave me the benefit of the doubt that the breakup in my marriage wasn't all my fault, and didn't make snide comments about my weight when I'd reached for that third, or fourth, slice of pizza.

I made a few comments of my own when I squeezed into the shower. The stall was large enough to hold my body, barely. I definitely didn't have room to move a washcloth, or lean against the wall to shave my legs. I had to turn off the shower and open the door to lather up. That done, I just stood under the pouring water for a while rinsing away the soap and just a bit of my hangover.

I could have spent all day in the shower. The hangover was a bad one and even with the air conditioning unit blasting at full speed from the moment I'd arrived, the trailer had barely cooled down at night and was already heating up like one of those aluminum solar stoves we'd used when I'd been a Girl Scout Leader in Leah's troop. All too soon, though, a knock on the door called me back to reality.

Wrapping a towel around myself, I peeked out the front door. For a change, instead of cops, Tina stood on my doorstep.

"Thought I'd offer you a ride to the StrongGirls orientation," she said. "If you show up late for your community service, they can throw you in the can."

Now that I thought about it, people living in trailer parks would probably know more about that than I would. Somehow, I'd fallen into the right hands—at least in terms of making the best of my bad circumstances.

I'd rinsed my shirt and underwear the night before and hung them in front of the air conditioner to dry (the humidity was so high that they wouldn't ever dry otherwise), but I hated the idea of getting back into the same clothes. Normally I'd have jumped at a chance to go shopping but the few dollars Leah had given me were gone on essentials and I hadn't even had enough money to pay for my share of the pizza the previous night.

Nick had been unhelpful the last time I'd talked to him, but that was because he'd thought I was trying to make him pick sides. Of course he'd lend me some money if he knew how badly off I was. I'd definitely have to hit him up for a loan—after my day with StrongGirls.

"I'm not ready."

"What would Rush Limbaugh say about someone who got sent to jail because she was too concerned about their fashion sense?"

Given what Tina had said about Rush, I knew she was making fun of me. Still, she had a point. It generally took me an hour or so in the morning to do my hair, apply my makeup, and make sure that my outfit was right for the events of the day. Since a prison-orange jumpsuit wouldn't be right for me no matter what the events of the day might be, I set a record pace, pulling on my clothes and only applying a minimum of makeup.

"Hurry." Every minute or two, Tina would look up from the game she was playing on her cell phone and nag me.

I had to tell myself not to smear my mascara when she handed me a ten-dollar bill so folded and crumpled it looked like it had gone through the wash with my bed linens.

"You can pay me back whenever," she said as she ushered me into the passenger seat of an ancient Geo Storm.

It took a couple of false starts but I finally squeezed my body into the tiny car. Then Tina started it up and headed toward the school where the StrongGirls orientation was being held.

Her faded-yellow car sputtered and groaned as it climbed Sylvan, but I was surprised it ran at all. No one I knew had a car more than three years old, but this thing had to be nearly as old as its driver.

Since I'd lost the Escalade, I didn't have a lot of room to criticize. I thanked Tina for the ride and struggled out of the low seat when she'd pulled into a standing zone near a portable building at the back of Nathan Forrest Middle School.

She gave me her cell number and told me to call her if I needed a ride home.

It surprised me that she was so nice. I had to think that maybe what had happened was part of some higher plan. Maybe I was being sent to this part of Dallas to help people like Tina. Obviously she had potential. Equally obviously, she'd somehow stepped off the right path, ending up in a horrible trailer park.

My thought that I could be helpful cheered me up. As I climbed the shaky stairs leading to the classroom and opened the door, I felt better than I had since losing the NTWRL election.

The woman giving the orientation, a pretty blonde, looked disgusted with me as I scurried in, barely five minutes late. She checked my name off a list and gestured to the desks where half a dozen other *volunteers* were seated.

The skinny metal legs looked like they'd crumple under my weight. The faux-wood writing surface was attached so close to the flimsy plastic of the seat I doubted I could fit a thigh between them, let alone my body. Very clearly there was an engineering mismatch between these desks and my body. I suspected that both I, and the desk, would come out of any confrontation bent and bruised. Instead of trying it, I leaned up against the back wall.

It wasn't comfortable, but at least the air conditioner circulated a steady stream of frigid air past my body.

The blonde looked at me, at the chair, then nodded. "I'm sorry. The classroom facilities were designed for middle school students, not for, well, large adults."

"I wasn't complaining." I was going to be sore later, though and I wasn't sure I could stand up for an entire day.

"Fine. Back to StrongGirls. Each of you will be assigned a student mentor," she explained.

"Excuse me. You mean a student to mentor?" I asked.

"Ms. Montag, right?"

"Mrs."

She made a note in her pad. "*Mrs.* Montag, then. Before *you* can mentor the young women we're trying to reach, you have to understand their world. Your mentor will help you with that and when she decides you're ready, you'll begin your work with the other girls."

"But--"

"I don't know about you but when I was in school, teen pregnancy was relatively unusual, and almost everyone graduated. In this part of Dallas, graduation rates are lower than the percentage of young women getting pregnant."

"They should 'just say no,'" I explained. I couldn't think how many lectures I'd been to that reinforced that obvious point.

"Like you do at the dinner table?" someone said in a stage whisper.

I looked around, horrified at the rudeness. These women were going to be teaching impressionable young girls? But everyone except the instructor seemed to be snickering.

"We're all going to be working together so let's dispense with the personal attacks," the blonde said. "It turns out, Mrs. Montag, that the *just say no* approach works better with wealthy donors than it does for the actual girls we're dealing with. The StrongGirls program helps with what happens *after* they say no. It is designed to offer positive alternatives rather than a purely negative message. The purpose of the mentor relationship is to help each of you learn about the realities these young women face every day of their lives. Here in the city, trouble doesn't equate with difficulties finding the perfect dress for the prom or getting ready for your debut cotillion. It's not about deciding whether to attend college at SMU or TCU. Here they worry more about the drive-by shootings, getting caught by immigration and sent back to Central America, or being evicted by crack dealers who want to use their apartment for a retail outlet."

I nodded. I thought I saw her game. The StrongGirls' mentor program pushed responsibility on the girls, letting them think they were being mentors to the older women when, in reality, we would be providing an example for them. It was clever thinking. My estimation of the program I'd been *volunteered* into helping went up a couple of notches.

For the next two hours, the blonde lectured us on what we'd be learning.

The next hour consisted of girls and young women coming in and telling us how StrongGirls had changed them.

The *we don't need men* message was a bit harsh, but overall, I was ready to get behind this program.

Finally the blonde brought in the founder of the program, a woman not much older than Leah, who gave us an inspiring welcome, and the two of them introduced us to our "mentors."

Since today was a half-day due to teacher in-service, we could spend a couple of hours getting to know them.

My mentor was a Latina girl named Lupe.

Lupe wore a white blouse and a gray-plaid pleated skirt that was similar enough to the skirt I'd worn when I'd attended Hockaday that I recognized it as a school uniform. She was a skinny kid, with little stick-figure legs and arms, but with gorgeous dark hair caught up in a thick braid that ran all the way down her back to her upper thighs, and with beautiful dark-brown eyes that glowed with life.

She couldn't hide the momentary disappointment that crossed her face when the blonde told her I was her assignment, but she covered it up quickly with a bright smile.

"Hola."

"I'm sorry. I don't speak Spanish." How was I supposed to help her if we couldn't even communicate?

This time her smile looked real.

"I can help you learn Spanish. It's a mentor's job to help her protégé."

She certainly didn't need me to help her with her English. Lupe spoke with television-perfect diction. Her English lacked even the slight Texas drawl that I still had from growing up in a time when Dallas was a far smaller and far more southern city.

"Although most of the girls in the StrongGirls program speak English," she explained, "there are a few who have only recently arrived in this country and speak only Spanish. You'll want to be able to communicate with them to gain their trust. Even if they speak English, many of our parents haven't learned much and it's important that you be able to talk to them."

The girl couldn't have been over thirteen but she delivered her message with so much emphasis that I had to believe she was speaking from the heart rather than reciting a line.

"I'd like to learn Spanish." Unlike some members of my group, I wasn't an English-only advocate. Texas's economy depended on labor provided by our immigrant population.

Lupe reached out a hand to me and dragged me from the classroom. Since my legs felt like they were about to fall off from standing in one place for four hours, I was happy to go along with her.

* * * *

Outside, the heat was unbearable. It had to be over a hundred degrees, and it so humid that beads of sweat clung to my body rather than drying off. My thighs sweated into my hose and all of a sudden I felt like I was walking through sandpaper with the rough nylon rubbing together and making a swishing noise with every step. My feet didn't squish in my shoes, but I feared that was only a matter of time.

We headed away from the middle school campus, Lupe dragging me by the arm and me following as quickly as I could while wiping the sweat from my forehead every other step. I was sure I was getting blisters. I hadn't worn practical shoes to the League meeting and was still wearing the same clothes and shoes.

I tried to take in the neighborhood as we walked. Squirrels dashed through live oak trees that created a near-complete canopy, wood-frame houses with fading paint butted up against car repair shops, and sidewalk concrete had dates stamped into them from the thirties and forties. From what I could tell, no one had done any maintenance work since, either.

"Shall we be first-name, or formal?" Lupe asked.

First name? With a child? "Well. I don't—"

"I'll call you Heather, of course, because I'm the mentor and you're not. But I would be fine if you wanted to call me Lupe. Ms. Gonzaga is a bit much, don't you think? Considering that I'm still quite a bit younger than you."

I nodded, suddenly uncomfortable when I remembered that I'd called Maria by her first name for years and never even offered to allow her to call me Heather.

"Thank you, uh, Lupe."

"You're very welcome, Heather." She changed direction, heading down an alley I would never have dared enter on my own. Half a dozen young men waited at the other end playing some sort of game in the grass and dirt of the alleyway.

I stiffened when they looked up at us and rattled something in Spanish. I didn't want to believe Lupe had led me into a trap, but that possibility seemed both unavoidable and frightening.

"Speak English," Lupe commanded. "Heather here doesn't know much Spanish yet."

"You're pretty fat, aren't you," one of the boys said. He and the others wore navy slacks and white polo style shirts, so I belatedly realized they weren't hoodlums but must be students from Aaron Burr, the local high school.

"I guess I am."

"Must be hard when it's so hot."

"Yeah, it is."

"You know the funny thing?"

I shook my head.

"Lupe here is part of the StrongGirls program and she's smart. Real smart. Doesn't matter, though. Sooner or later, she's going to end up working as a maid for someone like you who isn't as smart as she is, just because she's Mexican."

I got my back up. "She doesn't have to end up working as a maid. There are lots of opportunities for intelligent, well-educated women these days."

The guys all laughed. "Oh, we forgot. She'll probably go to Harvard, right? Like that happens to anyone from our neighborhood."

Lupe tugged on my hand. "Come on. They're just being mean."

The guys made hissing sounds as we walked by and I noticed Lupe squaring her shoulders.

"What's that about?"

"They think I should leave the StrongGirls and hang out with them. As if I was ready to start having babies."

"But you're just a kid."

She pulled me to a stop and looked up into my eyes. "You don't get it, do you? Three girls in my class have gotten pregnant this year. If it weren't for StrongGirls, more would have. I know things are different from when you were a kid. But if you're going to become a StrongGirl yourself, you've got to understand how things really are."

I didn't say anything for the rest of our walk to the neighborhood 7-11, but I wondered if I was StrongGirl material. I'd gone to college, but my major goal there hadn't been to get a degree or to broaden my education. I'd been caught up in the effort to find a man I could settle down with. Sure I'd been older than Lupe and her classmates, but when the girls in my sorority and I had giggled about the M.R.S. degree, had we been involved in the same sort of *rescue-me* mentality that the StrongGirls program was designed to confront?

I fished out the ten-dollar bill Tina had given me but Lupe made me put it away. The StrongGirls program had supplied her with two coupons for free beverages. She poured both of us frozen coffee drinks.

"You're too young for coffee." The words sounded hollow even in my own ears when I remembered that three little girls in her class were already pregnant, but I'd been a mother too long not to speak up.

She flashed bright white teeth. "Are you worried it would stunt my growth? I'm already almost as tall as my mother."

If so, her mother must be a midget because Lupe wasn't even five feet tall.

The clerk recognized Lupe immediately and greeted her with a burst of Spanish before switching to English.

"That last lady you mentored doing okay, Lupe?" he demanded.

"Everyone I mentor does okay. I'm the best."

"I think you are, too." He took the coupons she offered in payment for our drinks.

"You listen to my cousin," he told me. "She can help you become a StrongGirl yourself."

"He's your cousin?" I asked as we left the 7-11, drinks in hand.

"Yeah. He's okay. He's taking classes at Mountain View. He wants to be a nurse but it's real hard to get into the program. Nurses make big money. An experienced nurse can earn a thousand a week. Maybe more."

Surely they earned more than that. A thousand a week wouldn't cover what

Martin and I had spent on clothing, let alone our full living expenses. Yet Lupe spoke as if a thousand dollars was the kind of money it had been when I'd been a child.

The neighborhood gradually deteriorated as we walked past frame prairie style homes, into an area filled with what had once been nice houses that were now chopped up into multiple informal apartments. The tall trees gave the area the feel of a richer and more genteel area than it really was.

I kept quiet thinking about what the 7-11 clerk had said. Did *I* need to become a stronger woman?

Lupe lived in an apartment carved out of a beautiful stone home on Tenth Street. Tenth Street had once been a trolley route and hints of the old brick road peeked through the modern asphalt in several locations. I couldn't really imagine a time when Dallas professionals had stepped out of their homes and hopped onto a trolley to take them downtown for work, but I knew it had once been that way, before far-out suburbs had become fashionable.

Lupe's home was one of six apartments in the once-elegant home.

My legs screamed in agony as my mentor led me up the stairs to her home. Between walking through the neighborhood and standing for hours during the StrongGirls orientation, I'd worked them harder than since I'd given up tennis while pregnant with Nick.

Lupe fished into her blouse and came up with a silver chain that carried a small figurine of Mary and a key to the apartment.

She used the key to open the door and ushered me inside.

Despite the cold drink from 7-11, I was ready to flop on a couch and enjoy some quiet and air conditioning.

That dream was instantly dispelled. A pair of oscillating fans circulated hot air and a television blared in the corner of the room. Every chair, and every other flat surface, was filled with children.

I would have taken Lupe's mother for her sister. She couldn't be much older than Leah, but Leah was still exploring life and deciding whether it was time to settle down. That decision had long before been made for Lupe's mother, Elizabeth. Elizabeth sat surrounded by children with one at her breast and another, if the swell of her abdomen meant anything, on its way. A girl maybe a year older than Lupe held a couple of younger children in her arms. She looked to be as pregnant as her mother.

Claustrophobia clamped down on me like a vice. The television's cacophony of incomprehensible sound, the simultaneous shouting, crying, and screaming of children, and the sodden air frightened and intimidated me.

A pair of bunk beds and the television dominated the living room. Two open doors led to a single bedroom where a double bed and several cribs were set up, and to a tiny bathroom that all of these people must share.

"I can't stay here," I whispered to Lupe.

"What?"

I was panicking. "I, uh, I have claustrophobia."

Lupe looked like she'd heard that before. Which made sense if she were a regular mentor.

I took a deep breath and grabbed her arm. If StrongGirls could help Lupe, I was all for it. That didn't mean I could stay there. Not without panicking.

"Take Pedro," Elizabeth told Lupe as I dragged her toward the door.

Pedro was a cute kid, maybe kindergarten age.

The three of us headed for the North Oak Cliff Library. My mind whirled with what we'd just left.

My mother's family had lived in the south for generations, coming across from England during the days when Georgia was still a prison colony. But my father's family had come from Eastern Europe during the early twentieth century. They'd landed in New York and made their home there in the garment district. I still had *Yankee* cousins in Manhattan and New Jersey. Once, when I'd visited my paternal grandmother, she'd dug out some crumbling photos that showed the tenements her parents had lived in when they'd first arrived.

At the time, I'd considered those to be ancient history, no more connected to modern life than were stories of Christians battling tigers in the Roman Coliseum. Apparently history was repeating itself, but it was doing so in a way that was hidden and unknown to those of us who lived in the far northern suburbs. I wondered if the Americans of the early twentieth century had been as blind to the conditions of the new immigrants as my friends and I were today.

* * * *

Pedro scurried into story-time at the library while Lupe and I sat at a table.

In the public building, hard-working air conditioning cooled us. Muffled conversation and the clicking of keyboards and computer mice created a low rumble as both students and adults took advantage of the library's high-speed Internet access to do homework, job searches, or simply to chat online with others.

Unlike the largely deserted libraries of my own community, this branch of the Dallas Library appeared to be a center of activity. Boys flirted with teenaged girls, a pair of older men in blue overalls scratched their heads over a business plan for a printing business they hoped to open, and mothers stretched their legs and caught up on gossip while their children enjoyed the story-time.

"Are you going to tell me what you're in trouble for?" Lupe demanded. "I am your mentor, after all. Maybe I can help."

"Trouble?"

"You think they don't tell us which volunteers want to be here and which are doing community service? It's for our own safety, you know."

"Oh." I'd assumed my past would be my own secret. Apparently I was wrong.

"Well, I appreciate the offer but I doubt if there's anything you can do to help me. My husband was trying to divorce me and when I went to talk to him, I found out I'd violated a protective order. Which got me in trouble. Plus, I might have tried to hit him." The events of the previous few days had gotten a little confused in my mind but I definitely remembered losing my temper and swinging at both Martin and the cops who'd dragged me off.

"A StrongGirl learns that violence is a last resort," Lupe instructed me. "Since we're strong, we don't have to rely on force to protect ourselves or those around us."

"I'll remember that," I promised, wondering if this girl had ever been provoked to temporary insanity, as I had been.

"Divorce is a problem," Lupe said seriously. "It's against what the church teaches, of course, but some women are divorcing their husbands now, even in the Catholic community. Some men beat their wives and no woman should have to accept this. Some husbands like to drink or party with younger women even if they are married. A StrongGirl learns to take care of herself."

I looked closely at Lupe to make sure she wasn't an adult midget disguised as a middle school student. After a bit of thought, I realized that she might just have experienced more of the world than I had. I'd been lucky all my life—well, until the past few days, anyway. My parents had been affluent and we'd lived in a nice neighborhood in far north Dallas. I'd met Martin in college and he'd taken care of me ever since. I hadn't needed to be a StrongGirl.

One thing I wasn't going to do was get into a debate with a teenage girl about divorce—even a possibly wise teenage girl like Lupe. The past few days had shaken the certainties of my life and I didn't know where I stood any more.

Many of my friends had gone through divorce with disastrous results for themselves, their children, and even their husbands. It seemed that every few weeks, another rumor would circulate around the League. Someone's husband was having a midlife crisis. Someone had spotted him out with a hot car, with newly implanted hair plugs growing from his bald head, and eventually with a younger and dumber bit of arm-candy clutching for a sugar-daddy as he grasped for his lost youth.

Almost as soon as I'd decided to avoid the topic, my mouth opened and I started talking about it, all of my resolutions apparently unable to stand in the way of my need for catharsis.

"I'd always assumed divorce was for other people and not for us. Martin was in his fifties. Men are supposed to be past their mid-life crisis by that time."

Lupe patted my hand. "Do you want him to stop divorcing you? I don't know if I can help with this, but I can see what I can do. As your mentor, it's my responsibility."

Poor Lupe. She looked at me so seriously, with such concern on her small face. I hadn't noticed the way one of her front teeth edged in front of the other —a tiny imperfection that would have been ruthlessly eradicated in my neighborhood but that was apparently ignored here. A girl her age should be worrying about the latest boy-band and wondering if the right guy from school would call her, not feeling responsible for fixing other people's problems.

"It's too late for that. Someone murdered him."

"Oh, murder. That's very bad."

"It is bad." It struck me abruptly that I hadn't really mourned Martin—not unless that had been what my beer-drinking and pizza-gorging night had been about, or maybe the writhing on the kitchen floor in Leah's condo. My cake-eating marathon had clearly, in retrospect, been mourning the death of my marriage.

And I needed to mourn Martin. Sure I'd been mad at him. If he'd really needed to divorce me, he could have done it with a lot more sensitivity than simply locking me out of my home and making off with all the money. Still, I'd spent thirty years with him, loving him. He was the only lover I'd ever had. He was the father of my children. Instead of dealing with the loss, I'd acted as if I'd wake up and all this would be a dream.

That wasn't going to happen.

Tears welled up in my eyes. Martin was gone and my last words to the man I'd shared my life with had been filled with anger.

"It wasn't you, though, who killed him. Right?" Lupe insisted. "I don't think they'd let a murderer do her community service with StrongGirls."

"No. It wasn't me."

"Good."

I couldn't let her stay relieved. "But the police *think* it was me. Killing Martin made me heir to his estate. If he'd gone through with the divorce, I wouldn't have ended up with much at all. It gives me a motive."

Lupe stepped away to check on her brother, then returned, carrying the boy on her hip. She looked horribly serious. "I understand now. My role as your mentor is to help you discover the truth about your husband's death."

Chapter 5

I think I learned more about the real world during the three hours I spent with Lupe that afternoon than I had from thirty years of League lectures.

In my Frisco neighborhood, it was rare to see a pedestrian. People drove their children everywhere until the children turned sixteen. Children expected a new car as a sixteenth birthday present, as if it were some automatic birthright. If we wanted exercise, we drove to an air-conditioned health club. You could live in a house for years without ever meeting your neighbors because front doors were more ornamental than useful—the garage was the normal means of access. Even within our homes, there was so much room that an entire family could spend hours at home without ever seeing one another.

Lupe's world was completely different.

Most families in her neighborhood had a single car. Which left the children and one spouse walking anywhere they wanted to go. Without enough air-conditioning and with housing too small to hold more than beds and a television, families spent their time out on porches while their children played soccer or baseball in the streets.

For me, it seemed a frightening world, made more disturbing by the trucks rumbling down the street with their stereos turned up so loud they shook the buildings and the muscular men lounging in old-fashioned undershirts, looking like thugs from a gangster movie.

My assigned hours for the day were long over, but Lupe wouldn't let me leave, and I didn't really want to go back to the loneliness of Leah's trailer, either. So I let myself be convinced to stay, helping her with her homework, and feeling like a visitor from another world.

At six o'clock, Lupe's father pulled a shabby pickup truck in front of their apartment, hung his straw cowboy hat on a hook near the front door, kissed Lupe's mother and tousled the hair of all of the kids he could catch, and then grabbed a beer and went out on the porch to chat with neighbors. A few minutes later, Lupe's mother stepped outside with a huge steaming pot that smelled like heaven on earth, announced it was dinnertime and invited me to join the family meal.

I was tempted. Despite her pregnancy, the heat, and all of those children, she'd cooked a real meal rather than just ordering take-out.

Lupe's father, Mike, poured glasses of milk for the children and iced tea for the teens and adults, including Lupe's sister's fiancé who'd arrived a few minutes after he had, and offered me a choice of tea or beer (*cerveza*, he called it).

Although it looked like a lot of food, I'd hosted enough teen parties to know how hungry children could be. If I stayed and ate their food, there wouldn't be enough for them.

When I turned them down, Lupe handed me a folded piece of lined notebook paper. Written out in Lupe's neat script were instructions for catching a bus that would take me to the trailer park.

I had to swallow back the tears.

Earlier that afternoon, Lupe had asked me where I was staying and I'd admitted to being in the Shady Rest Trailer Park. I'd thought it was just casual conversation but apparently not. My mentor had been taking care of me. It was humbling to realize she *thought* she was more responsible than I was. It was doubly humbling to realize she might be right.

"You will need three more days of mentoring before you're ready to participate in the StrongGirls program," she explained. "Many of the volunteers only come once a week but, since you don't work and since you need to get your community service hours, you should come by the school at two o'clock on Monday."

"Okay." She was right about me not having a lot of alternative things to do with my time. Assuming, that was, that the cops didn't arrest me over the weekend.

"You should have plenty of material to study on the CD-ROM they gave you," she concluded. "I'll review that with you on Monday so be sure to spend some time with it."

"I don't have a computer," I admitted.

She wrinkled her nose. "That's one reason I took you to the library. To show you where it is so you could do your work. You'll need to show them proof that you live in Dallas and get a library card. The library is open all day Saturday. You'll be fine."

"Okay. I'll see you on Monday." I stepped off the porch and headed toward Jefferson where I was to catch my first bus.

At Jefferson and Tyler, where I made my connection, I spotted a sign advertising a clothing sale at a Salvation Army Thrift Store.

I was desperate for something new to wear and walked in, only to discover another world I hadn't imagined.

I knew about consignment stores where you could pick up a gently used Oscar de la Renta for practically nothing. I was expecting something like that. Instead, I found that you can buy used underwear. Just the idea gave me goosebumps.

I backed away from that rack so quickly I ran into another shopper, a woman with a missing front tooth and what looked like a developing spot of skin cancer on her ear.

"Oh, sorry."

"No problem." She fingered a pair of boots. "I don't much like the idea of wearing someone else's panties, either."

She didn't look like the kind of woman I'd talk to in Frisco, but I was still in tourist mode. "Where would you—"

"Family Dollar down the street sells that stuff cheap."

"By down the street you mean—"

"Less than two miles. It's on Jefferson. You can't miss it."

I'd already walked more that day than I had in the past five years. There was no way I was going to walk another two miles. And I only had what was left of Tina's ten dollars anyway. I decided I could rinse out my things one more day until I could borrow some money from one of my kids. I thanked her for the advice and turned back to checking out clothes.

At least the clothes smelled clean. Most of them were horrid, though. People had bought them cheap, worn them hard, then donated them when they barely had anything left to give. Near the back, though, I found a small rack of plus-sized clothes that looked familiar. To my surprise, they were things I'd asked Maria to get rid of. My own clothes from a couple of years before.

I paid seven dollars for what had cost me seven hundred at the Neiman Marcus near my home, plus a couple of practical muumuu-style dresses and headed toward the bus stop.

The wind wafted scents from the Mexican restaurant across the street my direction and my stomach gurgled. I knew it would be wrong, but I wished I'd taken Lupe's mother up on her offer. The steaming tamales and mounds of vegetables had looked delicious and I was hungry. The coffee drink from the 7-11 had been a long time before and I couldn't remember the last time my stomach had felt so empty.

If Martin hadn't gone nuts, this would be just another Friday night at home. We always had steak on Friday, and Martin always tried to get home, no matter where he'd be for the rest of the week. Maria would bake a cake or pie, and I'd make a salad while Martin grilled the meat. But the single dollar I had left wouldn't buy the worst cut of meat in the world.

I found a little shop that sold me four cartons of off-brand Chinese noodle dinners for that last buck.

My second day of being a widow had been rough. But I felt as if I was getting a bit of traction. I'd bought some clothes. I had something to eat. I was completing my hours of community service. I thought Rush Limbaugh would be proud of the way I was pulling myself up by my bootstraps.

Naturally, things took a turn for the worse.

* * * *

The cops were waiting for me when I arrived at my trailer.

A cop in the rumpled suit took the lead with uniformed officers spilling from their SUVs.

They stopped me before I opened my trailer door. "Mrs. Montag?"

"What?" I wanted to soak my feet in cool water. I would have settled for minor torture rather than put up with hours of police questioning.

Detective Rumpled Suit got in my face, his onion-breath nearly knocking me over.

"Mrs. Montag, we have been unable to confirm your alibi for the night of the murder. Unless you have some proof of your claims, I'm afraid we'll have to treat them as suppositions."

Since my alibi was that I'd been by myself in Leah's home, this wasn't a surprise. Unless they'd interviewed the dust mites. "Telling you the truth is the best I can do. I still didn't kill him."

Rumpled Suit pretended I hadn't said anything.

"We spoke to Mr. Montag's attorneys and were able to get a copy of his will. He left the bulk of his assets to your son, Nicholas, but both you and your daughter received considerable sums. And you are the beneficiary of a significant life insurance policy. That constitutes an additional motive."

I wanted to sink into the ground. By concentrating on me, they not only made my life miserable, they wasted the energy they should be using to catch the real killer.

"If I wanted to kill him for his money, I somehow don't think I would have blabbed my intentions to the entire world."

Rumpled Suit glared at me. "We don't advise that kind of flippant response, Mrs. Montag. We'd really like to know more about your movements the night of the murder."

I opened the door to my trailer and discovered the air conditioner must have blown a fuse—oven-hot air rushed out.

So I led the parade of cops over to the picnic table under the live oak trees and flopped down.

"Well, Mrs. Montag," Rumpled Suit demanded.

Barry, my briefly court-appointed lawyer, had warned me I wouldn't be getting any money while the police still considered me a suspect but refused to arrest me, so I wasn't too surprised that Rumpled Suit didn't hand over a check. "I've told you everything."

Rumpled Suit gestured to one of the cops who brought over a large sheet of posterboard. He studied it, careful not to let me catch a glance.

I was tired enough that I didn't really care.

Finally he got tired of waiting for me to ask what he was doing. "Mrs. Montag. We've taken the liberty of creating a timeline for your claimed activities during the night of the murder. I wonder if you would step us through everything that happened from the moment you discovered that Mr. Montag had filed for divorce to your initial interview with us yesterday morning. And this time, I mean *everything*."

"Can I see the timeline?"

He raised an eyebrow. "But it's simply a tool for the police. Surely *you* don't need it, Mrs. Montag. After all, you were there. Or are you stating that there might be some inaccuracies in your earlier claim."

His grin was as fake as his toupee.

"Aren't you supposed to be reading me my rights, giving me a lawyer, that kind of stuff?"

Rumpled suit smiled again and shook his head. "Oh, no. Not at all, Mrs. Montag. We do those for people we arrest, for suspects, if you will. At this time, you're merely a person of interest. A witness. It's your duty as a citizen to help the police in their investigation of this horrible murder. Unless, of course, you are guilty."

More of the lectures at the League came back to me, this time of earnest prosecutors and aspiring politicians explaining how criminals game the legal system, claiming that they'd been denied their rights, using legal loopholes to keep them out of jail and costing society countless tax dollars. Like the other members, I'd been profoundly unsympathetic with the lowlifes who took advantage of the Constitution and with the activist judges who expanded rights for the guilty without apparent care for the victims. We all feared criminals. None of us even considered the possibility of being accused ourselves, let alone falsely accused of murder.

But Barry had opened my eyes a little. Just as I'd been a tourist in a strange world when I visited with Lupe, so I was a visitor in a strange land when I was a suspect rather than a fearful victim of crime. What I would have called proper police behavior back when I'd been sitting in a League meeting felt like intimidation to me now. Certainly I hadn't ever really considered that any innocent person would *really* be put on the criminal side of the debate. The police go after the guilty, right?

When Rumpled Suit got worn out from shouting at me, trying to trip me up in my story, and generally giving me a hard time, another cop, this one a world-weary woman dressed in a khaki suit that wasn't nearly as nice as one I'd seen at the Salvation Army thrift shop, took over, pretending to be sympathetic and suggesting she had just "one more question." Until *she* got tired and Rumpled Suit came back at me.

An hour of tag-team attacks later, they were still going over my story, trying to pick holes in my timeline, jumping backward and forward in time until I started to get confused myself—which was something considering that all I'd done during the eighteen hour period was sit in a holding cell, talk to my lawyer, agree to the community service, do a little shopping, eat cake, and sleep.

I think they might have gone at me all night, but my new landlady, Tina, came to my rescue.

All the male cops stopped looking at me when *she* emerged from her trailer. Her cut-off jeans were so short she could have gotten a job as stunt butt for Daisy Duke, and her tight t-shirt advertised her unbound breasts and a game called Grand Theft Auto—an unfortunate choice for dealing with cops, I thought.

"You guys have harassed Heather for long enough," she announced. "So, why don't you run along?"

"Or what?" my cop stared at her small breasts, then walked over to her until his chest butted up against hers. "Maybe *you'd* better run along and mind your own business."

I think I would have crumpled if a policeman had glared at me like that, let alone the physical intimidation.

Tina just gave him a stone glare. "This is private property."

"You going to call the cops on us?" one of the younger cops demanded. That generated a laugh from the rest of them.

"You think that's funny, do you?" She looked at the row of police SUV's, proudly proclaiming the Frisco Police Department. "From what I hear, Dallas city cops don't think too highly of you suburban cowboys. I wouldn't be surprised if they don't get a kick out of running the lot of you in for trespassing. You'd get sprung, of course, once Frisco found out what had happened. But I've known the DPD to lose prisoners for days."

She wagged a finger in front of the young cop's nose. "And we all know how the inmates treat pretty young boys like you in prison, don't we. Especially if word gets around that you're lily-white suburban cops."

When Rumpled Suit got between her and the kid-cop. "Are you trying to make trouble? We're investigating a murder ere."

"And Heather has given you all the answers she can. So, arrest her or buzz off."

I closed my eyes. Tina might be trying to help, but her efforts seemed more likely to get me put in jail. And she'd probably get arrested as well. If they didn't just beat her up with their sticks.

"Your threats don't scare us," Rumpled Suit declared. "We're on a murder investigation. We have a perfect right to interview our primary witness wherever she may be."

"I thought you suburban cops handed all of the hard-core crime over to the sheriff's department. That you spent your time rescuing cats and catching shoplifters."

"Give us a break, lady."

Charlaine chose that moment to step out of Tina's trailer and hop onto her shoulder and the cops used that as an excuse to go into a huddle.

"Mrs. Montag?" Rumpled Suit glared at me seriously.

I braced myself for the arrest. "Yes?"

"I understand you're doing your community service here in south Dallas. I want you to notify the Frisco Police Department if you intend leave the Dallas area. When we come looking for you, you'd better be here."

That was it? "Okay. I can do that."

"Come on guys, we've got what we were looking for. Who wants to go to Gloria's for some dynamite El Salvador food?"

The cops climbed back into their SUVs and roared off leaving me, Tina, and the chicken alone.

"I thought you were going to get me arrested," I said.

Tina shook her head. "You can't let the cops walk over you, Heather. If they can't finish asking all their questions in an hour, they aren't really trying. And if they were going to arrest you, they would have Mirandized you. You were giving them a voluntary interview and you had the right to terminate it at any time."

Yikes. Benny had told me pretty much the same thing and I'd fallen for it again. "But they are the police."

She raised an eyebrow. "I noticed that. Otherwise I would have been out here a lot sooner."

"I guess I have a hard time with that kind of casual contempt for the law."

Tina actually laughed at me. "Contempt? You're kidding, right? I love the law. What I don't like so much is cops who ignore the law and harass people instead of doing their jobs. I happen to know that the police sometimes stretch the law. It's every citizen's job to make sure *everyone* follows the law, even the police."

That wasn't how I thought about it—it certainly wasn't the kind of attitude that the League looked for in its leaders. Still, Tina's position wasn't irrational, wasn't criminal-friendly the way all those lectures had implied it was. I *knew* the League was right, but I didn't think I'd convince her of that tonight—not after the intimidation I'd gone through. I wasn't even sure I could convince myself.

Tina looked into the little shopping bag I'd dropped on the wooden steps leading up to my trailer when the police had stopped me—an invasion of privacy no NTRWL member do.

"Are you really planning on eating that noodle slop for dinner?"

"It was a bargain. Four for a dollar."

"And eight hundred percent of your daily sodium allowance. If you're going to eat unhealthy, you might as well enjoy it." She pulled Charlaine off her shoulder and put the chicken down on the parking lot.

Could she really be saying what I thought she was? "You aren't going to cook your chicken?"

She gave me a look of absolute horror. "Charlaine? Of course not. She's my baby. Come on. I'll take you to Norma's."

"I really don't want to owe you—"

She reached for me like she was going to tow me there—then realized that would be like a rowboat towing the Queen Mary and turned to wheedling. "They have the best chicken-fried steak in Texas. Plus meringue pies so light they float."

My stomach made more gurgling noises. Those little packages of Chinese noodles certainly didn't sound as appealing as they had in the dollar store. Especially not if I could have the best chicken-fried steak in Texas. "Only if you let me pay you back when I have some money."

"When you get money, it'll be your turn to pay."

She'd persuaded me. I knew being easy to persuade was a part of the reason I hadn't been able to lose those extra pounds, but I'd been working hard all day and figured I deserved some kind of break.

"What about your friend, Angie? Will she want to join us?"

"It's Friday night. She's out hustling."

"She… she panhandles?" I asked, horrified.

Tina laughed. "No, silly. She's a hooker."

A bird could have built a nest in my mouth it hung open so long. "Angie is a prostitute? I've never known a prostitute before."

"She probably wouldn't use exactly those words, but yeah, she goes out on a lot of dates and the guys are always so grateful. She'd say that women who get married to have a guy take care of them are a kind of hooker too—she's just more upfront about it."

I knew what Dorothy must have felt like. I definitely wasn't in Kansas, or Frisco, any more.

* * * *

I was going to have to stop waking up like this.

It was a sugar headache, not an alcohol hangover like I'd had the previous morning, but it still made me want to crawl back into bed and stay there.

I definitely shouldn't have had both the chicken fried steak dinner (a big slice of fried, breaded steak, three vegetables, gravy, rolls and cornbread), plus that huge piece of coconut meringue pie I'd inhaled afterwards. But I hadn't been able to stop myself. Besides, Tina had kept up with me.

I've never been able to understand why it is that two people can eat the same thing and yet one of them ends up a hundred pounds heavier than the other. Sadly, that was the story of my life.

What was also the story of my life, at least over the previous few days, was that people wouldn't leave me alone in the morning. The knock on the door sounded again and it wasn't going away.

I hoped it would be Nick, whom I'd called from the restaurant using Tina's cell. I'd had to whine a bit, but he'd promised he would stop by his bank and lend me a couple of thousand dollars to help tide me over until I had access to my own money again.

He had made a snarky remark about hearing restaurant noises in the background and figuring out loud that at least I wasn't going to be wasting away.

I let him get away with it. I'd never felt as poor as I had over the past few days. Two weeks before, a couple thousand dollars would have been mad money—something I might have spent on a new suit or at Las Vegas Night with the NTRWL. From my new perspective, it sounded like the difference between misery and just a small degree of self-respect.

But it wasn't Nick at my door. It was Lupe.

"I thought I was going to see you on Monday." I invited her in, but she took one look at the trailer and decided she'd stay outside. Tina had found a circuit breaker and got the air conditioner running again, but it still hadn't caught up with the heat.

"I'm not here as your StrongGirl mentor, I'm here because you need help."

How was I supposed to explain to her that, StrongGirl or not, I was the adult and she was the kid? "Are you sure it's okay with your parents that you're so far from home?"

She looked at me as if I'd gone crazy. "Why wouldn't it be? If I could get directions for you to take the bus, I certainly could follow them myself."

That made sense, in a way. Again, though, it pointed out how alien the city way of life was. As youths, Nick and Leah had never just gotten on the bus and ridden off to visit someone. I suspected they hadn't done it as adults, either. I wondered if they even could.

"But why are you here?"

"Because you need me," she repeated. She pulled a thin yellow volume from her backpack and showed it to me.

I recognized the cover from my own young reading days. It was *Nancy Drew* and something or other, one of the ancient editions from the fifties or sixties.

"After you left last night, I did some research," Lupe explained earnestly. "Let me show you where Nancy was able to find who—"

"Lupe, honey. Nancy Drew is fiction."

She put her hands on her hips and glared at me. "Well I know that. But she's very smart. And one thing Nancy never does is wait for someone else to solve her problem. In a lot of ways, she *is* a StrongGirl. Like me."

And unlike me. *That* message came through loud and clear. But I couldn't argue with her. I hadn't been raised to be a StrongGirl and I didn't know how to go about becoming one. I'd laughed off the idea of a little teenage Latina being my mentor, but it obviously wasn't as farfetched as I'd initially imagined.

Then again, she was still a girl. "Have you had breakfast?"

"Uh, I left early."

And there probably hadn't been enough even then. Hunger had definitely not been a part of my world, but I recognized the signs of it. Scrawny little Lupe wasn't starving, but anyone in Frisco schools as thin as she would be sent to talk to a counselor about possible eating disorders.

I didn't have anything interesting in the trailer, but Tina had lent me another five dollars. It was all she'd had left after springing for dinner the previous evening. I got the feeling that supporting me was biting into Tina's reserves, but I couldn't exactly tell Lupe I was going to eat and she would just have to watch.

Besides, when Nick showed up, I'd be able to pay Tina back and my financial problems would be pushed off for a bit. In the meantime, the Chinese noodles didn't look any better for breakfast than they had for dinner the previous evening.

"Come on. There's a deli not far from here. We can get a donut or something."

"That isn't very healthy food. You should be eating more fruits and fewer fats and carbohydrates." Lupe's words were on track, but I sensed a certain lack of resolve behind them.

"How about you fix my diet *after* I'm a full-fledged StrongGirl, huh?" Not that she wasn't right. I needed to eat more healthy food. I also knew my blood sugar had crashed from the pie the previous night and that I needed something to get me going again. Donuts and strong coffee should do the job perfectly.

"Well, all right. Just this once."

StrongGirl or not, I suspected Lupe preferred donuts to fruit. I didn't blame her—I felt the same way.

"Give me half an hour to get ready," I told her. "You can come in and watch TV if you want." I assumed the TV worked.

"It's okay. I'll sit out here and re-read the Nancy Drew book. I read it back when I was in fourth grade, but I wasn't doing research then. There's a lot that Nancy does that's really smart and gives me great ideas to work on your case. I've always wanted to be a detective like Nancy, but most of the crime we have around here is stupid."

"I think just about any crime is stupid."

She rolled her eyes. "That's not what I meant. I meant, it's like, who poked the holes in my cousin's Miata top? You just ask around and someone will tell you."

From what I'd seen from Detective Rumpled Suit, that seemed to be the way the police investigated murder, as well. Except they'd decided that I was the person with the answers they needed—and they weren't willing to accept the answers I could give them.

"Do you want to be a police officer when you grow up?"

She shrugged. "Maybe a forensic pathologist."

I only knew what she was talking about because Leah had gotten me hooked on CSI. "That sounds like a good plan. You'll have to study hard and get good grades, though."

"Yeah, sure. Is there any way you could hurry so we could get the donuts? I'm sort of hungry."

Put in my place, I headed for the bathroom and my wrestling match with the shower.

I'd asked at the Salvation Army Thrift Store and been assured that they washed their clothes after they'd been donated. Still, even knowing that the outfits had once been mine, I had a hard time with the idea that other people had touched them, maybe even worn them.

I swear it hardly took me any time at all to shower, dispense with shaving once again, put on the bare minimum of makeup, and then gritted my teeth to put on my used clothes.

* * * *

"Hey, you. Leave that chicken alone." It was Tina's voice.

"I was just—"

"I know what you were *just* doing. Did someone pay you to catch it? Or were you planning on eating it?"

I opened my door in time to see Lupe duck behind a bush. Sure enough, she had a chicken, not Charlaine, in her arms.

"Nobody seemed to own it. Chickens are for eating, you know."

"Not these chickens. These are rescued chickens. Now let her go."

Lupe reluctantly obeyed. Once I was sure they weren't going to hurt each other, I cleared my throat loudly. "Anyone want to bring me up to date on what's going on here?"

"Everyone knows there are wild chickens here near the river," Lupe jumped in with an answer before Tina could say anything. "If you can catch one, you can eat it. That's the deal. I caught one."

"They aren't wild, they're liberated." Tina's explanation made even less sense than Lupe's.

Still, she was the landlord. "Okay, so no chicken-catching in the trailer park. Got that, Lupe?"

Lupe nodded glumly.

"You know her?" Tina demanded. "I caught her hanging around outside

your trailer. She won't tell me what she's doing here."

"Lupe is my mentor," I explained.

Expressions chased themselves across Tina's face until she caught one that satisfied her and put on a look of pensive approval. "The StrongGirls program, right?"

"You know about StrongGirls?" Lupe asked.

"My ex-husband contributes money to it. And he paid me to write a little computer game to give them some publicity and communicate the message."

Lupe's eyes widened. "*You* wrote *StrongGirl Roundup*?"

Tina took a step backwards. "Hey, it might not be the best game out there, but I didn't exactly have the hundred developer teams Electronic Arts has either."

"But it's a wonderful game. Two of my friends wouldn't even talk to me about StrongGirls until they played it. Then, all of a sudden it was like, hey, this is so cool. I mean, most games are shoot-shoot-kill-kill. Boring, right? But *StrongGirl Roundup* lets you, you know, relate. My friends are going to just piss in their pants when they hear I met the person who wrote it and that she's a StrongGirl too." Lupe paused. "You are a StrongGirl, aren't you?"

"She chased off a bunch of policemen last night," I said. "That seems pretty strong to me."

Lupe nodded. "Okay. I guess that makes you a StrongGirl."

Tina had grinned like a chimpanzee when Lupe had complemented her computer game. Now, though, her expression got serious. "Even fellow StrongGirls don't get to steal my chickens."

"Okay. Hey, we're going to get donuts," Lupe gave a reluctant look at the bush where the chicken had headed after she'd let it go. But her words were said so seriously she could have been talking about going to confession. "If you want to, you can come too."

Nobody had to twist Tina's arm and the three of us set off.

We walked.

The strange sense of having slipped into an alternate universe returned. In the suburbs, nobody would even consider *walking* out for coffee and donuts. For one thing, our zoning rules meant that restaurants and bistros were kept quarantined in their own districts. For another, shopping was about getting in cars and driving to huge malls, not finding little mom-and-pop delis on the side of the road. Being in an older, established, city was like going back to the 1950s or something. I halfway expected to see James Dean roar by on his motorcycle.

"Heather is in trouble with the police," Lupe told Tina as we headed down Fort Worth Avenue toward the deli. "Since I'm her mentor, I decided I had to help her."

"That's why I had to chase them off last night. They were giving her a hard time."

"Oh." Lupe glared at me. "You didn't tell me the police were looking for *you*."

I hadn't told Leah or Nick, either, I realized. "I'm not exactly proud of it."

Tina grabbed my arm to keep me from stepping out into the street in front of a huge truck. "You're ashamed of the cops hassling you? What's that about? I thought you were innocent."

"It has nothing to do with innocence or guilt. If the police suspect you, you're tainted. I'd just as soon everyone not know exactly how much they suspect me."

"That doesn't seem right," Lupe said.

The truck kicked gravel and dust into the air and I was coughing and wheezing as we finally crossed into the gas bays in front of the deli.

I couldn't argue with Lupe. Police suspicion probably shouldn't translate into social stigma. It went against the whole innocent-until-proven-guilty thing. But I knew my friends. In *their* eyes, being suspected was nearly as bad as being convicted. O.J. Simpson had convinced them that a sharp lawyer could get an acquittal for even the most guilty. Even if someone else eventually confessed to Martin's murder, there would be plenty in the League who remembered that I wasn't above suspicion. If word got out, I might even be asked to resign from the membership.

The really horrible thing was, I would have been first on the blackball list if it had happened to anyone else. At least, I would have until I'd experienced the suspicions myself.

* * * *

Even early in the morning, the deli smelled of fried chicken, hot dogs, and stale sweat.

The strong scent of freshly brewed coffee overlaid all of that, though, and my stomach gurgled.

I thought about remonstrating with Lupe when she filled three oversized Styrofoam cups with coffee, carefully adding shots of amoretto flavoring and cream. But it looked good.

I assuaged my conscience a little by stopping her when she started pouring sugar into my cup. I might have a donut, but I didn't need the bonus calories of sugar in my coffee.

"Since the cops think Heather killed her husband, they won't be looking much for other people," Lupe told Tina. "It's up to us to help her out. So I've been researching what to do. Nancy Drew always drives around and talks to people." Lupe held out the yellow library book as evidence in support of her proposition. "There's always someone who saw something. We'll just have to do the same thing."

Tina looked interested and I decided to head this off before it got silly.

"People talk to Nancy Drew because otherwise Carolyn Keene wouldn't have anything to write about. We don't have an author to make sure things come out just right, so why would they talk to us?"

"Well, it doesn't matter anyway," Lupe concluded. She continued to look downhearted even as she bit into and chewed an enormous apple fritter. "Frisco is so far out, it isn't even on the DART route map. My parents don't like it when I hitchhike."

I was glad to hear that her parents had *some* restrictions. I'd heard enough League lectures to be concerned about urban kids running around wild, with no parental supervision at all. Although Lupe seemed like a good kid, and although the StrongGirls program gave her life some structure, it still seemed to me that she was off doing things no middle school student should do.

It sounded like Lupe's idea of heading north and investigating would die in the bud.

Not to be.

Tina blew on her coffee, looked longingly at a chocolate éclair in the pastry shelf and then decided on a plain glazed donut. "I could drive."

"Really?" Lupe's smile lit her face. "That would be great. We'd be able to go everywhere if we didn't have to wait for buses all the time."

I'd already finished one donut and had taken a bite out of a second and we hadn't even paid for them yet. But this conversation was going completely the wrong direction.

"Look you guys, I know you want to help, but we can't do this. If I go snooping around, people are going to want to know why. And when they find out that I'm a suspect, they aren't going to talk with me anyway. I know these people. They're going to back the police no matter what I tell them."

Also, by bringing myself to their attention in that way, I would guarantee that they'd never forget that I had been a suspect. Not only wouldn't they talk to me about the case, they would probably never talk to me again about anything else.

The *only* solution was to hope that the police discovered the real killer—and did it before it leaked out that they'd even considered me a suspect.

The five dollars I'd borrowed from Tina didn't quite cover the donuts and coffee so we all had to dig in our pockets for change. I was imagining getting hauled off by the Dallas Police for shoplifting when I finally spotted a quarter on the ground where it had been halfway kicked under the huge case holding scratch-off lottery tickets. That quarter, a dime and four pennies Lupe dug from her purse, and a dollar coin and a couple of quarters from Tina pushed us up to the amount we needed.

I borrowed Tina's cell again as we walked back out into the heat—already baking at some ridiculously early time in the morning—partly because I wanted to check with Nick and see if he was on his way with the money he'd promised me, and partly because it was the first thing I thought of to head off this crazy discussion about heading up to Frisco and bearding people in their homes.

"Hello?"

"Nick? It's your mother."

His silence went on too long.

My donuts threatened to revisit me and I swallowed hard. "I was hoping you could come by this morning with the money you promised you'd lend me. Frankly, I'm a little strapped, and I don't have a car so I can't come up to Frisco to get it myself."

"We could—"

I shushed Lupe. I wasn't going to let them use this as another excuse to go up north and start digging around.

"I'm really sorry, Mother. I—"

"Oh, don't worry that you didn't make it first thing this morning. I know you're busy. If you could get here before lunch, though, that would be a big help."

Another long pause. Could my son really be planning on going back on his promise?

Nick sighed loudly enough I was sure he intended that I hear him. "That's just it, Mother. The police came by last night."

"Really?" I mean, what else was I supposed to say.

"They said that you're their primary suspect in Dad's murder."

I knew they thought that, but I couldn't believe they'd tell my son.

"Believe me, I didn't kill Martin."

"Well, of course you didn't. But remember that Laci Peterson case? How Scott Peterson tried to get his family to give him money so he could get away. The whole family looked implicated. I wouldn't want—"

I rubbed my forehead with my free hand. "I'm not trying to get away, Nick. I'm trying to get by. Heather lent me her rental trailer so that helps, but I don't even have money for food or bus fare."

"It wouldn't hurt you to miss a few meals. As for bus fare?" He laughed as if I'd told him some sort of joke. "Don't worry about that, I can get you a monthly pass. At least the Dallas bus system won't let you roam too far."

"As it turns out, I'd appreciate a monthly pass. I could use it to get to my community service. But I need more money than that, though. Despite what you think, I do need to eat. Then there's—"

"I'll put the bus pass in the mail then. As for the rest, you've always preached self-reliance. Why not try some of that?"

Chapter 6

"At least you have a place to stay," Lupe consoled me when we got back to the trailer park and huddled under the shade trees at the picnic table.

I took a sip of coffee and finished my third donut. "As Nick pointed out before he hung up on me, I'm not exactly going to waste away and starve any time soon."

I had no idea why my son was all over me about my weight now, when he hadn't commented in the twenty-eight years since he'd been born. Maybe the police had told him *he* was heir to the Montag fortune and he felt he could get away with things he wouldn't have tried while his father was still alive. Maybe my weight had bothered him all those years and he was just now letting it out.

"You'll need a job," Lupe decided.

"I think your young friend is right," Tina said. "Do you have any useful skills?"

"I used to be a pretty good typist. Do you know anyone who needs a secretary?"

Tina shook her head. "They're called admins these days, and everyone pretty much does their own typing."

I knew that. I just hadn't put it together with my own problems.

"Maybe you could be a cook," Lupe suggested. "Everyone needs to eat and wherever you worked would feed you."

My red velvet cake might be famous in Frisco, but I didn't have the experience or background to get a cordon bleu chef job anywhere.

"I was thinking more like McDonalds," Lupe said when I told her that. "Except you'd have to know Spanish so you could talk to the other people who worked there. Around here, pretty much everyone has to be bilingual."

I could hardly believe my life had come down to looking for a minimum wage job, but Leah echoed her brother's refusal when I hit her up for a loan and even had the nerve to ask me if I'd be able to start paying her rent for her trailer soon. I heard her boyfriend giggling in the background and egging her on, so I guessed he saw this as turnaround time for whenever I'd been less than perfectly polite to him.

I was sure Rush Limbaugh would have an answer for what to do next, but he hadn't called it in and I didn't have a clue.

"At least, since I've got to start looking for a job, we won't have any more silly nonsense about heading up north to Frisco and making like Nancy Drew." I tried to keep my voice upbeat.

Tina shook her head. "Not so fast. Don't you think it's a little odd that your own son won't lend you a few bucks? I mean, I lent you money and we're not even related."

"He said that the police—"

"Right. I'm so sure the police said 'Oh, no. Please don't give your mother even a couple hundred dollars so she could go grocery shopping.' They don't work like that. He was using the cops as an excuse not to help you."

"He said he'd give me a monthly DART pass." My words sounded unconvincing even to me.

"Last of the big spenders, isn't he? What I'm wondering is, maybe he doesn't *want* you to have too much freedom. Maybe he's happy with the police closing in on *you* for the deed. Maybe the reason he likes you as the police suspect is that *he* killed Martin himself."

"I don't think I've ever read that kind of plot in a Nancy Drew book," Lupe observed. "But on TV, it happens all the time. If you watch the Oxygen Network—"

My breath caught in my throat. This was Nick we were talking about, my darling son and first-born child. I'd carried him for nine months, raised him through all of the crises of school and broken hearts. Could they really think—

"Come on, you guys. I know Nick. He loved his father. There's no way he would ever do anything to hurt—"

"Someone killed your husband," Lupe growled. "And everyone knows murder usually stays in the family."

"The butler only does it in old English TV shows," Tina agreed.

"Well Nick didn't kill anybody and I didn't either."

"If that's true, it's probably the other woman," Lupe said.

Tina looked thoughtful. "If I was dating Martin on the side, I wouldn't kill him until he married me."

"No wonder your marriage didn't last."

Tina looked at me. "You have no idea."

That's when Lupe and Tina got into a debate about whether we should investigate or start me out job-hunting. Ignoring my opinion, they finally agreed that my lack of money shouldn't impact our next step—a trip up to Frisco.

* * * *

Tina took Oak Lawn Avenue up to Preston Road and stayed on the surface streets all the way to Frisco.

Avoiding the freeways let me see something I'd never noticed before. There was an invisible boundary line somewhere north of downtown Dallas.

Below that line, homes mixed with businesses and pedestrians strolled around, many with parasols to keep the brutal summer sun from their faces. Houses came in wild colors and oak, hackberry, and even a few ancient elm trees were large enough to prove they'd been in place for generations. Children played in the streets, ice cream vendors pedaled through in bicycle-based carts, and human sounds filled the air.

On the north side of that line, houses stayed in designated residential areas, lawns were green but maintained by chemicals and professional lawn services and the trees increasingly newly planted rather than old-growth. Other than the lawn care professionals, the only people I saw north of the line were driving in their cars—many with televisions blasting to further abstract them from the reality around them. Pedestrians seemed extinct.

Any children in these northern neighborhoods remained well hidden behind closed doors.

I felt like I'd come home.

"Where are all the people?" Lupe asked.

We'd phoned her mother for permission, of course, before loading Lupe up in the tiny back seat of Tina's Storm. Still, I thought how brave she was being to head into the unknown with us. I'd thought myself horribly brave to ride the train down to Leah's trailer, but I was an adult. Lupe was just a kid.

"They don't like to come out where there's no air conditioning," Tina explained.

Which was part of it. But the other part was fear. I'd never really seen it that way before, but a couple of days in south Dallas had given me a new perspective. Homes out here might be castles, but they were castles where the lords and ladies of the manor barricaded themselves behind elaborate security systems and eight-food privacy fences against a frightening world.

"How are we going to talk to people?" Lupe continued. "I mean, if they're all locked up in—"

"You're right. That's what I've been trying to tell you," I jumped in. "We're just wasting time."

Tina ignored me, kept driving, and eventually turned into the parking lot for Montag Industries.

The parking lot was surprisingly full for a Saturday and we had to park well away from the four-story glass building where Martin had worked. I guessed that the boss's death had motivated a lot of people to put in some extra hours —both to impress whomever would take over and out of morbid interest.

"Always start where the crime took place." Lupe's voice held approval. "That's what Nancy says, anyway."

I let the two of them bulldoze me along even though I outweighed both of them put together and should have been able to push back. I figured they'd learn better in a couple of minutes when security turned them away. Sure enough, Joe Moses, the man who'd guarded the door ever since Martin had moved here from the tiny office suite where he'd started the company, met us at the door.

"Hi, Mrs. Montag. I'm sorry, but I can't let you in."

"He was her husband," Tina said. "I think she has a right to see where he died."

"Yeah? So who the heck are you and why should I care?"

Joe was a decent guy but he looked scary. He had to weigh close to three hundred pounds, had ebony-dark skin and wore these black sunglasses and a black do rag that made him look more like a gangster than a security guard.

"I'm a friend of Heather Montag. She's asked me to help look into Martin's death. Do you have a problem with that?" If Tina weighed in at a hundred and ten pounds, it would be because she'd stuffed her pockets with quarters. But she didn't let Joe intimidate her.

"The police have been through there. If there was any evidence, it's gone now."

"Is the crime scene still quarantined?" Lupe asked.

Although his eyes were covered by the wrap-around shades, I still saw the crows' feet of his squint. "Who the heck is this, a midget? You babysitting for your cleaning lady's kids, Mrs. Montag?"

Lupe's face fell and a surge of shame shot through me. Had I ever asked that kind of question?

"Lupe happens to be a StrongGirl," I told him.

The wrinkles in the back of his skull shifted as he looked down at her. "A StrongGirl, huh? No kidding? I've been thinking about signing my daughters up for that. I mean, we move all the way out to the suburbs and there's still pressure to do drugs, have party sex, the whole bad influence thing. Can't get away from problems."

"StrongGirls is an excellent program to help young women deal with those issues." Lupe might be parroting the official line, but she clearly believed what she was selling.

Joe nodded slowly. "That's what my girls need all right." He looked at me, glared at Tina, then looked back at me. "Gary French told me not to let you in. Said you'd caused trouble last time you were here and he had to call the police. You know Gary is my boss. I can't go against him."

Although I'd resisted coming, now that we were here, turning tail and running seemed wrong. "I was just trying to find out what Martin thought he was up to. Things got a little out of hand that day. You know I'm not a violent sort of person."

"I wasn't there and I don't know anything. Like I said, I have my orders and I can't violate them. So, here's the deal. You guys aren't allowed in here. Get out of here and stay out."

"But?" Tina asked.

"There's no buts here. I'm going to be taking a coffee break now and I definitely don't want to hear that you guys snuck in while my back was turned. You're not allowed in the building and certainly not in the conference room behind Mr. Montag's office where he got shot."

I realized I hadn't even known where the murder took place.

Joe followed that cryptic proclamation by heading for the men's room.

"I think he meant for us to sneak in now." Lupe's voice was practically a whisper. "This is so exactly the kind of thing that would happen to Nancy Drew."

The elevator had a security pad to get to the top floor but Martin's code still worked. The door whooshed shut before Joe returned from his break and we were on our way.

Phones were ringing on the executive floor and I heard a couple of loud but muffled male voices playing some sort of dominance game behind closed doors. Fortunately, nobody was in the hall.

I don't think I would have fooled anyone in my out-of-style dress and comfortable shoes, but I pretended like I belonged there and strode down the hall to Martin's corner office suite in as good an imitation as I could of the person I'd been only a few days earlier.

I choked up when I saw Martin's name still on the door. *Martin Montag, CEO*. He'd been a good boss, built a company from nothing through hard work and a bit of seed money from my parents. He'd been a good father. Until lately, I would have said he'd been a good husband as well.

Oddly, his name had been scratched at with something sharp. I didn't think it was the cleaning crew trying to ready the office for someone else. To me, it looked petty—and personal.

"Can't wait to find out who takes over next, can they?" Tina asked.

Was I the only person in the world who mourned Martin? Sometimes it seemed that way.

"I'm sure a lot of the managers and the old timers are sad about Martin dying. Realistically, though, it's a big company. All of the executives will be more worried about whether Martin's death gives them a chance to move up or if one of their enemies will get the top job and force them out."

Just as with the League, fortunes could change quickly with a shift at the top.

"It would be tough to be unemployed after having an office like this." Lupe's eyes were huge as I used my key to open the door to Martin's office and the three of us stepped in.

"It isn't as bad as it sounds," I explained. "Once you're an executive, the old-boy club takes care of you. They won't have to worry about money, but if they lose their jobs, they lose power. In their world, power is what matters."

"I'd rather have the money."

"Yeah." Tina closed the door behind us. "Power is overrated."

I made sure the door was all the way closed before turning on the overhead light. The plush carpeting would keep any light from leaking out into the hall and giving us away.

This first part of Martin's office was where his admin, Betty, worked.

Unlike the executives, she wasn't working today. Betty probably had better things to spend her weekend on than worrying about which of the mostly-male egos would take over as her boss. Who knew, maybe she even missed him.

"I'm going to check out the conference room," I said. "Lupe, I'm not sure —"

"I'm going. So don't try to stop me."

"Let me at least look in first and make sure the police cleaned things up."

"I've seen enough blood. I'll check out your husband's office," Tina volunteered.

I nodded. I should have been concerned about corporate security and all that stuff, but I was too numb with the realization I was about to walk into the place where Martin had breathed his last, where someone had killed the man I'd spent my adult life loving, and, if I'd understood the questions the cops had been asking me, done it with my own gun.

I put my hand on the conference room door but found myself unable to take the next step. Almost as if Martin would still be alive somewhere as long as

I didn't open the door.

"Are you afraid?"

"Yeah, Lupe. I guess I am."

But Martin wasn't Schrödinger's cat. The only thing opening that door would kill was my irrational ability to ignore the fact that I'd lost my husband of thirty years.

Considering that the marriage had been as good as over even before Martin had been murdered, I needed to move beyond my fears.

I pushed the door open.

* * * *

The police had come and gone.

Thankfully they'd taken Martin's body with them—I definitely would have lost it if we'd walked in on his corpse.

They'd also cut out and carted off a substantial section of one of the walls and a strip of the rug.

From the angle of the blood spray, I figured the missing chunk of wall was where the bullet had gone. Considering the blood they'd left, I didn't want to think about what had been on the strip of rug they had taken.

No gun remained on the floor to accuse me of murder. Assuming that it really was *my* gun they'd found here and the police weren't just trying to panic me, they'd taken it with them as well.

"Gross."

"You were supposed to wait outside until I gave you the all-clear," I reminded Lupe.

"I must have forgot. Sorry."

I let her polite lie pass.

"He was sitting here." Lupe pointed to the head of the table where a chair was missing. The chair Martin had been sitting in.

"It looks like that."

"So, whoever shot him had to be here." She pointed to the closest chair—one just to the left of where Martin must have been seated.

"Generally people sit across these conference tables, not side-by-side."

She shook her head firmly. "Not this time. Look at the angle of the blood spatter."

Blood spatter? Lupe must have been watching crime shows in addition to reading Nancy Drew.

I heard Tina clicking on Martin's computer when I went back out into Betty's office and found a yardstick.

Back in the conference room, I aiming the yardstick like a rifle, lining it up from where Martin must have been sitting to the hole in the wall. Extending that line back to where the shooter must have been led exactly where Lupe had said it would. To the chair next to Martin's.

Picking the center of the missing wall bit, and assuming Martin had been sitting up straight, I got a slight upward trajectory on the bullet. Which might mean the shooter was shorter than he was. It might not mean anything, though, as the impact with the skull could change the bullet's angle. Still, it was all we had to go on, and all the cops had to go on too. Another reason they were looking to me. I might weigh as much as Martin had, but I was definitely shorter than he'd been.

"If I were sitting at a table with one of my sisters or a friend, she'd sit next to me, not across from me," Lupe observed pensively. "Maybe your husband was sitting with your so—, uh, a friend."

She and Tina hadn't given up on Nick being the killer.

"Or a girlfriend," I said.

"Maybe. But Tina says a girlfriend would want to keep him alive until she can marry him."

I'd been thinking about that. "Could be. But what if he had more than one girlfriend? If he was divorcing me to marry someone else, he would have had to let the losers know they'd dropped out of the running. One of them might have gotten mad, figured she didn't have anything to lose."

Lupe wrinkled her nose. "There was this guy I hung out with last year. After a while, though, he started hanging with another girl and it hurt my feelings cause he didn't even talk to me about it. But I didn't even think about killing him."

Hanging out and thinking you were in line to be the next wife were two different things. If getting dumped was enough of a motive to make the cops suspect me, it seemed enough of a motive for me to suspect another girlfriend. Who was I to argue with police logic?

"The only problem is, how would a girlfriend have gotten *your* gun? I'll bet Nick has a copy of your car keys, right?"

He didn't. But he knew I used my birthdate as my password for just about everything. He could have guessed the key-code to get into my car.

"If it was a girlfriend," I said, "Maybe she knew how to break into a car. I hear you can do it with just a coat hanger."

Lupe looked disgusted but she didn't argue. I could tell though, that she still hadn't given up on Nick as the killer.

After a couple of awkward moments of silence, she shook her head in a manner that proclaimed I wasn't a StrongGirl yet. Then she got down on her hands and knees and inspected the pattern of blood spatter on the floor.

On the exit wound side of Martin's chair, blood soaked thickly into expensive Persian rug I'd bought for this room. On the entry side, I couldn't see anything. Considering I wasn't wearing my reading glasses and the rich colors of the rug, that didn't necessarily mean a lot.

Lupe's young eyes, though, were better than mine. "Nick, uh, if it was Nick. Or the girlfriend. Anyway, whoever it was, he would have been covered with blood."

"Wouldn't the bullet push the blood the other way?"

"Not really. It's more like a splash. Throw a rock in a stream and water comes back at you. You get wet."

I would have used a swimming pool as the example but I understood

Lupe's point. "So somebody has a bloody outfit now. Maybe blood in his—*her* car, too."

"Could be. But he got the gun from your car first. That means forethought. Maybe he laid plastic across his car seat to be sure not to get blood on it."

When Lupe had first told me she was my mentor, I'd barely suppressed a laugh. Although I hated my vestiges of prejudice, I'd assumed I would be the leader and she would be the follower both because I was the adult and because I was Anglo while she was Chicana. Instead, she'd been right. She was being a mentor to me—she and Nancy Drew.

Still, I wasn't going to roll over to her belief that Nick had been the killer. There was no way Nick had killed his father. Despite the inheritance angle, that had to be impossible. The dumped girlfriend seemed a much more likely possibility.

I explained Sherlock Holmes's line to Lupe about eliminating the impossible and ending up with the truth, however unlikely, and how that meant it was the girlfriend.

"That's stupid. Nobody is *impossible*. This Shurlip Homes character doesn't sound nearly as smart as Nancy Drew."

It shocked me she didn't know who I was talking about. But we didn't get a chance for a literary discussion because Gary French burst into the conference room trailing several of his guards including a very angry-looking Joe Moses.

"What is the meaning of this, Mrs. Montag?" the security director sputtered. "This building is private property. Mr. Moses tells me he specifically ordered you out, so I know that you were aware that you aren't welcome."

I'd known Gary in the days Nick would drag him home for school breaks. If you've done someone's laundry, it's hard for them to intimidate you.

"If you think you or anyone else was going to keep me from seeing where my dear husband was murdered, you have another think coming."

"But...but he was divorcing you."

I thought my laugh sounded convincing. "Divorcing me? He would have changed his mind. There's never been anyone for Martin but me." I was laying it on a bit thick, but Gary couldn't know that.

"Hey boss. Look what I found." One of Gary's beefy security guards dragged Tina into the conference room, her arm twisted behind her back in what had to be a painful hold.

"Would you care to explain this?" Gary demanded.

"There's nothing to explain. This was my husband's company. My friends and I have a perfect right to be here."

I put all the conviction I could manage into my voice. If Gary didn't know about the will yet, he wasn't going to learn it from me.

"Want me to throw them the hell off the property?" Joe Moses demanded.

Gary looked at Joe like the man had just pulled his fat off the frying pan. "Yeah, do that. And Joe, I'm not especially happy with you going off on a break and letting these three females past you."

Joe simply stared at Gary, his black sunglasses looking like alien eyes.

"I guess you're entitled to a break sometimes." Gary wilted under the stare, his voice trailing off into a giggle. Joe might work for Gary in the corporate organization chart, but clearly all his weightlifting and college football experience didn't make Gary tough enough to confront Joe.

"Consider them gone, then." Joe abstracted Tina from the guard who was twisting her arm and turned his gaze at me. "Mrs. Montag, we can do this the easy way or we can do it the hard way. I'd prefer the hard way, but that's up to you."

"We'll come without a fight," I squeaked. I didn't think Joe would hurt us, but he was awfully convincing.

"Up to you," he repeated.

Joe held Tina's arm behind her back, but that painful look she'd had when the other guard had been twisting it went away. In fact, she winked at me.

"If I see you again, Mrs. Montag, I'm going to have the police come down on you like a ton of bricks." Gary was imitating Joe, trying to be Mr. Tough Guy. But he lost the effect partly because he wasn't Joe and partly because had to shout the words. Joe was already hustling the three of us down the hall.

"I told you to stay out of here and I meant it." We'd gotten onto the elevator and Joe was talking not to us but to the corner of the elevator.

"Microphone?" Tina mouthed the question, gesturing toward where Joe was talking.

Joe nodded.

Tina grinned. "Ouch. Can't you let me go now? It's not as if I can get away from you on an elevator, anyway?"

Since Joe had dropped his grip on Tina's arm the instant the door had closed, this had to be a big act.

"Keep talking doll-face. You're not Mr. Montag's wife. Nobody is going to care if I hurt *you*."

"But—"

Joe slammed his right fist into his open left hand. The collision made the sort of noise boxers make when they hit each other.

Lupe let out an involuntary squeal of fright and I almost wet myself even though I knew this was just an act. Gary and most of his guards played at tough. Joe really *was* tough.

"Sorry," Tina whimpered. Of the three of us, she was the only one who instantly figured out what was going on and how to play along. Of course, Lupe's squeal probably helped convince anyone listening better than anything.

"Just shut up."

Joe was playing a game, but he wasn't smiling.

A chill went through me when I realized what that meant. The security guard was ignoring his boss's rules because he wanted to. At the moment, he was only playing at hurting us. I suspected he would take his actions from game to reality for a nickel.

When I looked into the alien darkness of Joe's shades, I suspected that if Joe ever had a reason to kill someone, that someone was as good as dead.

Could he have had a reason to kill Martin? He might harbor anger at Martin for hiring Nick's friend Gary as Corporate Security Director. Other than being Nick's college frat brother, Gary had no real qualifications for the job. Maybe it should have gone to Joe. Maybe it *would* have gone to Joe except for the subtle racism that pervades the south no matter how far we think we've gone to put it behind us.

As a motive for murder, frustration over not getting a job didn't seem like much. But Joe didn't look like the kind of guy who needed a lot of motive.

The elevator walls seemed to close down on me.

Chapter 7

"I thought he was nice," Lupe said as we pulled out of the Montag Industries parking lot.

"I think he's scary," I confessed. "He never takes off his sunglasses. Even in the middle of the night, he's wandering around looking like one a Men In Black. And that do-rag makes him look like something from a gangster movie."

"He let us sneak in and he got us away from Gary," Lupe said.

Both Lupe and Tina laughed when I admitted my suspicion.

"Why would he have let us in then?" Lupe asked. "And why would he let us get away?"

"Why not? He didn't want to raise any suspicions."

"Are you sure you aren't reacting to his skin color?" was Tina's take.

I'm a baby-boomer. Which means I'm part of the generation that saw segregation finally outlawed. But it also means I grew up with prejudices and fear in a way that many younger people have never experienced. There'd still been *whites only* drinking fountains and restrooms when I'd been a kid.

I considered Tina's words, considered whether I would have felt the same if Joe had been white. I couldn't decide. In the south, color wasn't just something you could take away—it was a basic part of who Joe was, at least for me.

"You might be right," I admitted. "I just don't think we can afford to write him off the list."

"Speaking of the list," Tina said, "I have a couple of new prospects for you."

"What sort of prospects?" We were well outside of the Montag Industries property now, but I still lowered my voice as if fearing to be overheard. Or maybe I just feared her answer.

When I got that answer, I feared it even more. In fact, my heart sort of seized up for a moment and I saw big black spots.

"Girlfriend prospects," she told me.

It turned out she'd penetrated Martin's e-mail account. And found that Martin had long and intimate correspondences with *three* separate women: his admin, Betty; Kayla Switzer, my replacement at NTRWL; and a Caitlin Leitmol.

I made Tina repeat Caitlin's name a couple of times before it connected. Like seeing a tennis pro at the grocery store out of uniform, she just didn't fit. Caitlin wasn't a friend of Martin's. She was a friend of Leah's from college, barely older than I'd been when Martin and I had gotten married.

The idea of Martin sharing a bed with someone so young and perky churned my stomach.

"I could see Caitlin doing it," I concluded. She was a shallow thing, always comparing herself to other girls, wanting to have the best phone, the best car. "He might have slept with her but there's no way Martin could marry someone a year behind his daughter in college. He'd be a laughing-stock every time he walked into a business meeting with bimbo arm-candy as a wife. As long as he

64

was married to me, he could play her. But when he settled on one of the others, Caitlin killed him. Plus, she could have gotten my car keys from Leah. Which would explain how she got the gun."

"I saw his picture in his office and Martin wasn't *that* old," Lupe said. "A lot of girls go for an older guy with money and nice stuff. One girl in my school is dating a guy in his twenties."

"Hate to say it, but Lupe's right," Tina said. "I've seen plenty of older guys dragging young things around with them. The only grief they got for it was when other guys wanted to know if they got volume discounts on Viagra. Which was more jealousy than anything else. Guys are like that."

Maybe guys were like that. I'd never imagined needing any man other than Martin—nor of not having him available. His betrayal seemed to grow larger with every passing hour. I should be able to mourn him, but everything I learned had me resenting him instead. Still, someone like Kayla would have been a much better choice for Martin. Kayla would be able to play hostess, help him with his business, reinforce his political connections. I wasn't sure Caitlin was even a Republican.

"Let's go and see her."

I should have realized Tina and Lupe wouldn't just go along with my suggestions. First they had to talk things over. Then Tina insisted that we get something to eat. As the only one of us with a working credit card, she charged up the fast food meal. It took almost an hour and a half before we pulled into the Turtle Creek condo where Caitlin lived.

"Nice." Tina ran a finger along the tapestry-covered chairs in the lounge area where we waited while the security guard called Caitlin. "A couple of my ex-husband's junior executives live here. Can't even get an efficiency in this place for less than a couple thousand a month. What's this Caitlin do, anyway?"

I tried to remember what Leah had said the last time she'd mentioned her friend. "I think she does fundraising for a literacy program."

"Non-profit fundraising isn't exactly known for its high pay. I wonder how she affords this, and how she'll be able to afford it without a sugar daddy."

Apparently Caitlin was wondering the same thing. The first thing we noticed when we finally got buzzed through security was the stack of cardboard boxes near her front door.

"Mrs. Montag? What are *you* doing here?"

Caitlin was pretty in a Goth sort of way. Her hair was jet-black, but I suspected its natural color was a medium brown. Her skin didn't look like it had ever been touched by the sun and the emerald-green of her eyes just had to be cosmetic lenses. Her breasts were cosmetic, too-big cone-shaped things sticking out of an anorexic body. Had Martin paid for those, like he'd paid for everything else?

"I thought I'd talk to you about the funeral." I put on my League face, all kind and sweet. "Since you were special to Martin, I wondered if you'd like to say something."

"I'm sorry. I have no idea—"

I forced myself to laugh. "Surely you didn't think Martin and I kept secrets. I wasn't able to satisfy his sexual needs, so he looked elsewhere. But we talked."

Caitlin looked at Tina and Lupe, who stared back at her. "Can we talk alone, Mrs. Montag?"

"We'll wait outside." Tina grabbed Lupe and headed for the door. "Just call if you need us."

We waited in silence until the door snicked shut.

Caitlin stared at me for a moment, her chin trembling, although I couldn't tell whether rage, fear, or some other emotion drove her.

"Martin thought highly of you." I finally broke the silence.

"But he always said—"

"What? That he was going to marry you some day?"

She nodded glumly. "My friends warned me I was nothing but his mistress, his sex-toy. He was always nice to me, though. Gentle. And he was so grateful for anything I would do for him."

"I haven't actually seen the will yet, but I understand there's nothing for you there. Nick gets almost everything."

She blinked. "Oh. I hoped—"

Caitlin sounded too ditzy and disorganized to be a cold-blooded murderer. I tried to remember Caitlin's major. Had she been in theater? Could this be a compelling act?

"By the way, I was wondering if I could pick up the spare set of keys you borrowed from Leah?"

"I don't—"

"I'm afraid I'm going to have to insist."

Caitlin's augmented chest heaved. "You are mean, just like Martin said you were. He told me you didn't understand him, you wouldn't satisfy his needs, would fight him if he tried to get a divorce. I thought maybe he was justifying having an affair, but he was telling the truth, wasn't he? You didn't love him at all. You just used him as a money pump, buying whatever you wanted with the money he made. At least I gave him something in return for the money he spent on me."

"That's fine. But—"

"I think you're horrible." She fisted her hands.

"Calm down, Caitlin."

"I just lost my boyfriend and you want me to calm down? How am I supposed to pay the rent here? Just the rent is higher than my salary. Martin was making payments on my Jaguar. How am I supposed to keep those up? And it isn't just the money, we had plans."

I looked at an antique French Empire clock on the wall. I could sell that clock for enough money to live for months. "I thought you just accused me of using him for his money. How are you different."

"I made him happy, which you didn't. And I didn't kill him."

"Meaning what?" I demanded.

Caitlin sighed. "Come on, Mrs. Montag. He was divorcing you and he was

66

going to marry me. You knew you were out, but you wouldn't settle for a nice spousal support, would you. You wanted it all, so you killed him. It's no secret. It's in the paper—the cops say you're a person of interest, but we all know what that means. What I don't understand is why you're still running around on the streets instead of in jail. And why the cops are letting you bother me."

I lost my temper. "You perfect little bitch. I hope I'm still around when you do trap some innocent man into marriage and he starts straying on you. Then —"

Lupe and Tina broke through the door and kept me from doing anything rash.

I felt like an ocean liner being pulled by a couple of little tugboats when Tina and Lupe combined to drag me out of the apartment before I tore that skinny little thing with the oversized boobs into shreds. Caitlin followed us down the hall to the elevator, all the while screaming that I'd murdered her great love and that she was going to sue me, and the estate, for what Martin had promised her.

"I don't think Nancy Drew would have screamed and gotten mad like that." Lupe spoke gently once we'd gotten into the elevator and out of range of Caitlin's screeching, but I could tell I was a big disappointment to her.

"Nancy Drew was a lesbian," I fired back. "So nobody was sleeping with *her* husband."

"Nancy Drew was not a lesbian, but even if she was, she still had class," Lupe answered.

"I think we've also established that your husband wasn't exactly a class act," Tina said. "Carrying on with a wife and three girlfriends at the same time definitely qualifies as jerk material."

"He wasn't carrying on with me, he was married to me. Why would he want someone fat and disgusting like me when he could have someone skinny and perky like Caitlin. I mean, even her name. Don't you just hear *perfect* when someone says Caitlin?"

The more I'd thought about it, the more I realized that Martin had gone a long time without coming down to my bedroom. For the first couple of years after I banished him for the snoring, he'd made a regular pilgrimage to my bed, but that had tailed off a long time before.

"You're not disgusting," Lupe said.

I noticed she didn't try to correct my comment about being fat. Well, what had I expected? I was fat. Being in denial about it hadn't helped me at all.

"Whether he was sleeping with you or not, I think my point still stands," Tina said. "He was married to you and he was carrying on with other women."

"Anyway, Caitlin didn't do it," Lupe said. "She wouldn't have been so mad at you if she'd been the one to do it. And she sounded real certain about you being the killer."

"She was a theater major at SMU." At least that's the way I remembered it. "She's supposed to be good at that histrionic stuff."

"I don't know what histrionic means," Lupe admitted, "but she seemed pretty broken up to me."

I didn't want to admit Lupe was right, but she was. Caitlin had been *very* convincing. My conscience started nagging me. Was I really certain she'd been a theater major? Maybe it had been something else, like music or dance.

"Besides, even if Martin was going to marry one of the others, he would probably still have carried on with Caitlin," Tina broke into my introspection. "She could have kept her nice apartment and her Jaguar. As it is, she's out on the street. If she didn't mind doing it with Martin when he was married to you, why would she complain if he married someone else?"

"Let's not talk that way in front of Lupe," I said. Admittedly I was a little late remembering, but Lupe was a teenager. She didn't need to be exposed to the filth involved in adult sexuality.

"You've got to get over some of your hangups," Tina fired back.

I gasped, and Tina concentrated grimly on her driving as a long silence opened.

"Okay, I've got to get home now to take care of my little brother." Lupe finally said. "Tomorrow, we can go and talk to the other girlfriends. I'll go to evening mass tonight so we can start early."

I shook my head firmly. I might be late in getting there, but I was not going to continue letting Lupe wallow in this filth. "You're too young to be exposed to the type of sexual intrigues we're discovering."

"I'm old enough to look at blood spatter but I'm too young to know who's sleeping with whom? What's that about?"

Put that way, it did seem like a strange rule. Still, I'd spent a long time working with the League to keep sex out of the schools and away from our young people. I would be a complete hypocrite if I then invited a teen to come along while I explored the depths of my own husband's depravity. "Hey, remember? I tried to keep you away from that too. But sex is different."

Lupe turned red. "I'll bet that's why Caitlin is in her situation. Nobody ever talked about sex with her at an adult level. So, then when a man came along, treated her nicely, took care of her, she fell for it because that's what people always told her was the right thing to do. Nobody taught her how to be a StrongGirl, so she's a wimp."

"Nobody told her to have an affair with my husband, either. And you're still not coming with me."

"I bet *somebody* told her, like maybe your husband. Tell you what, Tina. Let me out here. I'm the one who suggested we investigate and now this woman wants to keep me out. I don't need that grief."

Tina reminded her that *she* was driving, that *she* hadn't been the one saying Lupe couldn't come, and that *she had* promised Lupe's mother to bring her safely home.

"I don't care."

"You're both being immature," Tina announced. "We'll discuss our plans tomorrow morning. Until then, I'm going to take both of you home and that's

68

that." She paused a beat. "Don't even think about trying to jump out of my car, Lupe. For one thing, you might get hurt. For another, you'd probably knock out the window and I can't afford to get a new one put back on.

We spent the rest of the trip in silence, occasionally glaring at each other, but with no one willing to apologize or admit that they might possibly have been, even ever so slightly, in the wrong.

* * * *

The next morning, a pickup truck roaring through the trailer parking lot woke me up way before my body was ready to move.

My watch informed me that it was six in the morning. Looking at the gold and diamond instrument on my wrist also gave me an idea I never would have come up with before moving into this strange neighborhood of tiny cafes, stores specializing in music I'd never heard of, and pawn shops.

I snuck out of the trailer park, making sure Tina didn't spot me, and headed up to Jefferson where there was a whole lineup of pawnshops. Including several who advertise twenty-four-hour loan availability.

I was huffing and puffing by the time I'd made the two-mile walk, but I was grimly proud of myself. I hadn't depended on anyone else to drive me, to lend me bus fare, to intervene at all. I'd done it by myself.

It turns out that Rolex watches are highly counterfeited. The first two pawnshops I went to offered me ten dollars outright for the watch that had cost Martin ten thousand when he'd bought it for me years before.

The third, though, recognized it as genuine. I pawned it for a thousand— and agreed to pay twelve hundred to redeem it within two weeks.

Somehow I doubted I'd be redeeming it. Even if I magically found the money to get it out of pawn, the watch would always remind me of Martin, remind me of Caitlin's accusation that I'd just used Martin for his money rather than truly loving him.

I *had* loved him once. When we'd been in college, there had been so much passion in our relationship that I thought I'd combust every time I kissed him. When we'd first married, we'd made love almost every night. Neither of us could get enough of it. When the children came, we'd settled down to what I'd assumed was a more comfortable, long-lasting love. But maybe *I'd* been the only one who'd settled down. Martin, it seemed, hadn't. Not until someone had settled things for him in a permanent way.

With money in my pocket, I expected things to be better. I found a payphone and called a car rental company that delivers cars directly to you.

Typical of the way my life had turned lately, nothing was easy. Even with money, if you don't have a credit card, you aren't really a person. No working credit card, no car rental. Martin had made sure I didn't have any working credit cards before someone had killed him.

For the first time, I understood why the cops were so sure I'd done the deed. He'd been so petty, so grasping, I kept getting angry with him even though he was dead.

I ended up having to spend eight hundred of my thousand dollars buying a car that even the housekeepers in my Frisco neighborhood would have scorned. Its air conditioning had been broken so long I thought I spotted dinosaur prints across the vents, and there was more primer than paint on its body.

But it ran. And I had two hundred dollars left. I wasn't completely dependent on Tina any more.

A week earlier, I could have gone through two hundred dollars in a single restaurant visit, and twenty times that much in an afternoon of shopping. But I'd learned some painful lessons since Martin had been killed. I figured two hundred could last me a better than a week if I was careful. By then, maybe I'd get access to my jewelry. I could pawn that too, keeping me going until I was able to clear my name and get whatever I had coming from Martin's estate.

I was on my way toward becoming self-reliant.

Just in case Tina had gone back to the local hangout for breakfast, I avoided the convenience store gas station where Tina, Lupe and I had gotten donuts the day before and filled up my new old car at a place a couple of blocks away.

The gas ate a big hole in my two hundred. Always before, gas had just been a matter of putting it on my credit card and letting Martin worry about it. It seemed like everything cost more since I'd lost Martin, but I knew that could just be a change in perspective. Credit cards had never really seemed like spending money to me.

At least I'd bought a tiny car so it only took twelve gallons to fill it up.

"Hey, you're Mrs. Montag, aren't you?" People without credit cards have to go into the shop to pay for their gas. I hadn't known that.

I looked at the handsome Hispanic youth who was working the counter. He didn't look familiar, but he was giving me a huge grin.

"Yes. But I'm afraid—"

"I'm Lupe's cousin Jimmy. I saw you guys at the library. I was talking to Lupe at church last night and she told me she was helping you investigate a murder. Is she in your car? She said you guys were going out today. What a junker, by the way. Did you see the way it's burning oil. I think you need a valve job."

I stared at him to make sure he wasn't talking dirty to me, but he looked innocent.

"I don't know what a valve job is."

"It's probably going to cost you a thousand dollars," he said.

Getting a sound system upgrade on my Escalade had cost more than that, but the idea of spending another thousand on my new car practically drove me to tears.

"I hope it'll keep running for a while without that."

"You'd better buy a couple of quarts of oil, then," he said. "I'll show you."

I tried to beg off, but Jimmy dragged me out to my car, showed me how to check the oil, and poured a quart into an opening right on top of the engine.

"The way you're burning oil, you need to check the level every morning," he explained. "Otherwise you'll throw a rod."

Throwing a rod sounded as nasty as *getting a valve job*. I couldn't help but wonder why it was that male things always seemed to have sexual connotations.

"Lupe can help you with this. When she started being a StrongGirl, she asked me to show her how to change a tire, and how to check oil levels. You want to drive an older car, you've got to learn to take care of it."

I didn't really *want* to drive an older car, but what I wanted hadn't mattered a lot over the past few days.

I thanked Jimmy for his help.

He looked at me strangely. "You're dumping Lupe, aren't you?"

"I'm not dumping her. I'm working with her for my community service. That doesn't mean it's right to drag her into some of the situations I'm involved in. She is a child."

"Those are nice words," Jimmy observed. "Too bad you're hurting Lupe's feelings."

I paid him for the oil he'd poured into my engine and for a couple more quarts he put in the back seat and then headed out. I'd been to psychologists who charged me five hundred dollars for a fifty-minute session. I definitely didn't need free advice from an eighteen year-old pump-jockey.

This time, I noticed the cloud of blue smoke that followed me down the street and onto the freeway. Maybe I had needed his advice after all. About the old car, at any rate.

Smoke or not, the car was running.

Chapter 8

I took advantage of my new wheels to head for Betty Rope's Plano home. If anyone knew Martin's secrets, it was his secretary. She'd been working for him for more than ten years and the two had spent more time together than he and I. She'd even accompanied him on business trips to be sure he had everything he needed for the executive presentations he would do for customers and business partners. While not as young as Caitlin, Betty was slim and attractive. If he was going to step out on me, Betty was definitely a convenient target for his lusts.

She also treated Martin like he was some sort of genius, always repeating back what clever things he'd said, admiring his taste in clothes (as if I hadn't been the one who'd picked all of his suits), and giggling at his bad jokes. Once I even heard her admiring the way he brushed his teeth. Sycophantic talk like that made me sick, but Martin had enjoyed being fawned over.

No one answered Betty's door when I knocked, so I went back to my car and waited.

It wasn't even ten o'clock in the morning and I had all of the windows rolled down. Still, I was covered in sweat within a couple of minutes. The Texas sun beat down on all that primer paint and turned my car into an oven.

I wished I'd bought a bottle of water when I'd filled my car's tank, but I hadn't, so I sat and sweated.

Until I finally had a memory of being a little kid, running wild on the streets all day without any supervision at all.

Back then, we would grab drinks of water from garden hoses.

I hadn't drunk unfiltered city water in at least twenty years, but if it came down to unfiltered water or dying of dehydration, I figured I could swallow the water.

I found a faucet on the side of Betty's house, turned it on until it ran cold, cupped my hands under the stream and drank deeply.

"Hey, you. What are you doing there?"

I looked up, sputtering.

Betty looked like she'd just come back from church.

"Hi, Betty. I thought we should talk—about Martin."

She looked at me, then her eyes darted toward her house. Fortunately, she'd parked in front of her house rather than driving directly to the garage because she didn't look like she would have opened the door for me if she'd been able to get inside first.

She drew back toward her car. What did she think I was going to do? Attack her?

"Why would I want to talk to you about Mr. Montag?"

"Because he was murdered."

"I've talked to the police. It's *their* job to track down the killer. Right now, I wish they'd been a bit more active about locking you up, too." She edged further away from me but she kept looking toward her house. If she got into her car, she wouldn't have anywhere to go.

I made sure I stayed between her and the door to her house. She might be quicker than me, but I had the angle on her. "When you were talking with the police, did you happen to mention that you were sleeping with him?"

Betty stiffened. "What I told the cops is none of your business."

"Funny. I think it's very much my business. It must have been painful for you to set up Martin's schedule, blocking in time for each of his mistresses when all the while you wanted to keep him all to yourself."

Betty's attempt at a chuckle wouldn't have fooled a devoted cocker spaniel. "I'm not going to feed your fantasies, Mrs. Montag."

"You probably weren't too threatened by Caitlin Leitmol. I mean, *that* was obviously just about the sex."

I studied the perfect summer-weight suit Betty had worn to church and noticed her little shudder when I'd said the "s" word. Martin might have been sleeping with her, but Betty had never seemed like the sex-for-fun kind of woman and that shudder confirmed it. If she gave him sex, she expected other considerations from him.

I could sympathize with that attitude. So I decided to switch my tactic and try a little female bonding. "Letting Martin satisfy his physical needs with someone like Caitlin just took the pressure off of you, didn't it? But when he got serious with Kayla, that changed things. I mean, how could it not? Kayla is younger than you, and anxious to get ahead. With her education, connections and energy, Kayla is the kind of woman Martin could actually marry. Naturally Martin wouldn't understand how it would hurt you to have to set up his meetings with her. He probably assumed you were perfectly okay with whatever attentions he could spare for you. I can only imagine how it must have hurt you."

Betty's chin wobbled a bit. My guesses had obviously hit home.

"I think you should go now, Mrs. Montag. I don't need to listen to your tasteless implications."

"Don't you think it's unfair that a latecomer like Kayla pushed herself in front of you? Just because she had that animalistic need for sex all the time while you were more—"

"Get out of here!" She ran at me, her fists flailing like the arms of a Kitchenaid Mixer. "Martin wasn't like that. He was special. He *needed* me. He would never have replaced me with some other woman. I knew someone like you would make it sound like it was all about sex, but that was never what Martin saw in me."

My nose stung from where she'd landed a fist on it. I swiped at it and my hand came up bloody. Betty's punches had been wild, but they hurt where they'd landed. "I do understand, Betty. But Martin was a man. And men have these needs, you know."

"Ohmigod. You're bleeding. I hurt you."

I stopped myself before denying being hurt. Betty had been the ideal admin partly because she was a perfectionist who took responsibility for everything. If she felt responsible for me, I might have the chance to get her to open up more.

"You don't know your own strength."

Betty's hands fluttered. "I'll get you fixed up. Come on in the house and we'll get some ice for your nose. Oh, and look at your eye. I'm afraid you're going to have a black eye, too. I've never actually hit anyone before. I'm so sorry."

"It's been an emotional time for all of us."

I let her usher me into her home, sat down at her kitchen table, and took the washcloth filled with ice cubes she gave me to press to my nose and eye, then vanished to change out of her suit which I'd managed to bleed on.

Naturally I didn't just sit at the table and wait for her. The second she left, I got up and I snooped.

Her kitchen featured the latest appliances and slate countertops. But it was pretty much personality-free, so I headed out into the living room.

Where many women decorate their walls with wedding pictures or prints of impressionistic art, the walls of Betty's living room featured framed photos of Martin with Betty and Martin without Betty, intermixed with certificates of appreciation for all Betty had done for Montag Industries—for Martin. Yep, the woman had a fixation on him, all right.

Her house was one of those ranch style homes built in the sixties, but the modernization wasn't limited to the kitchen. She'd had the walls between the dining room and living room torn out to create a larger living space and had its walls artistically decorated with fake bricks painted to look like it was an Italian villa. All of her furniture was hand-made and expensive.

I flipped through the magazines in her magazine basket hoping to find one on firearms or murdering bosses. Instead I found Decorating Monthly and ten years worth of Montag Industries annual reports.

The click of her Italian designer shoes warned me as she left her bedroom and I headed back into her kitchen to get a few more ice cubes for my eye.

She joined me, wearing a pair of black slacks and a sleeveless blouse that showed more of a figure than I'd ever guessed she had. Even her upper arms were firm, which didn't seem fair. As long as I could remember I'd had a bit of softness in my upper arms. I'd thought of Betty as an efficient admin, but she was actually kind of hot.

I recognized that she had intentionally gone for the sexy look to show me up. Nobody had called me sexy at least since I'd gotten pregnant with Leah. Considering that I was wearing clothes from the Salvation Army Thrift Shop, and that they'd wilted out from me sweating on them, Betty didn't have to work hard to make me feel inferior.

My only choice was to stay on the offensive.

"You must be worried about what happens next at the office," I offered. "Has anyone said anything to you about what you'll be doing?"

"Nobody knows yet. Nick is supposed to inherit his father's stock, but Mr. Montag only owned about twenty percent of the company. That's not enough for Nick to vote himself the new CEO."

"If he does, would he pick you as his assistant?"

"Surely he wouldn't keep Desiree."

I'd never thought about it before, but Desiree was the world's worst assistant. She also had a perfect figure and giggled all the time. Was the entire Montag Industries filled with perverted guys and their bimbos? No wonder Martin hadn't left his shares to me.

"A new boss might want to make some changes. He might see you as too loyal to the former management."

"Oh." She paused and took a deep breath. "I hadn't thought of that. I've been the senior admin for so long, I guess I assumed I always would be. But if Nick keeps Desiree, I'd either have to settle for one of the VP's, or," she gulped for air again as if considering a worse-than-death possibility. "Or maybe nobody will want me."

I knew Martin had his self-image wrapped up in his job, but before I'd seen Betty's living room, I hadn't imagined a woman would be the same way. Women are supposed to get their identity from their families, not from business. Maybe Montag Industries was the only family Betty had.

"At least you've had the chance to sock away some serious money," I said. "You were one of the first employees, right? Didn't Martin give you part of your pay in stock in those early days?"

Betty giggled. "I never worried about that. Just stuck the certificates in a drawer."

Looking at Betty's home, I could tell she wasn't doing too badly. If she still owned all the stock she'd received from the early days, though, she wasn't just doing okay, she was rich. She also had to be one of the biggest stockholders in the company.

I told her that.

"You think?"

"Definitely. If you still have all those shares, you might want to stand for the board or something. Maybe you shouldn't be working for one of those guys, those guys should be working for you."

"I never thought of that."

I thought I'd softened her up, so I went back to my questions. "So, anyway, Betty, what I want to know is why Martin was still at his office the night he was killed. Martin always said you knew his schedule better than he did, so I know you're the person to ask. Who was he meeting with?"

Her eyes widened. "You know I can't tell you that. Mr. Montag's privacy is sacrosanct."

"You can't protect him any more, Betty. He's dead."

Her gaze refused to meet mine, slipping off to the left every time I tried to catch it. "I gave his entire schedule to the police. I don't have to tell *you* anything."

"You want to keep your job, don't you? When the police find out you were sleeping with Martin, everyone at Montag Industries will learn about the affair and how you did your job on your back. How likely is it you'll be able to stay on after that? Everyone you worked with would just be thinking about how you put out to get your stock. Your only hope is to give me everything you know and help me find the real killer before the ugly truth turns your reputation to filth."

Her face went pale beneath her artfully applied makeup. "Get the hell out of my house, Mrs. Montag. I don't need the kind of help your kind offers. For years, you weighed down Martin like an anchor. I don't understand what hold you had over him, but it must have been something ugly. I'm not going to let you blackmail me the same way."

"I didn't—"

She covered her ears. "I'm not listening. I'm not listening. I'm not listening." She repeated those words, loudly as she ushered me out of her home.

I outweighed her by a good eighty pounds, so there was no way she could have physically moved me out. But she could call the police if I refused, and I'd already gotten more face-time with the cops than I could stand.

* * * *

My car made plenty of noise as I headed back for my trailer, rattling, backfiring occasionally, and squealing like I was crushing a puppy in the engine. Despite that, I felt a sort of empty silence. I needed to talk to somebody about what Betty had said to me, how she'd reacted to my words. By sneaking out that morning, I'd as good as told the two people who believed in me that I didn't want their help.

For once in my life, knowing I was right didn't really make me feel better.

My new car's "check engine" light came on when I was a couple of miles from the trailer park.

I slowed down, gritted my teeth, and hoped that Jimmy's prediction about rod jobs or whatever he'd called it wasn't coming true.

Tina and Lupe didn't look up when my car sort of wheezed to a stop a couple of yards from where the picnic table where they were sitting. Tina wore a pair of cutoffs jeans that showed way too much leg and a ratty t-shirt that advertised something called a video card, whatever that was. Lupe wore a pink dress with a matching bow in her hair. She looked like she'd had to go to church in the morning after all.

I got out of the car and craned my head to see what they were doing.

To my surprise, each had a super-thin laptop computer in front of her.

"Ooh. It crashed again." Lupe sounded so near tears I wanted to run over and comfort her, the way I'd comforted my own children when they'd been younger.

"Did you get the hex-dump?" Tina's voice sounded confident and competent. "Let's have a look."

"What's going on?" I asked.

They ignored me.

"Okay, I think I found your problem," Tina's finger touched something on Lupe's screen. See this module here? You didn't assign a destructor for this object. That created a memory leak. Every time you invoke it, the system assigns more memory and never gets it back. That makes the program crash."

Tina's fingers flew over Lupe's keyboard for a moment. "You see what I did, right? It's not too hard, but you've got to stay organized."

"Can we run it now?"

I was close enough that they could probably smell my sweat, but neither looked up. It could have been that they were just so engrossed in whatever they were doing that they didn't notice me. But since my car had backfired three times after I'd turned off the engine, I didn't think that likely.

They were intentionally ignoring me. The worst part was, I couldn't really blame them after what I'd done to them.

Lupe clicked an icon on the screen and a game started.

I'd gotten hooked on computer bridge for a while, but I wasn't really much of a game person. Still, Nick had played games since he'd gotten a Nintendo machine as a child. Lupe's game seemed a bit simpleminded even by the standards of the games he'd played two decades earlier. From what I could see of it, the game consisted of a sketchily drawn girl who ran around a mostly empty screen making friends. Everyone she touched followed along behind her until she looked like that old fairy tale about the kid with the duck and everyone sticking.

Still, Tina and Lupe crowed like it was the greatest thing since Bill Gates.

"Very interesting," I said.

"You really like it?" Lupe looked at me for the first time since I'd arrived. Her deep brown eyes flashed with excitement.

"There was an old TV show from before when you and I were born," Tina said. "One of the characters would always say, 'very interesting, but stupid.' That's what she's saying. Right, Heather?"

From before they were born? That was a low blow. Tina must have been even madder than I'd guessed.

"I'm sorry. I didn't mean to insult a game you enjoy. Maybe you can tell me what it is?"

"Why bother?" The joy had evaporated from Lupe's face like water on a Dallas street. "You don't care about us. You only care about yourself."

I couldn't hold back my gasp. This was so unfair. I'd left Lupe behind to protect her, not because I was self-absorbed. "You're too young to be exposed to the sex and corruption. It's the same reason why you aren't allowed to go to R rated movies."

"What? Keeping us ignorant has worked so well half the girls in my school get pregnant before they even get to high school."

"Maybe you can explain it to her," I said to Tina.

"You've already explained your position perfectly," Tina answered. "You don't respect us or want to have anything to do with us. Well, that's your right. We *agreed* we'd talk things over in the morning. You would have had a chance to explain your reasons, let everyone know that you thought it would be better or safer or whatever for Lupe to stay away from some parts of the investigation.

But you didn't do that. Instead, you decided that you knew best. Well, okay. Montag was *your* husband. It's *your* neck the cops are clamping down on. If you think *you* know better, then just go for it. It turns out that Lupe is interested in game design and I'm helping her learn some basic 'C' coding. She appreciates *my* help, so that's something I'm interested in doing. You don't need our help. That's fine. We're certainly not going to push ourselves on you. You might want to put ice on that eye, though. You're getting a monster of a shiner."

I told myself having the two of them back off was exactly what I wanted as I stepped into my trailer.

The fan my trailer's the air conditioning unit was still blowing, but it had given up even pretending to cool the air before pushing it around.

With the sun beating down on its aluminum skin, I felt like a baked potato.

I considered calling Leah to see if she'd have a workman repair the air conditioner, but I remembered the last message I'd gotten from her about paying rent. I suspected if anyone was going to pay for an air conditioning repair job, it would be me.

With what little I had left after pawning my watch, that wasn't going to happen.

I maneuvered myself into the shower and let lukewarm water drip over me. I was trying to get rid of the sweat and blood, but I also wanted to wash away the nasty feeling I'd gotten from both Lupe and Tina.

Since I knew I was right, I shouldn't have felt like the villain in all of this.

I still did.

* * * *

Tina and Lupe were still at the picnic table when I looked out after I'd finished my shower, soaked my bloody dress in the sink, changed to clean clothes, and cleaned up the trailer.

I was sweating again before I'd gotten even the worst of the mess taken care of, so I decided I'd finish cleaning after dark, when it got cooler.

I tried the TV, but nothing was interesting enough to distract me from the heat.

It was too hot to just sit in the trailer and I still felt bad for how my confrontation with Lupe and Tina had gone. For one thing, I'd insulted a game that Lupe was programming rather than just playing. I hadn't known she'd created it at the time, but still, I hadn't asked, hadn't given her a chance to show me. I definitely needed to apologize for that.

Just because Lupe shouldn't be exposed to Martin's disgusting sex life didn't give me the right to be rude.

I headed outside.

"I'm sorry if I insulted your game."

Lupe's eyes softened, but Tina cut her off before she could say anything. "*If?* What's 'if I insulted' supposed to mean? Are you trying to say we misunderstood you? That it wasn't really an insult?"

It took me a couple of seconds before I realized I *had* sounded like a politician, pretending to apologize without really admitting I was wrong. And I had been wrong. Lupe was just a kid and she had created something that was sort of clever and a lot different from the shooting and killing that seemed to be all most computer games managed.

"What can I say? You're right. Sorry, Lupe. Sorry, Tina."

"It's okay," Lupe said. "I know the game isn't very good yet. It's more what they call a proto…"

"Prototype," Tina put in.

"A prototype," Lupe continued. "And I'll have to put in a lot more work on it before it's finished. I'm not even sure how it's going to work and the graphics suck. I think it's cool to have a game about making friends, but a StrongGirl needs to know that you can't be friends with everyone. Some people just make bad friends and drag you down."

Why did I feel like she was talking about me? Maybe it was those soft brown eyes looking up at me like a puppy waiting to be kicked again.

I cast around for something to say, not wanting to have Lupe and Tina turn their backs on me again. "It must be hard to draw all of those little pictures."

"I drew them and Tina scanned them in."

"But they're walking and stuff. How can you draw that?"

She giggled. "They're different pictures."

Lupe reached into her backpack and took out what could only be the originals of the graphics I'd seen on the screen. Each character was drawn multiple times from front, back, and each side—sometimes with their legs straight down, sometimes with the right leg forward, sometimes with the left. Lupe had used graph paper to make sure that each drawing had exactly the same height, and that the widths were the same whether the character was seen from left or right, front or back.

"That's a lot of drawing."

Tina nodded. "People are looking for something more than Pac-Man style graphics these days, Heather. Lupe doesn't have much training as an artist, but some of her graphics are clever and fun."

I sat at the picnic table, a few feet away from where Lupe and Tina continued to work on Lupe's game. They alternated between running the game as it was, and discussing the software they were developing to make the images move on the screen—and to make the screens look something like the streets of the Oak Cliff neighborhood of Dallas where Lupe lived.

The sounds of them keying in what looked like nonsense computer symbols, like parentheses with nothing inside of them, and their soft giggles when something unexpected happened was peaceful and lulling. For the first time in longer than I could remember, I actually felt relaxed.

Creating a game was, I saw, an iterative process. With every step, the graphics became a bit more coordinated. Instead of a crudely drawn girl running around an empty screen, now she moved between buildings and in alleys. Cars drove by on the streets and the occasional cat or dog poked its head out of doorways.

"We'll go around the neighborhood with a digital recorder next weekend and pick up ambient noises," Tina promised. "Audio effects add to the game's simulation of reality."

"Does ambient mean what's around?" Lupe asked.

"Yep."

I knew that. I hadn't realized Tina did. From her living in a cheap trailer, having a dead-end job as a trailer park manager, I'd assumed she was uneducated. But she was teaching Lupe how to program computers—something I couldn't do—and her vocabulary was definitely up to par.

For just a moment, I wondered what other prejudices I might be holding onto, without even realizing I had them.

Lupe pulled a box of raisins from her backpack, offered a handful to Tina, then put it away. I didn't think she was excluding me on purpose. It was just that, while I'd been off on my own investigation, the two of them had created a bond that I wasn't part of. Lupe was so deep in her game that I wasn't even there for her.

I was only three feet away and I'd never felt so alone.

Almost an hour later, Tina looked up from her computer. "Lupe wants to create a game that girls will enjoy. So she doesn't want any killing or blood. But if it's just a matter of making friends, the StrongGirl message gets lost. Because one of the things StrongGirls learn is that people will take advantage of you if you are too dependent on approval from others. What do you think, Heather? Do you have any suggestions?"

I felt as if I'd been wandering in the dark and Tina had finally turned on a flashlight, welcoming me back into a friendship I hadn't even known I'd established. I thought fast.

"My son showed me a game called *The Sims* once. There wasn't any killing or fighting, really, but you still had to help your characters make the right decisions or they'd get sick or something." As I remembered, Nick had thought the game was boring for exactly that reason, but to me it had been more interesting than any of the more violent games he played.

Tina nodded. "The A.I. level required for a game like that is out of Lupe's league, at least for now. But it's a good suggestion, Heather. Maybe we can include activities like going to school and doing chores at home as choices. If you spend too much time with friends, you get in trouble with your family or the school. People need a balance in their lives."

"And some friends are bad for you," Lupe added. "I need some way of figuring out how to tell good friends from bad friends."

"Maybe the bad friends are red and the good friends are green," I said.

"Too easy. You've got to recognize good and bad from the way people treat you, not from their color or the way they dress or look."

'Out of the mouths of babes,' as it were. Lupe might be the one who was supposed to be learning here, but there seemed to be plenty of lessons for me, too.

Maybe there should have been a game like Lupe's a long time ago. Maybe if there had been, and I'd played it, my life wouldn't be such a mess now.

We spent the next half-hour brainstorming ways to tell the difference between good and bad friends. And how a game could show those ways without oversimplifying.

I enjoyed feeling included again. Tina and Lupe hadn't exactly forgiven me, but they were willing to let me back into their circle, at least on a provisional basis.

The more I thought about what it means to be a good or bad friend, though, the more I realized how bad a friend I'd been—and not just with Tina and Lupe. It was no wonder the women at the League had abandoned me the moment I no longer had the power and wealth of Montag Industries behind me.

It wasn't completely my fault, of course. Plenty of them had been as two-faced and self-interested as I had been. That didn't make me feel any better about my own flaws, though.

* * * *

My stomach gurgled and I looked at my watch—and found nothing. Oh, yeah. My watch had been magically transformed into my new car and a few bucks.

"It's five-twenty," Lupe said, reading the time from a little clock at the bottom of her computer.

"I missed lunch somehow. How about we go out somewhere. My treat."

"You have money?" Lupe asked. "You didn't rob anybody, did you?"

"Of course not. I pawned my watch. That's how I paid for my new car. I just have a little cash left after that."

"Wow. A watch that's worth as much as a car. That's so weird. Didn't you always worry you might forget it somewhere?"

Maybe it was a little weird. I'd always thought of Martin and myself as being comfortable. But perhaps a ten-thousand-dollar watch went beyond comfortable and into extravagant. Maybe if I'd thought about the money at all, I would have been worried about losing it.

"It was a pretty good watch."

"If you say so. You want to see a really cool watch, you should check out Tina's. It's really a computer."

Tina blushed for the first time since I'd met her. "I can't help it, I'm a nerd. Still, it seemed like such a good idea at the time."

I could see how having your appointments and to-do list there on your watch could be convenient. But when Tina showed me she could read a book that way too, I realized she was right—it was impossibly nerdy. If I wore something like that to a League meeting, my friends there would laugh at me.

Except, I didn't really have friends there. My brain felt like its muscles were straining to get straight on my new understanding of friendship. Every time I thought I had it, though, I saw that there was even more.

"Let's go to Peter Pan's," Lupe suggested. "I'm always hungry for pizza and I love the games th—" She paused and looked at the flashing lights approaching down the road. "Uh-oh. Looks like somebody's in trouble. Again."

Chapter 9

Squealing tires from a trio of Plano Police cruisers, accompanied by a single Dallas Police Department squad car, cut off the dinner discussion.

The Plano cops bounded out of their car, pulled weapons, and surrounded my trailer.

I tried to sink into the wood of the picnic table. Most of the cops ignored us, but one uniformed officer, who looked barely older than Lupe, got between us and my trailer and stood there, gun drawn, watching us.

"Oh-oh," Lupe whispered. "What did you do? Are you sure you didn't steal that car?"

"Of course I didn't steal it. I didn't do anything. Well, not lately."

"Doesn't look like they agree."

The two Dallas officers remained in their car watching as the Plano cops moved toward my trailer.

One of them pulled what looked like a shotgun with a big grenade on its top and pointed it at one of my trailer windows.

Another cop carried a piece of paper up to my door, knocked, and instantly raised his big boot.

"I'm here," I screamed. I didn't think the cops would pay to replace my front door or side window if they broke them and I had an instant mental image of my remaining hundred and fifty dollars being swallowed by trailer repairs.

The cops whirled around. The young one who'd gotten between us and the trailer dropped into a crouch, pointing his pistol right at me. The guy with the shotgun's finger tightened on the trigger so much his knuckles turned white.

I was glad I was sitting down because I felt wobbly all of a sudden. They were pointing guns at *me*.

"Mrs. Heather Montag?" Although he was only twenty feet from me, the plain-clothed cop shouted into a portable loudspeaker. Might as well let everyone in the trailer park know the police were after me.

"Yes. That's me." My voice was barely a squeak.

"We have a warrant to search your home. Will you open the door or must we break it down."

"It's," I cleared my throat and started again. "It's not locked."

"Better ask to see the warrant," Tina whispered. "Cops lie."

"But surely—"

"We'd like to see the warrant," Tina said.

The couple of seconds where she'd been polite and talked to me first rather than insisting were long enough for a couple of the cops to have the door open and enter my trailer. It was too late to withdraw my permission even if I'd been convinced that was a good idea.

"Get Lupe home," I whispered to Tina. "I don't know what's going on, but it can't be good news."

"Why Plano Police, though?" Tina wondered as she shut down her computer. "Martin was murdered in Frisco, right? I'm sure it was the Frisco cops last time."

I hadn't thought about it, but it seemed to me that cops generally only work the crimes committed in their own towns. Martin *had* been in killed in Frisco and that's where I'd had my own run-in with the police. Frisco cops had burst in on me at Leah's Richardson apartment. Frisco cops had questioned me here in the trailer park.

But Betty lived in Plano. Had she reported me for trespassing and drinking water from her faucet? She'd been angry enough to do something like that when I'd left her, but it was hard to believe a judge would issue a search warrant for that kind of offense.

I knew Plano prided itself on its low crime rate and rapid response to citizen complaints, but a guns-drawn reaction still seemed extreme for stealing a drink of water.

"What's this about, officer?" I wanted to focus their attention on me and away from Tina and Lupe.

He snarled at me. "It's detective, not officer. I'd like to see some I.D."

I reached for my purse and every gun within sight was pointing at me.

"I'm just getting my driver's license."

"Move very slowly."

I couldn't have moved fast if I'd wanted to. My hands shook like a San Francisco earthquake and I had to squeeze hard to keep my bladder under control. I dropped my wallet a couple of times before I finally had it out.

"Don't move. Shove it toward me."

I tried, but it only went about two feet.

"Jeez. Women." The cop, or detective as he wanted to be called, stepped in and picked it up.

He checked out my driver's license, peered at the thin stack of bills, and latched onto the pawn ticket, sticking it into a plastic bag he stuffed into a hip pocket.

"Hey, I'm going to need that."

"Your property will be returned to you in due course."

"But I only have two weeks to get that watch out of pawn."

His smile told me he was enjoying this. "Really?"

I didn't have any idea how I'd get the money to get the watch out of pawn, I'd washed my hands of the bauble when I'd pawned it, but having the ticket taken from me like that put a finality on my decision, like closing the door on me ever having money and nice things again.

"If you don't—"

"Mrs. Montag, we are investigating a crime here and I don't have time to listen to your complaints. Right now, I want your account of your activities over the past eighteen hours."

"Why?"

His eyes narrowed. "Who cares why? Have you done something illegal, something you can't share with the police?"

I stood, then froze when at least ten guns followed me up. I would have sat back down, but my legs froze in place.

"I'm just—"

"Don't *just* do anything, Mrs. Montag. Stand very still. Put your hands on your head. Officer Greene, would you please check Mrs. Montag for weapons?"

Officer Greene looked younger than Leah but she moved with an assurance I wished Leah would cultivate. She stepped up to me, being careful, I saw, not to get between any of the pointed guns and their target.

She patted me down quickly. "She's clean."

"All right, Mrs. Montag," the detective said. "Let's start with your schedule."

I forced my knees to unlock and sank back to the table. "I might be able to help you more if I knew what you were looking for."

I thought about signaling Tina to get Lupe out of there, but I realized the cops would notice—and anything I did would backfire.

One of the cops ran out of my trailer, his hands filled with a dripping dress —the dress I'd bled on when Betty had smacked me in the nose. "Blood. There's blood on these clothes."

I'd thought the detective looked angry before. He scowled harder when he saw my wet laundry.

He switched on a small digital recorder. "This is Detective Richard Luscombe interviewing Mrs. Heather Montag." He quickly gave the date and time, then the location. "Mrs. Montag, would you care to explain the blood on what appears to be a dress found in your trailer?"

"I got a bloody nose, offi—uh, detective."

He stepped closer to me.

The detective was tall, maybe in his early thirties, and had wiry black hair that stood straight out from his head. His suit was strictly off the rack, from one of those discount suit places. And while his tie might be silk, it looked like it had been through a couple of world wars after the silk worms had gotten finished with it.

His skin could definitely have used an industrial strength exfoliation. I suspected there were moon craters smaller than some of the pores on his face. And his eyebrows grew together in the center. I remembered one of my college friends telling me that the unibrow was a sign of a werewolf. Looking at the detective, I had my suspicion she hadn't been pulling my leg, for once.

"I'm sorry. I didn't catch your name."

"Luscombe. Detective Luscombe. Want my badge number, too?"

His breath smelled like mint gum but a rotten odor lay under it. I suspected he had put off needed dental work.

"That won't be necessary. As I was saying, Detective Luscombe, I got a bloody nose and bled on my dress. There's no great mystery here."

"Greene, get a shot of Montag's nose." He turned back to his recorder. "Mrs. Montag's nose appears to be slightly swollen. She also has an abrasion on her upper cheek, and what looks like the beginning of a black eye. I have asked

Officer Greene to photograph the apparent injury."

I felt like the subject of a TV commentary.

"Detective," Tina said, "I don't believe that Mrs. Montag should answer any more questions until you tell her what this is about."

The cop whirled toward Tina. "Who the hell are you and what business is it of yours."

"I'm the manager here. And if you're going to pull a bunch of cars into my parking lot, you'd better have a reason for it. It isn't as if you're Dallas Police. You're out of your jurisdiction."

"We're interfacing with D.P.D."

"Calm down, Tina." I used every bit of mental telepathy I possessed to tell her to go away and to take Lupe with her. I didn't know what the cops wanted, but I knew they hadn't come down to tell me everything had been a big mistake.

For once, Tina seemed to pick up on my message and shut up.

"We'd like you to come to headquarters with us," Detective Luscombe said. "It would be easier for us to ask you questions there."

A week before, I would have agreed to that request without thought. I wasn't sure if I'd gotten more cynical since then, or just smarter.

"I'm afraid I am going to have to know what's going on before I agree to anything."

"We can *make* you come down with us."

"Am I under arrest?"

"Is that the way you want it, Mrs. Montag?"

Since telepathy wasn't doing the job, I had to take the risk and come right out and say it. "Tina, why don't you take Lupe home and I'll talk to the detective here. He doesn't seem to want anyone listening in."

"Don't say anything without a lawyer."

"I didn't do anything wrong, so I don't need a lawyer." I knew that was my old ways speaking. Still, I couldn't help the words slipping out. Even more than in my comfortable Frisco existence, I had a pathetic need to believe that the police were looking for the truth, that they wanted to find criminals rather than make my life miserable.

Lupe, rather than Tina answered that. "Come on, Heather. Even you can't be that naive."

Hearing that from a thirteen-year-old was something of a shock. I'd never thought of myself as naïve, just sensible.

Detective Luscombe and I waited until Tina finally dragged Lupe away, promising her that she'd take her to the pizza place Lupe had suggested.

Once Tina's beat-up car chugged out of the parking lot, Luscombe turned back to me.

"Tell me about your relationship with Ms. Betty Rope."

"She reported me for trespassing, right? I was just getting a drink of water from her faucet."

"You are voluntarily stating that you met with Ms. Rope today. Is that correct?"

"This morning, I'd think. I don't have a watch any more, but I got started early and went up to her place as soon as I'd bought my car."

"If you think she accused you of trespassing, you must have had some sort of confrontation. Is that correct?"

"You could say that. That is how I ended up with a bloody nose, after all."

"How did that happen?" Detective Luscombe was making sure his recorder caught every word.

"She got mad when I accused her of sleeping with my husband."

"You're kidding me?" The detective seemed confused as to where to go next for a moment. "And, was she really? Sleeping with your husband, I mean?"

"Yes. She was his admin and had spent the past decade traveling with him so she could take care of things for him. Apparently one of the things she took care of was his sex drive."

"Why did that make *her* angry? I'd think you would be the aggrieved person."

"I guess it wasn't the accusation that made her mad. It was when I suggested that Kayla Switzer was replacing her in Martin's love life."

"And, ah, was this, uh, Kayla Switzer also your husband's lover?" He had me spell out her name.

"Oh, yes."

He narrowed his eyes. "Most women would find listing their husband's lovers to be a bit emotional. It doesn't seem to bother you very much, Mrs. Montag. Can I ask why?"

It was a good question—one I had been careful not to ask myself. I decided to give it my best answer. "In the past week, I learned my husband was divorcing me, lost him to murder, lost my home, my car, everything I own, have been dumped by my friends, had to move into a tiny trailer in a part of Dallas where I wouldn't have been caught dead before now, and was sentenced to community service for violating a protective order. I think I've gotten a bit numb."

Luscombe digested that for a while.

"Still, you must have been angry at Ms. Rope."

"For sleeping with my husband?" I thought about it. Betty knew better, of course. But Martin did too. Why should it be just women who are supposed to say no all the time? Betty was single, after all. *She* hadn't promised to be faithful. Maybe she *should* have been able to sleep with whomever she wanted, so long as they were willing too.

Martin, on the other hand, *had* promised to be faithful when he'd married me. I wasn't the most liberated woman on the planet, but the double standard, the always blaming the woman thing, didn't seem right at all. Martin had needed to keep himself in check and he hadn't. I didn't think that Betty had just stripped down for him at the office one day. He'd pursued her, seduced her. And if Betty hadn't volunteered for the job of handling Martin's libido, it would have been someone else. In fact, it *had* been several someone elses that I knew about already. I wondered how many other women he'd slept with over the years, and how long after our wedding before he'd first become unfaithful.

"Why wouldn't you be mad at her, after all?" the detective continued when my mind wandered away from his question.

"Well, sleeping with someone else's husband isn't polite. But I don't think she killed him. Is that the angle you're working on? I don't think she would have killed him even if he'd told her he was marrying Kayla. Working at Montag Industries and being admin for Martin was Betty's whole life. I think she'd rather die than give that up, even if he cut her off for a while. Sex didn't seem like that big a deal to Betty."

"As it turns out, we aren't considering Ms. Rope as a suspect in Mr. Montag's murder."

I'd been certain I was on the right track. "Oh. If that isn't it, what *is* this about?"

"I'd like you to go over the timing of your visit with Ms. Rope. Starting with when you got up this morning."

I took him through my morning, the pawnshop, buying the car, my chat with Jimmy at the gas station, my wait outside Betty's home, our confrontation, and our conversation.

"You must have been pretty angry when she refused to listen to you and threw you out."

"I was okay." I didn't like the way he kept going on about how mad I must have been.

"So, what did you do next?"

"Then I came home."

"And Ms. Rope was fine when you left?"

Uh-oh. All of a sudden, I thought I'd figured out what this was about—and the news wasn't good. "She seemed fine. Why shouldn't she have been fine?"

"And you're certain you pawned a valuable watch in the morning, *before* you visited with Ms. Rope? Not after? There's no time on the pawn receipt, you know."

"I'm positive." Had Betty claimed I'd stolen something from her? "Martin gave me that watch ten years ago. He might have given one to Betty, too, for all I know. More likely, he had Betty buy it for him to give me. But the watch was mine."

"I'd like to take a DNA sample from you." He called over a technician and handed me a cotton swab. "Rub this along the inside of your cheek nice and firmly."

I'd already done it and handed it back to him before I realized he wouldn't be asking me to do this without giving me a reason. And the reason couldn't be good.

"Something happened to Betty, didn't it? Is she going to be all right?"

"What makes you think that, Mrs. Montag?"

"You aren't here questioning me because I trespassed and drank from her faucet. You aren't even here because you think I might have stolen my own watch. You're here because something happened to her after I'd left. I'm learning that I've been pretty ignorant about the way the real world operates, but I'm not stupid. All of these cops wouldn't have made the drive down from Plano if it was just Betty complaining about me annoying her."

"Maybe you should be the detective instead of me, Mrs. Montag." Luscombe sighed. "Betty Rope is definitely *not* all right. A friend discovered her body a couple of hours ago. Ms. Rope had written your name on her notepad but it was hard to spot, what with all of the blood on it."

"Someone killed her."

"That's our preliminary assessment."

"And you think *I* did it?"

"Let's just say that we're investigating all the possibilities. You seem to have a motive, and you're known as a violent offender."

A violent offender? Me? I closed my eyes in horror.

* * * *

They didn't arrest me. Yet.

Detective Luscombe spent hours going over my morning and got the Dallas police to promise to stop by the pawnshop where I'd left my watch and talk to the owner to confirm whether I'd pawned the watch before I'd visited Betty.

When Tina got home, they nailed her on what time I'd returned. Then Luscombe sent his cops door-to-door in the park, trying to find anyone else who'd noticed what time I'd come home. I doubted anyone would keep that close tabs on their neighbors, but I had to hope we'd have at least one busybody.

Tina's friend Angie popped out of her trailer at around eight in the evening, and all of a sudden, Luscombe and Officer Greene, the female cop, were the only ones who had any attention left to give me at all. All of the other males were trying to make time with Angie.

"Doesn't it bother her that guys drool all over her all the time?" I whispered to Tina.

"Are you kidding? Why do you think she chose that business?" she reminded me.

Tina and Angie waited with me until the cops finally left around midnight —after first warning me not to leave the Dallas area without notifying them.

"Well that's a relief," I said when the caravan of cop cars finally turned off their flashing lights and headed north.

"Don't get too relaxed. They still think you did it," Angie said. "They just need to figure out how you were able to get back so quickly. Did you see that one guy measuring the temperature of your car's engine?"

I'd missed that. I didn't even know how you'd go about taking a car's temperature or what you'd do with it even if you could.

"Angie's right," Tina said. "You're the prime suspect in two murders now. They're going to keep looking for evidence that you did it and ignore anything that points the finger away from you. The way I see it, if you want to beat a lethal injection, you'd better come up with the real killer."

"So far, every time I try to detect, I get into more trouble."

"Naturally it would be ridiculous to ask for help."

"I don't get you, Tina. Lupe is a kid. Of course we can't expose her to sex."

"She's a teenager. She's going to school with a bunch of guys whose hormones are rampaging. Pretending sex doesn't exist makes things worse, not better."

"I still don't want to share my husband's infidelities with her."

Tina finished the glass of wine Angie had brought her and handed the wineglass back to her friend. "Tell you what, Heather. You think about what you'd like me to do, what you'd like Lupe to do. Then you tell us. If it makes sense to us, maybe we'll play along. But if you want to do your own investigation, go running off places where you can get in trouble, where you can get accused of more murder, then you can leave us out. Think about this, will you? Someone killed your husband. Unless there's a really freakish coincidence going on here, that same someone killed Betty Rope. I'd just as soon not end up next on that killer's list. You might not want to, either."

"Time for me to get to work," Angie said. She fluffed up her hair and headed out from the trailer park.

"Is she just going to walk the streets?" I asked Tina.

"Nah. One of the Plano cops is waiting for her."

"Isn't she afraid he'll arrest her?"

Tina looked at me like I'd grown horns. "For someone who doesn't want anyone interfering in her business, you certainly stick your nose into a lot of other people's concerns."

I stared at Tina with my mouth open in shock. I'd been trying to be helpful.

"Don't forget you've got StrongGirl training tomorrow," she added before I could get my lips around an answer. "Lord knows, if anyone needs help in becoming a StrongGirl, it's you."

Chapter 10

"In 2000, over thirteen percent of Hispanic teen girls, and over fifteen percent of Black teen girls became pregnant. We aren't talking about newlyweds here. Almost none of these girls intended to become pregnant at the time. And most of those who were in middle or high school at the time ended up dropping out."

These were statistics I was familiar with and I nodded along with our StrongGirl instructor. Next up was the essential 'virginity until marriage' creed —a tactic that had certainly helped me land Martin. Although, given what had happened, maybe landing Martin hadn't been as wonderful as it had seemed at the time.

"We encourage girls to recognize that sex is their responsibility, a choice," the instructor continued, stepping way outside of the script I'd expected her to follow. "StrongGirls know that a healthy relationship is a partnership, rather than a matter of subservience."

I stopped nodding and started thinking.

I had always thought about my relationship with Martin as a partnership. He would never have gotten to where he was without my help. My parents had been his initial investors. My good taste had put him on the list of Dallas best-dressed and made sure he would fit in with the elite group of business leaders. My efforts in raising our children had freed him to spend so much of his time building a business. For the first time in my life, though, I wondered if *Martin* had ever regarded our relationship as a meeting of equals. Or had I just been part of his support staff?

Now that I knew about his affairs, I understood how each of his women had filled one of his specific needs. Caitlin had been a purely sexual romp. Betty had been his organizer. I'd been the woman who raised his children and dressed him. Kayla had been destined to become the trophy wife who would look good on his arm as he moved his business to the next level, leaving me, fat Heather, far behind.

What kind of partnership was that?

"Did you have a question, Heather?"

I pulled my attention back to the instructor. "Actually, I sort of do. I'm not sure I know how to teach girls to be strong because I'm not sure I've ever been strong myself. I married the man my parents picked out for me. I played the traditional housewife role for him, raising the children, making sure food was on the table and entertaining his friends. I thought it was a partnership at the time, but now it looks to me like I was a glorified servant. Oh, and a servant who was expected to provide sexual favors." Not that Martin wasn't also getting sexual favors from the other female servants in his life.

"Is that what you wanted to be, Heather? A sort of servant to your man in exchange for his protection?"

I was enough of a woman of the times to want to deny it instantly, but I thought about the question, instead. "That's how I was brought up. My mother never worked outside the home. My sorority sisters and I joked about getting our M.R.S. degrees, but in a lot of ways, that's what we were in school for. We thought girls who studied engineering were nerdy and unfeminine. I majored in art history, for goodness sake."

"I'm glad you mentioned this, Heather." Our instructor, an impossibly perky blonde named Deb Sampson, perched on the desk at the front of the class. "The StrongGirl program recognizes that many of the problems facing our girls flow from a misapplication of traditional sexual roles. It isn't that those roles are bad in and of themselves. At the time those sex roles were developed, traditionally male and female activities were both essential to household survival.

"With the changes in our society, the power position flowing from these traditional sex roles has altered. Increasingly, those roles have become misapplied. Our middle school and high school girls are getting pressure to have unprotected sex so that they'll be accepted. Accepted as girlfriends, as cool people, as belonging. And it's part of our makeup as females to want to please, to create and fit into social structures and to define ourselves by those structures. Helping the girls understand the consequences of their choices, though, is important. Most important, though, is that they know there are choices, alternate structures that can lead to a better life."

"Like finding guys who won't pressure them for sex?" I asked. "Who'll wait until they're married?"

Deb had the grace to take my question seriously. The other women all giggled as if I'd said something completely off the wall.

"I don't think *marriage* is the first thing on the minds of our twelve- and thirteen-year-old girls. I'm talking about creating social structures that are supportive of them, that allow them to make their own choices."

It was interesting that my League friends had looked at the same information, said so many of the same things, and yet had come to such different conclusions.

I'd been completely convinced by the League approach, but Deb made a lot of sense too. Learning the truth about my husband had opened my eyes to a lot that I'd done my best to ignore until then.

As we broke for lunch, I realized that Deb might have been saying something to me that was a lot more immediate, and had a lot more to do with the rest of my life than just becoming a mentor for the StrongGirls. Because if there was anyone who needed a positive social structure right then, it was me.

* * * *

Rather than eat with the other StrongGirl prospects, I tracked down Lupe in the dining room. "Can I sit with you?"

She looked at her friends, all Latina girls with long braided hair and shortened school uniforms, then at me. "You don't have to get mentored by me until after school. Why would you want to sit with me now?"

It was time to grovel. "It turns out that you were right. I need a support structure and you and Tina are my best hope."

Her frown wasn't making this any easier for me, but I pushed ahead.

"Anyway, I'm sorry for standing you up yesterday. I'd like to start over."

She looked at me for a couple of seconds, then turned to the girl next to her and said something in Spanish. Both girls giggled.

"If there's anything you want to do to..."

I was talking to the back of her head, though.

Finally I got up. I might have been able to squeeze into the mentor table. If I'd been a size two, anyway. As it was, I had to sit at a table by myself.

A few minutes later, Deb joined me. "You look like you're in the dumps."

"Yeah."

"Want to talk about it?"

I realized I'd been putting too many eggs in the Lupe and Tina basket. Sure I'd messed up when I'd agreed to meet them and then blown them off. Mistake or not, though, I couldn't undo what I'd done. And Deb Sampson probably had all kinds of contacts. She was a trained psychologist. Much more so than a teenage girl and a trailer park manager, Deb could help me. Deb was the social structure I needed.

"The cops think I killed my husband and his girlfriend," I blurted. "I can't get anyone to listen to me, and I need help if I'm going—"

"Hold on, now. How, exactly, did you get involved in the StrongGirl program?" Deb demanded.

"I got assigned it for my community service."

"Community service for trespassing, not violent crimes."

"That was the plea bargain." I gave her the short version of how Martin had served me with divorce papers and how I'd confronted him.

"They sent you to us after you'd been arrested for assault?"

"My plea bargain was only—"

"And the man you attacked turned up dead a few hours later?"

"That had nothing to do with—"

"Look, Heather. I'm glad you explained this to me. I'm sure it's just as you described it and you had nothing to do with the deaths. Still, our program can't afford the negative publicity we'd get if word got out that we accepted suspected killers and convicted felons into the program. I know you'll understand that I have to call your judge and get him to reassign you. StrongGirls is definitely not the kind of program we want associated with violent criminals."

"I haven't been convicted of anything and I'm not a violent—"

"Even if you didn't actually kill all those people, you did assault someone, right?"

"But—"

"I'm afraid I have to ask that you leave the Dallas School System property. Now, Heather."

I left.

My new car conked out as I pulled into the trailer parking lot.

I turned the key in a futile attempt to restart the engine, but all I got was a sort of clicking noise.

I looked around at the crappy little trailers, the rusting pickup trucks that filled the parking lot, and my own pathetic little Toyota, and all of a sudden, I couldn't hold back the waterworks any more. My life had turned to shit, I'd lost everything and was practically homeless, and I'd just gotten fired from my second unpaid volunteer job in less than two weeks.

Tears had always worked for me before. When I cried, my kids responded, my husband bought me presents, and Maria, the housekeeper, had bent over backwards to provide me my favorite desserts.

Here, though, nobody cared. Crying just added to my general dehydration problem.

It took me a good five minutes, but I finally realized I wasn't making any progress sitting in the middle of the parking lot in hundred-plus-degree weather, balling my eyes out, and refusing to get on with my life.

I got out of my car and took about three steps toward my trailer when somebody honked his horn.

"You can't just leave your car there in the middle of the driveway." It was one of the tenants, a rough-looking man about my age who wore a cowboy hat and drove one of those big pickup trucks with the double-tires in the rear and a gun rack with what looked like both a shotgun and a rifle hanging from it.

Even from twenty feet away, his sweat was strong enough to make my eyes water, and as I watched, he brought up a 7-11 cup and spit a stream of tobacco juice into it.

In Frisco trucks like that were a fashion statement rather than a practical choice. Their gun racks were empty other than in hunting season and the beds were kept empty and pristine. This guy had his truck loaded with bags of concrete and other construction material.

"My car broke down."

He sighed. "Great." A long pause. "Want me to take a look at it?"

I'd been thinking negative thoughts about him. But he'd been out working, so what could be more natural than that he'd sweat? I didn't think anyone in the suburbs would offer to help a stranded vehicle. At best, they might call the auto club.

"Could you?" I didn't bat my eyes at him. I might, possibly, have lowered my voice just a bit.

A big sigh. "Might as well."

He popped open the hood on my car, stared at the engine for a moment, then told me to start it up.

I would have felt like an idiot if the engine had started, but I got the same click.

"Battery is dead," was his diagnosis. He spit on the ground this time as a sort of punctuation. It was still gross, but it didn't bother me as much now that he was helping me.

"Can you fix it?"

"Look lady. You don't *fix* batteries, you buy new ones. And it doesn't take a mechanic to put in a new one—it just takes a bit of care to make sure you're attaching cables to the right leads. *You* can do it yourself. Now let me push your car out of the way so people can get into their own homes."

I stood there with my mouth gaping while he dragged one of those blankets moving men use from the back of his truck, draped it over my car's bumper, and got back in his truck, pushing it up until its bumper touched my own.

"Get in your car and steer," he told me.

I obeyed, turning the car into an open parking space as he shoved it with his truck.

He stopped, retrieved his blanket, tipped his hat at me, and headed down to another trailer—one of the more run-down ones nearest the river.

I watched him go and wondered about myself. He wasn't appealing to me at all, but I'd still gone all helpless on him, exactly as I had when I'd been at SMU and dating Martin. There was something really wrong with me and I didn't even know what it was.

The mail had arrived before me and I was distressed to see an electric bill in my name. Leah had obviously operated quickly to get the utilities switched. Worse, the bill was for the previous three months, with a warning that if I didn't pay this time, they were going to cut off service.

There was a payphone outside the gas station at I-30 and Sylvan. I walked there, pumped quarters into the machine, and called my daughter.

"I'm letting you stay for free," she reminded me. "The least you can do is pay for the utilities."

"But I wasn't living here when that electricity was used. Besides, I only have about a hundred dollars left."

"Don't you think it's time for Nick to help? He's the one with the great job. He's the one who gets all of Dad's stock. Can you believe all I'm supposed to get is some sort of allowance from a trust? Barely ten thousand a month. Richard and I were counting on a lot more. We wanted to move someplace nice and out of this dump of a condo."

"I'll call Nick. But if you could just—"

"I already told you, Mom. *I don't have the money.* That ten thousand has to pay for *everything*. Richard needs a new motorcycle and you can't believe how expensive those things are."

My hand was shaking when I disconnected. Leah wasn't a bad child, but I'd never seen how self-absorbed she was. She wasn't hurting me on purpose, but I had to calm myself for a good ten minutes. Then I took Leah's advice and called my son.

"We're completely swamped with Betty's death, mother. Nobody had any idea how much we depended on her organizational abilities and the institutional memory she brought. With both her and Dad gone, we're overwhelmed."

"I understand you're busy. But I need—"

He interrupted me with a sigh. "Yeah, yeah, it's still all about you, isn't it? Tell you what, Mother. I'm free for lunch tomorrow. Come on up and I'll give you half an hour. You can tell me all about your problems and I'll see what I can do."

"Do you think you could send a—" The sound of a dial tone cut off my question. He'd hung up on me.

I'd eaten at Lupe's school, but I'd just been rejected by both of my children. I needed comfort food. Since I was only a few feet from the gas station food center, I stopped in and bought a big bag of Cheetos and a two-liter bottle of Diet Coke.

* * * *

I realized, as I headed back for the trailer, munching on Cheetos and swigging on the Diet Coke, that I'd walked more since I'd moved to the trailer park than I had in years. No wonder so many people in Texas exercise in nice air-conditioned facilities. Moving around in the summer heat was brutal.

Tina emerged from her trailer as I stumbled back into the trailer park, sweat dripped into my eyes. The sun was so bright it gave me a headache, and the only air movement came from cars and trucks whizzing by.

"I heard you got fired," she said.

I looked at Tina to spot any signs of gloating. She looked sympathetic.

"Yeah. They thought I was a dangerous influence."

"Them along with half the police departments in the state. Speaking of which, have you talked to your lawyer?"

"We've been through this. I don't get a court-appointed until I actually get arrested."

"I'm talking about the lawyer for your assault charge. Since you got bumped from your community service, you're in technical violation of your probation. If you don't get things rescheduled, they'll put you in jail."

"Jail?"

"I've been there. Trust me, you don't want to take that route."

"But I went to my community service. I tried to do it and they kicked me out. It wasn't my fault."

"You think your judge will care?"

All my life I'd heard about how soft the system was on criminals. Now, though, I was on the other side, and I wasn't even a criminal. Not really, anyway, no matter what trumped up charge I'd agreed to. Things didn't seem soft to me, they seemed like a horrible Catch-22. No matter what I did, things only got worse.

"Okay, you're right. I just got back from the Texaco station making calls, and I don't have the energy to walk there again in this heat. Can I borrow your phone?"

She stepped back into her trailer and I thought she'd decided to ignore me, just like everyone else was. But she was out again in a couple of seconds, cell in hand.

She handed the phone over and I left a message with Barry Levitz letting him know about me getting fired and asking his help in staying out of jail.

Tina gave me a funny look when I handed back her phone.

"What?"

"You sounded almost human there."

A part of me wanted to bristle, but at least Tina was talking to me. Which put her on a very short list.

"Thanks. I guess."

She shoved her phone back toward me. "I did some research for you. You might want to look at what I found under Betty Rope and Kayla Switzer."

I stared at the phone. It was a nice model with a big screen, but I still didn't know what she was talking about. "Huh?"

"Come on, Heather. You're not dumb, so don't put on the act. It isn't just a phone, it's a computer. I spent some time Googling those two and downloaded the files for you. The files are listed under their names."

Flushing, because I knew I occasionally put on the dumb female act, I fumbled out the phone's stylus and clicked my way into the computer part of the system.

What Tina had found was plenty interesting, all right. In less than a year, Kayla had gone from a junior associate at one of those divorce-for-$39.99 street-corner law places to being the managing partner of a multi-million dollar law office. It turned out that her entire firm's business was conducted for Montag Industries.

I saw Martin's hand in her success. He'd always believed in doing business with friends, and friends he could sleep with made for an added bonus. I wondered where Kayla's firm stood now that Martin was no longer around to send business her way.

Tina's information on Betty was every bit as interesting.

"I knew she was getting stock for pay in the early days, but she was still just a secretary. I can't believe that they gave her two million shares."

"They didn't," Tina answered. "It was just a few thousand shares in the early days, and worth almost nothing. But she held onto it. And the stock has split a number of times. Since Betty never sold any, she ended up with more. Lots more."

"With her dead, somebody is going to come into a nice inheritance." I looked further into Tina's findings. "I presume you noticed this. Betty doesn't have any close relations, which means there isn't any clear motive for someone to kill her. Unless she left a will, some distant cousins will divide up the money."

"Even if someone was going to inherit, we need someone with a motive to kill both her and Martin. I doubt that anyone will inherit from *both* of them."

"Good point. But who the heck would have a motive to kill both her and Martin."

"Besides you, you mean?"

I felt like she'd stuck an ice pick in my heart. Still, I tried to make a joke out of it. "Well, yeah. But I didn't."

Tina nodded and took back her phone. She was a lot quicker with her stylus than I was and keyed into the Securities Exchange site on the Internet.

"She didn't just own a *lot* of shares," Tina reported after a couple of minutes of clicking away. "She was the company's second largest stockholder."

"Lucky her."

Tina shot me a look. "You've got a strange definition of lucky. Anyway, as long as her lover was in charge of the company, I'm sure she voted the corporate line. But I wonder if she would have come up with other ideas once Martin was gone. You said that all of those executives were jockeying for position. Without Betty's support, they'd have a hard time coming up with the votes they need to select the next Chairman of the Board. Probably over the years there were more than a few of them who talked down to her, treated her like garbage because she was a woman and worked in an administrative job. Wouldn't they be surprised when it turns out that she has the power to ruin their careers? Mightn't one of them have realized she could screw their chances?"

"You're saying—"

"You already *know* what I'm saying. Your son, Nick, is the designated heir. But Martin's holdings were just under twenty percent of the company, and Nick owns maybe one percent on his own. Betty's holdings are almost ten percent. With the rest of the ownership spread everywhere, those two blocks, together, give effective control over the entire corporation. Separately, they can partially offset each other.

"If she opposed Nick, he probably wouldn't get the votes to become the new chairman. In fact, if she wanted to, Betty would have had almost as good a chance of stepping into that Chairman role as Nick would."

"But why would she oppose him?"

Tina shrugged. "Because he isn't his father? Because he didn't treat her well? Because she thought she could run the company better than he could? It's lucky for Nick that he won't have to worry about that. Since she's conveniently been murdered, there's one less obstacle to him taking control."

"Come on, Tina. You're making it sound like--"

"I'm saying that we've got someone with a much better motive than yours. Your motive is just revenge for your husband stepping out on you. Nick's motive is control of a billion-dollar company. Money trumps love in my book."

"Nick wouldn't kill anyone."

"I'll bet he tortured cats when he was a kid, right?"

"Of course not."

Tina laughed. "I was just kidding about that. But you do see what I mean, don't you? You're ready to dismiss him out of hand just because he's your son. Think about this, Heather. If he did it, he set you up to look like the killer. So, how much do you really owe him?"

"He didn't do it." Still, at the back of my mind, a voice demanded, *what if he did?* He was my son. Was I willing to take the fall for him?

If we'd been involved in a fire or an accident, there was no question in my mind. I'd save either of my children at the cost of my own life and think it was cheap at the price. I imagine most mothers would do the same. Who could live with herself if she knew she survived thanks to the death of one of her own children?

But murder was no accident. If Nick had killed twice, taking the fall for him wouldn't just save him. It would let a killer free. Someone who'd killed twice would think of murder as a way of doing business. Which meant, I'd be responsible for anyone he killed in the future.

But that was pointless speculation, wasn't it? "I just won't believe that Nick killed his father," I repeated. I could be in denial, but I knew Nick. He'd been a sweet kid. He'd had all of the athletic tools, but he'd never been a superstar in sports because he lacked the killer instinct. He'd toughened up when he went into the sales department at Montag Industries, but he was still my sweet son.

"The second murder is a tragedy, of course," Tina said, "but it's a big help for us if we want to figure out who really did it. Lots of people might have had a motive to kill Martin. But there can't be that many people with motives to kill both of them. Nick's motives are obvious. He killed his father to gain control of the company. When he saw that Betty was in the way, he killed her too. Your motive is equally obvious—you killed your unfaithful husband and one of his lovers.

"You say it isn't Nick, and we know it wasn't you. So, who else could it be? I don't see Caitlin killing her sugar-daddy. And Betty wouldn't have let her close. Not after you talked with her."

"Definitely not Caitlin."

"What about Kayla?" Tina asked. "I mean, she is a lawyer."

"I've been assuming that she was the big winner in keeping Martin alive. She was the one best set up to move into the wife position. But what if Martin didn't see it that way? What if she found out he was stringing her along?"

I caught a sudden memory of the way Betty's nostrils had flared when I'd mentioned Kayla to her. Betty might have dismissed my words, but she saw Kayla as the main threat. And with the stock she owned, she could make sure that Montag Industries cut its ties to Kayla's law firm—and spreading the word that Kayla had gotten her business on her back rather than through courthouse savvy.

"Betty hated Kayla. And once I talked to her about her stock, she might have realized she was in a position to do something about it. Kayla would have had to respond quickly to protect her business. But how would she have known?"

"Easy. Stock ownership is included in SEC 10-K reports. If Kayla had bothered to look, she would have found it. Lawyers know how to research. Of course, Betty might have called her and told her to haul her butt out of the Montag offices."

I breathed a sigh of relief. "So, Nick is off the hook, right? It's got to be Kayla."

Tina made a clicking, disapproving noise with her tongue. "Nobody's off the hook, Heather. Kayla might have had a motive to kill Betty, but why would she kill Martin? And as long as Martin was alive, Betty was no threat to Kayla."

I knew she was wrong. It *had* to be Kayla. I only wondered why it had taken me so long to realize this.

I opened my mouth, then shut it when I previewed what I'd been about to say. I wasn't just on probation with the courts, I was also on probation with Tina. She might not be reminding me of how I'd stood her and Lupe up, but she hadn't forgotten, either. If I just blew off her ideas, I risked losing her entirely.

Without her help, I'd be completely alone.

For the first time, I really understood the type of social pressure the StrongGirl program talked about. I *needed* other people around me. And frankly, to get the type of support I needed, I would compromise a lot of the high-minded ideals I'd spouted when I'd been safe and rich in Frisco. It's easier to know all the answers when you're talking about other people's problems. When you've got actual problems yourself, things weren't as straightforward.

"So that's two suspects," I said. "I don't believe Nick killed his father, but I agree that we can't rule out the possibility. Not yet, anyway. And I agree that we don't understand why Kayla would have killed Martin. So, that's a short-list of two. Who else can we add?"

Tina shrugged. "Nick is what, twenty-nine? Maybe one of the other executives thinks he could take over, that the board will think Nick is too young, too inexperienced. If Betty was planning to support Nick, that would motivate whomever is next on the list. And killing Martin would make sense because if they waited, Nick would be older, better positioned to move into the CEO spot."

In the early days, Martin and I had discussed the politics at Montag Industries a lot. I'd helped him when his first partner had tried to loot the company by demanding kickbacks from suppliers. Over the years, though, our conversations had faded to discussions about the children, about my decorating projects, and about contributing to candidates for local and national office. I was no longer up on who was battling with whom on Montag Industry's mahogany row, which is what they called the paneled top floor of the Montag headquarters building in Frisco.

"I'm having lunch with Nick tomorrow," I said. "I'll try to get his take on office politics."

"I guess that'll have to do it. What about your daughter, Leah?"

"She won't be there."

Tina sighed. "I mean, could she be a suspect?"

"I don't see why. She's getting less money now than when her daddy would write her checks all the time."

"Maybe she was angry with him for divorcing you and sleeping around on you."

I considered that—for maybe half a second. "Leah doesn't think that way. She's my daughter and I love her, but it's all about her."

"What about that boyfriend she has?"

"Richard?" I didn't like Richard, thought he was a horrible influence on Leah. He lacked even the morals of a rabid vulture, but I didn't see him having the guts to kill someone. Kick them when they were down, yes. Kill them, no. "Much though I'd like it to be him, I just can't see it."

Tina considered, then nodded. "You know these people and I don't so I'm going to go with your judgment."

Except when it came to my son. I didn't raise that issue with her—it was becoming increasingly obvious that I just wasn't a StrongGirl. Maybe it was for the best that I'd flunked out of the StrongGirl mentoring program.

"So, what are we going to do?" I asked.

"Why wait. Let's see if we can get with Kayla today."

It was six o'clock and I suspected Kayla would have gone home, but she answered her phone when I called her office.

I lied and told her I had some things to hand off to her in her new role as Chair of the League and she agreed to meet me at a Plano sports bar in an hour.

I'd hung up before I remembered my car was broken.

Tina looked at her own car for a moment, then shook her head. "We'll take the train. We'd better get going."

Chapter 11

Kayla had one empty margarita glass in front of her and a second that was only half full by the time we got to the bar. And we weren't late.

"Kayla." I did the cheek-kiss thing with her, exactly as if she hadn't stolen my job and my husband from me.

That I thought about it in that order probably said something, I realized.

"You look so, uh, relaxed and comfortable, Heather," Kayla responded. I could practically feel her disapproval of my thrift-store wardrobe.

She, of course, looked fabulous. Her jet-black suit would have been perfect for a funeral or a White House dinner, except it was just the slightest bit too short, highlighting legs that would stop traffic. Somehow, though, it seemed that she'd forgotten her blouse and a camisole peeked through the buttoned suit jacket.

Naturally the woman had a rack. I knew I was being catty, but I wondered if Martin had financed her breast enhancement, as he had with Caitlin. My husband, the one-man supporter of Dallas's plastic surgery industry.

I looked down at the muumuu-style dress I'd pulled out of my drawer that morning. I hadn't noticed the stain on the sleeve when I'd bought it, and the thrift-store lighting hid exactly how faded out the pattern had become.

I pretended to take her compliment seriously. "Do you like it? I've been simplifying my life and I was so afraid this might be over the top. Kayla, this is my friend Tina Anderson. I hope you don't mind me bringing her along."

Kayla rolled her eyes at Tina's ratty jeans and trade-show t-shirt. "I thought you wanted—"

"Anderson, as in ex-wife of Andy Anderson, second richest man in Dallas," I said in a stage whisper. If Kayla chose to believe that made Tina a rich potential donor, that was her mistake. Extreme wealth means you can dress however you want. Just look at Bill Gates's haircut.

Kayla blinked. "Andy Anderson Anderson? Oh, of course. Have a seat, Heather, Tina was it?"

"Thanks, Kayla. Let me get the next round." Tina headed off to the bar and I sat down across the table from Kayla.

"Andy Anderson has always supported the *other* party," Kayla whispered.

"Maybe putting his ex-wife on the stage on our side would help defuse that." It had always been an embarrassment to us that we were supposed to be the pro-business party but we couldn't count on the support of some of the biggest business leaders in town.

Kayla grinned. "Zing, in his face. I like that, Heather. You always had clever ideas. I'm glad you're on our side, and that you don't have any hard feelings about the election."

I waved a hand as if dismissing any possible pique. "Not just the election. I'm also grateful for your help with Martin. You cannot believe how tired I was of his continual sexual demands. Once you and the others stepped in, things

101

were so much easier for me."

"Others?" She squeaked a little when she said it.

My giggle sounded horribly forced to me—I had to hope that Kayla had drunk enough that she wouldn't notice. "Come on, girlfriend. We're all adults here. You know as well as I do that Martin wasn't the kind of man who'd limit himself to one woman."

"That's not..." she paused and chug-a-lugged the rest of her drink. "That is to say, I don't know what you're talking about and I'm distressed on your behalf to hear that Mr. Montag might not have been completely faithful. As you know, my connection with Mr. Montag was purely professional. I worked as lead outside attorney for Montag Industries when it had litigation requirements. I certainly never would have compromised that professional relationship—"

"Oh, Kayla, you are so sweet for trying to make me feel better, but it isn't necessary. I could understand lying if Martin was still alive and the divorce was an active issue, but with him dead, that just doesn't come up, does it?"

"Naturally I'm sympathetic with your grief." Kayla pretended to ignore everything I'd said.

I nodded, accepting her faked sympathy. "It has been hard for me, Kayla. Just as I'm certain it's been hard for you. With Martin's tragic death, you went from being the future Mrs. Montag to a cuttable expense item on the Montag Industries income statement.

She swallowed the rest of her margarita. "I'm not sure—"

"But I'm sure neither of us is worried about money at a time like this."

Kayla narrowed her eyes, as if the margarita interfered with her focus. "Everyone is saying you killed him. So why the hypocrisy?"

"I killed him?" I faked a laugh. "I was going to clean him out in the courts. You've seen the kind of settlements abandoned wives have gotten, lately. I'll have a harder time dealing with his estate."

"But if you didn't—"

"That's the thing, Kayla." I paused and stared at her for a good ten seconds. "I've been trying to think, though, who would have killed him?"

She slammed her empty glass down on the table. "I'm sure—"

Tina unobtrusively replaced the empty with another full margarita.

"Not you, of course, Kayla. You were the winner in the little dog-race that Martin set up between his various lovers. I was thinking of Caitlin."

"Caitlin?"

I laughed. "Oh, Kayla. You are so funny, pretending like you didn't know what was going on with Martin. You know as well as I do who I'm talking about. Little Caitlin Leitmol, of course. Martin's barely-out-of-her-teens sex-toy. When she found out he was going to replace me with you instead of her, she must have lost control. Horrible, of course, but young people have such a hard time learning self-control."

"But that's—"

"Don't tell me you didn't know about Caitlin."

She might not have noticed that Tina had replaced her drink, but she took a big hit from the new one. "I'm sure I have no idea what you're talking about, Heather. Mr. Montag's love life is a complete mystery to me."

"Other than when Betty was able to pencil you in, you mean? Of course, Betty couldn't give you too many slots. What with reserving as many as she could for herself."

"Betty is a bitch."

"Well, I certainly won't disagree with you there." Except about the tense.

Kayla finished her third margarita and grabbed at a fourth that had magically appeared. "Why are you telling me this stuff, Heather? What's your angle?"

"Not every woman is as understanding as we are," I said. "You and I understand the way men think. Men are like lions. The powerful ones gather females around them like a magnet attracts iron filings. For forceful leaders like Martin, sex with multiple women was simply claiming his due. You and I realize that's just sex. That even the master lion can be tamed by the Queen of the Jungle. But a young thing like Caitlin would believe in love. She'd think Martin cared for her, rather than simply seeing her as a reward for his wealth and power. When she realized the truth, that she was way down the totem pole, she might snap."

I watched Kayla's face closely and I noticed the way her jaw clenched when I gave her my description, all too accurate, of Martin's apparent personality disorder. I was using Caitlin's name, but I was describing the attitude I suspected that Kayla would take as well. Kayla was the one who had put herself on the line, the one who was in the best position to become the next Mrs. Montag. If Martin had told her she was going to have to continue to share his sexual favors, especially with younger women who didn't have to work so hard to maintain their perky perfect figures, she might have decided to sever the relationship—permanently.

Betty had refused to tell me who Martin had been meeting with the night of his murder. Although she'd claimed she had told the police everything, I was willing to bet that she hadn't told them that Martin wasn't just meeting with his lawyer, he was meeting with one of his lovers. After my talk with Betty, she'd probably called Kayla to confer, and maybe to threaten. Kayla would have realized she needed to strike before it was too late.

Everything was coming together. As Kayla sucked down a large mouthful of her next drink, I wondered if things were coming together *too* well. If I was right, Kayla had already killed two people. She might just decide that I was the next.

"Everything was going to be perfect." She slurred her words together, but I'm pretty sure that was what she said, anyway.

Kayla tried to bring two fingers together, missed, and managed to connect on her second go-around. "Martin and me, we were like this—*simpatico*. I was going to be on the corporate board. My business was set to explode."

I shook my head with as much sympathy as I could fake. "That sounds perfect, Kayla. And you'd worked so hard to make it happen."

"Then it all fell to shit."

"What happened, Kayla? Did Martin tell you he'd changed his mind?"

"Martin? That pussy-whipped fool? Are you kidding? I had him so wrapped around my finger, he asked permission before going to the bathroom."

"Did Betty get in your way?"

"She wanted to, the bitch. And Martin wouldn't fire her boney butt. But I was working on her."

"I'll bet you were. Still, things didn't go right. What happened?"

"You know what happened." She sprayed spit and lime juice as she talked. "Somebody killed Martin. Without him, I was just another whore in a company filled with whores. And all of a shudden," she stopped and blinked at me, "sudden, I meant to say, nobody would return my phone calls."

"But why kill Martin?"

"Thash what I want to know. Why would somebody kill *him*? I mean, sure Martin was trying to keep his money from you. But like you say, even a halfway decent lawyer would have cracked him open like a walnut. No way you were going to walk away with less than ten, maybe twenty million. Maybe a lot more. But the way he went tried to screw you... I wouldn't blame you for killing him, the bastard.

"You mean you didn't love Martin?"

"Love him?" She blinked at me. "Of course I didn't love him. I slept with him because that was what I needed to do to get the business. You grew up rich, Heather. You even have a rich-girl name. Not me—I was lower middle class. But as head of a high-dollar law firm, I was something. Now, though, everything is turning to shit."

The conversation had taken a turn I hadn't expected. "So, why *did* you kill him, Kayla?" It was worth a try.

Unfortunately, that ploy works better on TV than it did for me.

"You killed him, not me. Bartender!" she suddenly yelled. "'Nother drink."

"I let the bartender know she shouldn't drive," Tina said. "Do we need any more, here?"

"Darned right we do." I turned back to Kayla. "You're the only person with a motive to kill both Martin and Betty. You said yourself that Betty was ruining things for you. Why not kill her?"

"Never thought of it."

"Come on, Kayla. You're a lawyer. You think—"

"Don't feel so hot."

I leapt from my seat in the booth across from Kayla barely in time to avoid the projectile stream of vomit that extruded from her mouth.

The guy behind where I'd been sitting wasn't so lucky. He turned around, looked at the sheet of barf that covered the table, the bench, and his suit jacket —and promptly ralphed himself.

"Don't feel so hot," Kayla repeated to the suddenly quiet bar.

"I'll walk you to the bathroom." Cleaning up after the woman who'd stolen my husband from me was way down on my list of things I wanted to do, but I'd cooperated in getting her drunk. It was only fair that I cooperate in cleaning up the mess.

"Go-way. You killed Martin. I could be next." She swirled in a big circle, her purse out clunking into heads of anyone nearby until she stumbled and ran her hip into someone else's table.

The table had been loaded with beers and shifted when she hit it, empty and full bottles smashing to the floor.

She bent over and got sick again, this time missing everyone, but dropped her purse as she straightened herself back up. A small black handgun popped out of the handbag and slid across the floor.

"Gun! She's got a gun."

I didn't know who'd screamed, but it started a panicked run for the doors.

I kicked the gun away, toward the bartender.

"I'm calling the police," the bartender told me once he'd secured the weapon. "If you want to stick around, that's your call."

"Do you need help?" I asked Kayla.

"I wouldn't touch your help with a biohazard suit. Gimme my gun and I'll shoot you, just like you shot Martin."

She went after her weapon, but the bartender was too quick, sweeping it away from her and depositing it in a locked drawer behind the bar. "We've posted 'no weapons' signs so she'll probably be arrested," he explained. "If she's your friend, you might want to bail her out."

"Not my friends," Kayla shouted.

"Let's go home," Tina suggested. "As the Lone Ranger would say, 'Our work here is done.'"

I followed Tina out to her car with a sinking suspicion that we'd just crossed someone else off our suspect list. In margarita veritas, or something. Kayla had been very drunk and very convincing. If she hadn't done it, though, the only suspect we had left was Nick.

* * * *

When I woke the next morning, the bus still didn't run to Frisco and my car was still non-functional, sitting where my sweaty chewing-tobacco neighbor had pushed it.

I considered hitchhiking up to Frisco for my meeting with Nick—something I'd done often enough as a teen in the seventies, but I'd heard too much about stranger-danger since then. I just couldn't make myself do it. So, I went and groveled with Tina.

She had a cup of coffee in her hand and looked like she'd been up for hours. Her cut-off denim shorts and halter top were a lot more practical approach to the Texas heat than was my thrift-store dress, but they didn't make halter tops big enough to fit someone my size. At least, I hoped they didn't.

Tina stared at me as I ran through my request shaking her head the entire time until I finally ran down.

"Let me get this straight. You ruined your own car after owning it for two days and so now you want to borrow mine? Why would I agree to that?"

Good question. "Because you're my friend?"

"Jeez, Heather. You don't make being a friend easy."

Tina was right about that. I'd been high-maintenance since I'd come into her trailer park. I'd been high-maintenance before that too, I realized. It had seemed to be my lifestyle choice. In fact, many of the women in the League would joke about how much they demanded, as if that was something to be proud of. I'd never bragged, but I hadn't exactly showed the others a better example, either. The Rolex watch I'd pawned earlier was just one piece of evidence.

"I don't mean to be."

"Oh, really? Well, let's see what we can do. Because I'm *not* going to let you borrow my car."

What we could do was practically a miracle. As trailer park manager, Tina owned a full set of tools, and had at least some idea how to use them.

A quick trip to an auto parts shop and I was the proud owner of a new battery, although buying it drained my wallet down to the last six dollars of the Rolex pawning money. Of course, I hadn't asked Tina how much she'd paid for all those drinks when we'd been questioning Kayla. As my assets declined, my debt went up even faster.

Tina showed me how to remove the old battery, explained how to dispose of it (who knew you couldn't just dump it in the dumpster like everything else), and taught me how to hook up a new one.

As I wiped grease off my fingers with a rag, also courtesy of the auto parts shop, I had visions of getting a job in auto mechanics. Those visions became even more real when I stepped into the car, cranked the engine, and it started right up. I'd repaired a car and it worked. For the first time since Martin's murder, I felt like I'd accomplished something.

"Sounds like hell and you're burning oil," Tina commented.

"Can we fix that? A cousin of Lupe's told me I needed a valve job. I thought he was talking dirty at first."

"He wasn't talking dirty and you probably do. But that's major car surgery and I don't have a clue how to do that. And speaking of the devil, here comes Lupe now."

She was wearing her uniform and had her book backpack slung across her back, but she was a long way from school.

"You stood me up again. I went to the volunteer room and you weren't there. Were you afraid to show your face?"

"I got fired," I admitted.

"But I wasn't important enough for you to tell? How do you think I felt when I was standing there with all the other girls and they told me that my mentee was gone?"

"Mentee?"

"I'm a mentor. That must make you a mentee."

I was pretty sure that was wrong, but I didn't know the right word. One thing for sure, though. This wasn't the time to critique Lupe's English. She was steaming mad and she had good reason.

My exit from the school had been pretty abrupt, but I could have made an effort to let Lupe know. My work with the League had taught me to follow up, not to expect anyone else to do what they should.

"I'm sorry."

"You're sorry a lot, aren't you?"

I turned off my car and got out. There was something uncomfortable about having to look up to see a girl shorter than I was. Plus, she'd situated herself so I had to look straight into the sun to see her.

"I've only been sorry a lot lately." Maybe I'd had reason to be sorry before, but I'd never stopped to notice. Since starting my second life, though, I'd had plenty of opportunities to make up for lost time.

"Why'd they fire you?"

"They didn't want to expose impressionable girls to a possible murderer."

Lupe glared at me for a couple of seconds before she realized I was serious. Then she started to giggle.

She tried to get control of herself and failed, breaking out into new fits of laughter several times.

Finally I decided it was time for an intervention. "So, why aren't you in school?"

"School is stupid. I learned more working with Tina the other day than I have all year. None of the teachers knows how to program a game or anything like that."

"Considering that the school year only started a couple of weeks ago, it isn't a big surprise that you haven't learned a lot," Tina reminded Lupe. "They always start out with review. Anyway, you've got to go to school."

"Are you going to tell me that you never cut your classes?"

"*I* never did," I assured her.

"Well la-di-da. That's because you're a goodie-two-shoes. What about you, Tina?"

"I got this job at the trailer park because my ex-husband owns it. If you want to use me as a role model, you're setting your standards way too low."

"So, you did cut out."

"Heather has to meet with her son. And I've got to take you back to school."

Lupe's eyes widened. "You're going to let Heather meet with that killer all by herself? Think of the danger. And don't tell me he wouldn't kill his mother —he killed his father."

"Nick hasn't killed anyone." I kept my line even though I'd run out of alternate candidates.

"We'll write you a note," Lupe decided. "We'll tell him that we know you were going to meet with him and that we'll tell the cops he did it if you don't return safely."

"You know," Tina said. "I think that's a good idea."

Lupe reminded me to pour a quart of oil into the engine, wrote the note, reluctantly got into Tina's yellow Storm and the two of them headed off.

I followed a couple of minutes later. I would be early for my meeting with Nick, but I figured I could spend my time in the company cafeteria getting a sense of what people were thinking. I couldn't believe Nick was behind the dual murder, but someone had to be. And I had to believe that whoever had killed Martin and Betty had some financial stake in what happened. So, besides Nick, who were the big winners at Montag Industries?

I couldn't think of any.

My car looked like the ugly duckling amongst the gleaming SUVs, pristine extended-cab pickup trucks, and luxury sedans that were the swans of the Montag Industries parking lot.

I parked up front, though, in visitor parking, ignored the evil eye I got from one of the security guards, and headed for the front door.

Joe Moses guarded the main entrance to Montag Industries. As always, his shades were in place, his black-on-black uniform imposing, and his shiny bald head scary. He headed straight for me.

I squeaked. I'd forgotten about my earlier suspicions of Joe.

But if Joe killed me, Tina and Lupe would call the cops on Nick. And if Joe had reason to be angry with Martin, he had even more reason to be angry with Nick. After all, it was Nick's friend Gary French who'd been brought in to head up the security department. So, Joe could kill me and put Nick in jail. A two-for-one.

"Nice to see you again, Mrs. Montag." He pinned a visitor badge to my dress.

"Hi Joe." I had managed not to piss on myself, but it had been a close call. "Everyone must be pretty shaken up here, what with two deaths within just a few days."

I assume he was staring at me. With his black shades, he might have had his eyes shut for all I knew.

"You'd think that, wouldn't you?"

I would think that and Nick had said it. What was going on? "You mean things aren't all hectic?"

"Maybe it's a mark of how well organized we are. Martin always said that the company isn't about any one man."

It would never have crossed Martin's mind to suggest that the company isn't about any one *woman*. I wondered, though, if Betty's death might not have been a harder blow to the company than Martin's. Nick had spent his life training to take over for Martin. Nick's assistant, Desiree, had always seemed challenged by the alphabet. I didn't think she was going to be able to keep the whole company organized the way Betty had.

"I thought I'd wander around the cafeteria and visit with some of my friends here," I told Joe.

As if anyone in the company would admit to being friends with me considering that I was still the primary suspect in Martin's murder.

"I got special orders from my boss. Gary said that Nick is anxious to see you, and I should take you straight up to Nick's office. Shall we go, Mrs. Montag?"

Joe didn't twist my wrist or anything, but he made it very clear I had no choice but to go along.

He followed me into the elevator and punched the top floor button.

"Nick's office is on the third floor."

Mahogany row was the fourth floor, but Nick had chosen to office with his sales team on third rather than with the other executives.

"Nick has moved into the CEO's office."

"I thought there would have to be an appointment by the Board of Directors."

Joe's teeth glistened bright white against his dark skin. "Apparently Nick felt that a *fait accompli* would serve his purposes better than just waiting."

I reminded myself that I still didn't believe Nick was capable of murder.

Increasingly, I was less convincing.

Chapter 12

Gary French waited at the elevator exit. He shook Joe's hand, inquired as to my health, and wondered if Joe would like to take me down to Nick's office or turn me over to him.

"Guess I can manage a couple more steps."

"Good, good." Gary got a funny look on his face like he was trying to pass a kidney stone. "And I owe you an apology, Mrs. Montag. Mr. Montag said he was worried that you'd freak out when you got word about the divorce and I over-reacted in the meeting room. "I know you're not dangerous," he continued, "and I've called the police to see what we can do about dropping the charges. Unfortunately, they say you pled out and they can't do anything about that. They did take you off the hook when it comes to your community service, though. Again, I'm sorry for what happened. Please let me know if there's anything I can do to make it up to you."

I blinked a couple of times. This was the man who'd come down on me like a ton of bricks and had treated Joe like he was a field hand. But my mother had raised me to have manners, and lesson one was, if someone offers you an apology, you've got to accept.

"That's perfectly all right, Gary."

"I'll be in my office so don't hesitate to stop by if there's anything I can do. In the meantime, I know Nick is looking forward to seeing you."

Nick might have looked forward to seeing me when he'd been in elementary school. By the time he was a teen, though, he'd decided that moms were not cool. When I drove him to school, he'd always made me drop him off half a block away so he wouldn't be seen with me.

I was thinking I'd slipped into an alternate reality until Joe brought me down to the corner office where Nick had set up camp. Then things got back to normal.

Nick's assistant, Desiree, gave Joe one of those looks normal people reserve for when their cats drag still-living lizards into their houses.

Joe pretended not to notice. "Mrs. Montag is expected, Desiree."

Desiree looked up from her nail file. "Mr. Montag is on the phone right now, Mrs. Montag. I'll let him know you're here as soon as he hangs up."

Joe wandered over to Desiree's desk. I wondered why a guy would want to check out a woman who treated him like he was filth and wasn't surprised when Desiree wrinkled her nose as if she'd smelled something that had been left out in the sun for too long.

"Guess he's off the phone now," Joe announced, staring pointedly at her phone. "All of the lines are open. Must have just happened. Right, Desiree?"

Desiree fluttered. "His call was scheduled to go on for an hour but they must have finished early today. Let me get him on the intercom."

Joe stepped back to me. His gait was loose-limbed, as if he hadn't a care in the world, but Desiree was playing out of her weight class when she deliberately confronted the guard manager.

I wondered how she would have felt about Betty staying around, owning enough stock to guarantee herself a place of power, knowing where all the bodies were buried. If Desiree were the type to scheme, and she certainly appeared that way to me, Betty would have been a horrible burden. I wasn't prepared to claim this gave Desiree a motive for murder, but people have been killed for less.

As Desiree whispered into the intercom, I checked out Nick's assistant more closely than ever I had before.

Before, she'd just seemed like one of the dozens of beautiful young women that filled the corridors of Montag Industries. Which wasn't really much of a clue. Frisco is home to lots of beautiful women. Plastic surgery and cosmetic dentistry were big businesses here. Still, it seemed strange that I'd never noticed that virtually every woman employed by Montag Industries were unusually attractive.

Desiree could have stepped out of the mold. She was a pretty brunette with dark blue eyes and curves in all the right places. Her hair was unprofessional— hip-length, hanging loose. The kind of hair men fantasize about.

Her fingers were unadorned with either a wedding or engagement ring, and her makeup fell short of perfect only because her lipstick was smeared.

If Desiree wanted to join the League, she would have had to cut her hair and ditch her low-cut dress and wear something more businesslike. I made a note to myself to speak to Nick about the example he was setting for the rest of his organization by allowing his assistant to flaunt herself in this way. Then I wondered if I was just getting old. Like facial piercings, tattoos, and midriff-baring tops, maybe that kind of hair and cleavage-display were now mainstream business fashion. A moment later, Nick burst out of the office I continued to think of as Martin's.

He looked wonderful, of course. Unlike Leah, Nick had inherited my taste in clothes. His navy pinstripe was the perfect mix of conservative businessman and, with its Italian cut showing off his gym-sculpted muscles, pure style. His tie was a classy regimental design, but it seemed slightly askew, as if someone had tugged on it. And I thought I saw a hint of something red on his lips.

I tried not to compare the shade to Desiree's lipstick, but the evidence seemed incontrovertible. My son was making out with his assistant.

Nick was single, so this wasn't the same as Martin and Betty, but I could only see trouble brewing. And if I could see it, Martin would have been able to see it as well. Uh-oh.

"Guess I'd better get back to my post," Joe said.

"I appreciate you bringing my mother up, Joe. You up for our handball game on Friday?"

"Wouldn't miss it."

"You'd better watch out, then. You killed me last week, so I'm going to be looking for revenge."

"I'm shaking."

They did that sort of shoulder-punching ritual that guys do to show that they're manly, and Joe headed out, leaving me alone with my son and his admin.

Nick grasped me by my shoulders and looked me in the eye. "Mom, I'm so glad you're here. You know, it looks to me like you've lost some weight."

Even if I had, I doubted Nick would notice. This was how he always greeted me. Until then, I'd considered it a positive. I wondered, though, why he thought it was helpful to call attention to my weight all the time.

"I see you've moved into the CEO's office, Nick. Shouldn't you wait for the board to confirm you?"

He gave me that mischievous grin that had broken hearts through his high school and college career. "You know what they say about forgiveness being easier than permission, Mom. I figured, if I stayed down on the third floor, the board could look around and say, 'let's consider all the choices.' But if I was already here, they'd have to say 'can we afford to kick Nick out of his father's office?' I don't think they'll do that. It would look like a slap in Dad's face."

I didn't think Betty would have had any problems with Nick following in his father's footsteps. But she might have wanted a little more time before her lover was evicted from memory.

Surely, though, getting into the corner office wouldn't be motive for murder.

I reminded myself that I wasn't looking for evidence Nick was guilty. At one level, I was sure he was innocent. Lupe and Tina had gotten to me, though. I filtered everything he said through the possibility that he might have killed his father.

"Come back into Dad's, uh, my office. We can chat for a few minutes before we go down to eat."

"Great."

"Desiree. My mother takes her coffee with cream but no sugar. I believe we have some real cream in the refrigerator."

"No problem, Nick." She lowered her voice an octave and hip-twitched over to the coffee maker.

Nick stared after his assistant and I had to halfway drag him to his office.

"I don't want to hear about it," he told me the instant I sat down at the conference table in what had been Martin's office.

"Don't want to hear what, Nick?"

"You know you're just twitching to give me a lecture about how to treat women and how Desiree is trying to trap me into some financial disaster."

He was right about that. I straightened his tie and wiped the lipstick stain from his cheek. "How you treat your people reflects of how you run your whole organization."

"Dad always—"

"Your father was far from perfect."

"Dad was a great businessman. Gary has been trying to persuade me you couldn't have killed him, and I'm trying to give you the benefit of the doubt here, but I won't have you attacking him."

I guessed I owed Gary more than I'd known. "Saying he's not perfect isn't an attack."

"Yeah, sure. It's high praise. Anyway, I'm not doing anything with Desiree that she doesn't ask for, and she came onto me a long time before I responded. But I don't want to talk about her: I want to talk about you. How have you been doing? Leah tells me you've moved into her little bungalow downtown. What an adventure that must be for you. I've always thought downtown living would be cool. So close to all the culture, surrounded by the pulse of a real metropolis."

"It's not a bungalow, it's a trailer. And it's not downtown, it's in Oak Cliff."

"Really? Oak Cliff?" He paused for a moment, then managed to come up with an unconvincing laugh. "And a trailer. Then it *really* must be an adventure. I hope nobody in your League finds out. They'll drum you out if they discover you're associating with people earning less than half a million a year."

I wondered if everyone in the trailer park combined to earn that much.

"Very funny. The party does very well with middle class and lower middle class voters because we reflect their values."

"Sure, Mom." Nick hadn't really been paying attention to what I'd said. But then, I hadn't either.

My response was reflexive. Politics had been my life for years, since Leah had gotten old enough not to need her mother all the time. Since Martin's death, though, I hadn't thought much about politics, hadn't listened to talk radio, hadn't tuned into the *Fox Network*. I'd been too busy with real life. Being out there in real life had opened my eyes to a few things. The world seemed a lot more complicated from below than it had when I'd been on top.

"But enough about me," I said. "I want to know how you're doing. It must have been upsetting for you to lose your father right in the middle of your … disagreements. And now it's too late for you to negotiate through them. I know myself how hard it is."

Nick went very still. "I don't know what you're talking about."

I didn't know what I was talking about, either. Although I could guess that Martin wouldn't be pleased if he knew about Desiree, I couldn't be positive he had known.

Seeing Nick relate to Desiree, though, had inspired me to toss out the idea that father and son had been in conflict to see how Nick responded. I'd hoped he would laugh it off and I could finally cross him off of the suspect list.

Instead, though, he practically froze. His denial was about as convincing as Caitlin's artificial breasts.

* * * *

Nick used Desiree's arrival with coffee as an excuse to change the subject and he kept up a patter of stories about sales mishaps, business successes, and social engagements until it was time for us to go down and eat.

Martin had decreed that Montag Industries would have one cafeteria for all employees, eschewing the executive dining room concept that many more hierarchical businesses maintain.

I wondered if Nick would maintain that tradition. Certainly he didn't mingle with the employees the way Martin had, although he did call out greetings to some of the sales managers.

As he had for coffee, he had Desiree bring us our lunches. No mingling with the *hoi polloi* in the cafeteria line for Nick. Not that the mostly white well-fed and well-paid managers who made up the headquarters staff of Montag Industries could really be counted as working class.

"I've talked to our legal staff about finding someone to defend you in the murder trial," Nick confided after we were seated and Desiree and Gary French had cleared out all of the people eating within a couple of tables of ours. "They can't be involved themselves, of course. They're concerned that the company not be seen as taking sides."

"By legal staff, I assume you mean Kayla Switzer."

He raised an eyebrow. "Kayla and her team, of course. We've pretty much outsourced all of our legal activities to Kayla's firm. It isn't as if we're going to develop leading-edge performance in law internally."

"Kayla is hardly a neutral observer."

"Surely you're not suggesting—"

"I'm not suggesting anything. I have proof that Kayla and your father were having an affair."

He pressed his hands to his ears. "Please don't tell me any more. I don't want to hear anything that would give you more motive to kill him."

I didn't have time for this and I jerked his hands away from his ears. "I didn't kill your father and you know it."

Nick stared at me for several heartbeats. Then he picked up a steak knife and carved into what looked like a tender sirloin. I looked down at the small salad Desiree had selected for me. I was hungry and a few green leafs wasn't going to cut it. But I wasn't going to beg Desiree to get something else. For one thing, she'd limited herself to a small salad too.

I figured that with my seven remaining dollars, I could go through the cafeteria line alone, once I was done talking with Nick.

After making a substantial dent in his steak, Nick wiped his lips with a cloth napkin Desiree had found him (the rest of the cafeteria's customers made do with paper) and gave me a fake-looking grin.

"So, what's this you heard about Dad and me having problems?"

Since I hadn't *heard* anything, I couldn't exactly answer, but I knew my son. I'd known this question would be coming from the instant he'd denied having problems back in Martin's office. Since I hadn't been distracted by food, I'd spent my time trying to come up with a way of dealing with it that wouldn't expose my ignorance. While the Nick and Desiree thing could have been the cause, there might have been something even more substantial and I didn't want to give Nick an easy way out.

I still didn't want to believe Nick would kill his father, but I wished he could be a lot more convincing than he had been.

"I just wish you had come to me when you and your father first disagreed," I said. "You know I would have—"

"You couldn't have done anything," he interrupted. "Dad didn't just decide to divorce you last week, you know. He'd been building up to it for months."

And Nick had known the whole time. I wondered if I'd been the only person in Frisco who hadn't seen the breakup coming.

I swallowed hard. I knew Nick was counting on me getting defensive. But I'd deal with the issues of my husband dumping me once I'd found out who'd killed him—and cleared my own name.

"You've got to know that the police will be interested in your disagreements," I said. "If they think you were hiding it from them, they'll be more suspicious of you than if you're straightforward with them."

"Nobody knows of any disagreements. Nothing was written. Nobody spoke to anyone. What I'm curious is, who told you? And don't tell me that Dad did. I know the two of you were barely speaking for the past couple of years."

Couple of years? There was no way Martin and I had drifted apart for that long.

"I think you've made my point, Nick. I'm not the most connected person in this organization, but even I knew there were problems. With all of the political maneuvers over the next couple of months while the board of directors decides who to officially appoint as the new CEO of Montag Industries, you know it's going to come out. If you don't control the timing, one of your enemies will."

Nick looked down at his half-eaten steak and pushed away his plate. "A little disagreement over sales strategies is hardly going to give anyone leverage against me. Thanks to Dad's will, I'm the biggest stockholder in the company. Anyone who stands against me now will be outside the board looking in after the next stockholder meeting."

His look said he'd run up that sales disagreement thing to see if I'd go for it, or if I knew something else. He'd played stunts like that since he'd been a young boy, first learning how to lie. He'd tell part of the truth and then, if I challenged him on it, he would get all offended because he hadn't been lying at all. But Nick's definitions often stretched. Nick could construe an order from his father to stop sleeping with the sales admin as a disagreement over sales strategies.

Still, he had a point about the Board of Directors. They weren't likely to vote against the anointed son of the founder.

But his point made him that much more likely as a suspect. He'd as good as admitted that he and Martin had a serious disagreement about the way the company was going. And Martin was the kind of manager who required his employees to line up behind him. I couldn't imagine he'd actually fire his own son, but he sure could push him down in the organization, change things so he reported to a sales and marketing officer rather than to the CEO. Martin would have done that if he'd thought he needed to remind Nick who was boss.

Relying on Martin's block of stock to punish any internal opponents also increased Nick's motive for killing Betty. If he and Martin had feuded, she'd have known, and would have taken Martin's position.

I decided I would have to dig around at Montag to find the truth about the disagreement. One thing was certain, Nick wasn't going to tell me anything.

Since I had him on the defensive, I figured I would change tacks.

"I need some money, Nick."

He narrowed his eyes. "Are you talking blackmail, Mom? That you'd go to the cops if I don't pay you off?"

I fluttered my eyes. "Of course not, Nick. I just need some money for my living expenses. I've got an electric bill, food, clothes, that sort of stuff."

"Come on, mother. Your house has nine bedrooms and the closets in every single one of them are filled with your clothes. You need new clothes like Texas needs more dust storms."

Nick was not one to talk. I didn't recognize his suit's designer, but I'd spotted it as an Italian original. I did recognize his shoes—twelve hundred dollars, and his shirt was hand tailored. He didn't wear a Rolex, but his Rado was every bit as expensive, if a bit less ostentatious in solid black.

"Yes, I *own* plenty of clothes. But I can't get to those clothes, remember? Martin had me locked out of my own house."

"The house *is* corporate property. I had Gary look this up for me after you called me the first time. Dad sold the house to the business in return for a lifetime lease at a dollar a year. That was *his* lifetime, by the way. Which means that the house is now on the market. If you want to move back in, I'm sure the company would cut you a deal."

I didn't think the company would sell it to me for seven dollars, which was all I could offer them now. I was even more sure they wouldn't go for what I'd have left after I got something to eat for lunch. I pushed away the green weeds Desiree had brought me.

"The company may own the house, but I own my own property inside it. Surely the company could let me get my clothes and things."

"Clothes, yes. But what *things* are you talking about, mother? Your jewelry?"

"That would be a start."

He nodded, considering, then gave me the kind of grin that said he'd pulled a fast one on me.

"Okay. You keep your mouth shut and I'll have Gary take you over there. Don't try to take anything that doesn't belong to you. Do we have a deal?"

"We have a deal. I won't tell anyone what I know about your disagreement with your father," I said.

Since I didn't *know* anything, I thought that was a fair promise. It surely wouldn't cover anything I might learn in the future."

"Desiree." Nick raised his voice only slightly, but his pretty admin was instantly there.

"Call Gary and get him back over here. I want him to take my mother by the house, watch her while she gathers some stuff, and then lock up after her."

"I'd be happy to go over and clean up afterwards," Desiree said.

"Maybe I'll take you over there this afternoon. If you promise to be a good girl."

She giggled. "Are you sure you don't want me to be *bad?*"

I managed not to gag.

"With you, being bad is good."

I waited until Desiree sashayed away. "In all the years your father was having an affair with Betty, he never carried on like this." I'd have been better off keeping my mouth shut, but I'd been giving Nick advice since he'd been born and obviously it was too early for me to stop.

"I really don't want to hear about your motives for killing Dad," Nick said. "I think you'd better go before I change my mind. Ah, here's Gary."

Chapter 13

"My son tells me you're the one I should thank for his change of attitude, Gary."

We were in the entryway to the house I'd shared with Martin. Gary French had driven me over in his Hummer and opened the door with a freshly milled key.

"You don't owe me anything, Mrs. Montag. Nick took his father's death hard—and has taken out his frustration on a lot of people. I told him that if the police don't have enough evidence to arrest you, he shouldn't convict you in his heart. That's all."

"Still, that's better than most people have been."

Gary worked the toe of his shoe in the carpet. "Whatever. I need to be back at the office in an hour, so grab what you want quickly, if you can."

"I can be quick, but only if you help me."

I'd cleaned up after him when he and Nick had downed too much beer while watching bowl games on New Years Day, and given him money to tide him over when he'd bet on a sure thing that wasn't. With that background, it was relatively easy for me to put him to work climbing to the top of closets and fetching suitcases and boxes.

Martin had a large walk-in closet off the master bedroom, but the rest of the house was filled with my things. Tens of thousands of dollars spent on designer suits. Tens of thousands more dollars spent on shoes. I wished I could have a small percentage of that cash back now.

I flipped through the hangers, past hundreds of neatly dry-cleaned outfits, looking for anything that would fit with my new life.

I left most of my clothes behind. I didn't have room for them in Leah's trailer and besides, everything I'd owned was designed with air conditioning in mind. There's a reason for all those jokes about fat people and sweating—except it wasn't funny.

Still, I'd have underwear again—without having to hand-wash things in the sink every night. I picked half a dozen casual outfits that would be comfortable in the heat. I also gathered up several pair of shoes.

Gary stopped me, though, when I went into Martin's home office, took the wedding portrait of the two of us off the wall, and started dialing the combination of the home safe. "I'm sorry, Mrs. Montag. You know I can't let you in there."

"But Nick said—this is where we kept my most valuable jewelry."

"It's also where Mr. Montag kept his stock certificates, his gold coins, and his other valuables. Until the will is probated, I can't risk having anyone go through them."

"I can understand that concern. How about I describe what I'm looking for. If it sounds like something of Martin's, you just let me know. But I assure you that Martin never wore pearl necklaces or diamond earrings."

"I wish I could do that, Mrs. Montag. But Ms. Switzer was real clear on this when she took the security team through the details. If anyone even opens the safe, the whole inheritance gets a million times more complex. Even if it was me who opened it, that doesn't change things."

My big plan for pawning enough stuff to catch up on my bills was going up in smoke.

Naturally I had a lot of jewelry I didn't lock in the safe, and some of it was nice enough—eighteen carat gold designer bracelets, some of my smaller diamonds, one nice antique silver and turquoise necklace I'd worn to a function the night before my world fell apart and hadn't bothered putting back into the safe. I filled up a small suitcase with pawnable valuables, and a large one with clothes.

I nabbed a couple of Leah's old outfits that would look good on Tina, and one of her leather jackets Lupe might like once summer finally ended and we got some cooler days.

Gary helped me carry the loot out to his Hummer, but he made sure he kept me in sight the whole time.

"Why would Desiree want to come over here?" I asked him as he lugged my suitcase into the back of the SUV.

"She believes Nick is going to marry her. I think she just wants to play house. You know, do him in the master bedroom, that kind of stuff. Give him an idea of how good it would be if she moved in with him."

"You don't sound that enthusiastic."

He shrugged. "Desiree is okay. She's pretty enough. She's not even stupid, although she sometimes puts on a pretty good act. Nick can do better, though."

I watched as he locked what had once been my house, set the alarm with a code that had been changed since the days I'd lived there, and then got into his Hummer with him.

As we drove away, I had the feeling I was looking at my past for the last time. No matter what happened in my life, I wouldn't be coming back.

If there was anyone who would know the secrets of a conflict between Nick and his dad, it was Gary. Gary had adopted Nick when Nick had been a freshman and Gary a sophomore, but Nick had always seemed like the big brother, looking out for Gary and making sure he was protected when things got tough.

The two had shared dreams, spent one summer working construction together to toughen up, another summer bumming around India, and had finally both stepping into executive positions with Montag Industries.

If Martin and Nick had fought, Gary would know about it, and would be on Nick's side.

I couldn't press too hard, though. Just as Nick had no secrets from Gary, Gary kept nothing from Nick. Whatever I asked him, or he told me, Gary was certain to report back to Nick.

I'd been focused on how Desiree could have been the source of conflict between father and son. With Nick as protective of Gary as he was, they could also have fought about Gary. I wondered if Martin had reconsidered having Joe

Moses working for Gary, for example.

"I'll bet things are horrible in security right now." I was trying to sound friendly and concerned. "Are all the managers calling you and wanting to be protected since you've had two murders of key Montag employees?"

"Don't make light of it, Mrs. Montag. I know the police have got you on their radarscope, but that doesn't make a lot of sense to me. I figure you would have done fine with the divorce—at least as well as you're going to do out of Mr. Montag's death. And that means that there's a killer out there somewhere who the police aren't even looking for.

"When I signed on as security director, I assumed I'd be dealing with the cleaning service stealing, with prospective employees faking qualifications on their resumes, and with guarding the physical plant. I never counted on someone gunning down our senior managers."

He was at a red light so he rubbed his hands into his eyes. It looked to me like he'd been missing sleep lately.

"And those other problems don't stop just because a big new problem drops into your lap, do they?"

"Darned right. Just last week, we found one of the cashiers pocketing money in the cafeteria line. She'd ring up the orders all right, but she'd cancel things out once the customer had left. She got away with more than three thousand dollars before we caught her. When I called in the police, they laughed and told me to fire her." He shook his head angrily. "Sure I fired her. But she should be in jail, not applying for a cashier job at another company. And if I tried to blackball her in the business league meetings, she'd probably sue me."

Could a disgruntled cashier be the murderer? That would be the ideal solution in a lot of ways. She wouldn't be anyone I knew, anyone connected with my life. Having an unknown third party kill for reasons of her own would be sort of like having the butler do it in those English mysteries I used to watch as a guilty pleasure (guilty because they weren't really American) on television. But even if the cashier were crazy, how would she have known to track down Martin and Betty? And why them? Why not, for example, Gary and Joe Moses? Unless the killing wasn't over yet. Could someone really be mad enough to wipe out the entire executive management of the company—for getting fired from a cashier job?

"So, *are* you hiring more people to guard Montag executives?"

Gary was driving, but he took his eyes off the road for long enough to stare me straight in they eye. "You know I can't answer that, Mrs. Montag. I don't *believe* you're the killer, but I'm not the investigating officer. So, I'm not going to tell anyone other than Nick himself what we're doing to protect the management team. It's basic *need to know*—the heart of any security system."

Since Gary had majored in physical education, I figured he must have been taking security lessons from Joe Moses.

"If you'd just help me load up my car," I said when he pulled us back into the Montag Industries parking lot, "I'd really appreciate it."

"I'm sorry about your other jewelry," he said. "I don't suppose you know if

Nick has the combination to that safe."

"I'm sure he does. Why?"

He rubbed his hands on his face again. "Oh, great. Maybe Desiree does want to go over and play house with Nick. But she's also interested in *bling*, know what I mean? I've seen the diamonds you've worn to the Christmas parties and she has too. Wouldn't little Desiree just love to sink her claws into that kind of loot? And Nick just might figure giving her your stuff would be a lot cheaper than having to spend his own money buying things for her."

I wasn't sure I'd ever be wearing diamonds again, but letting Desiree make off with them didn't have any appeal, either. "Maybe you should remind Nick about what Kayla Switzer told you," I said. "Make sure he doesn't mess with what's inside the safe before the probate is taken care of."

"Yeah. There's only one problem with that."

"Sounds pretty straightforward to me. You get on the phone and talk to him. You'd be doing your job as a security director."

"Maybe. But Nick doesn't like it when people bring problems to him."

"Who does?"

Gary laughed. "You got that right. I guess I'll remind Desiree that Nick will be pissed if she messes up the probate. Appealing to her greedy side is generally the way to work it."

He loaded up my car without making any of the rude comments I'd expected about the poor little thing, then got back in his Hummer and waited.

He made sure I made it to the Montag parking lot exit, then pulled up next to me at the stop sign and lowered his passenger-side window. "Mrs. Montag?"

My window was already down. It was hot, my car had been baking in the sun, and the blower only blew engine-heated air in at me. "Yes, Gary."

"I just wanted to tell you that Nick doesn't want you wandering around in the headquarters building. He's asked Joe and me to keep you out. I wanted to make sure you knew that, and that you wouldn't take it personally when we do our jobs. I suggest that you make it easy on all of us by staying away."

"No problem, Gary."

He looked relieved. "Good. See you later, Mrs. Montag. And remember, I *still* believe you're innocent. I'm working on convincing Nick of that, too."

Learning that my son needed to be convinced didn't make me feel better. I tried not to think about that as I headed for the Tollway. I was halfway there when remembered if I paid the toll, I couldn't afford gas, so I turned around to drive toward Highway 75.

* * * *

"Real leather? I love it. This is so cool" Lupe set the leather jacket carefully on the picnic table, threw her arms as far around me as they would go, and hugged me.

I tried to remember the last time anyone had really hugged me. Nick had sort of fumbled with my shoulders when I'd been in his office, but it hadn't been a real hug. Before that final day when he'd turned away from me completely, Martin used give me a peck on the cheek every morning. It had been years since he'd really taken me in his arms and squeezed.

The women I'd associated with before losing everything and being sent into the purgatory-world of trailer-park living were air-kissers, not huggers. Touching could smudge carefully applied makeup and was so, well, common.

Lupe's hug sent a jolt of peaceful pleasure through me, like what I used to feel when the kids were young and thought I hung the moon.

"I guess you're forgiven," Tina whispered.

I nodded, then wiped the tears from my eyes. "I hoped you would like it, Lupe. And I hoped you'd like some of the outfits I brought you, Tina."

Her smile was as fake as the million-dollar bill Martin used to keep taped to his desk in the early days of his business, back when a million dollars had seemed like a very big deal to him.

"They're really nice. I recognize a lot of the designers."

Uh-oh. "But?"

"But I'm here for a reason, Heather. You know I could have dinged Andy for a zillion dollars when we split up. If I'd wanted the professional big-business life, I would be living it. The reason I wear jeans and ratty t-shirts is because this is what I feel comfortable in. I'm trailer trash and I'm not ashamed of it."

"What did happen to your marriage, Tina? Did Andy bring in the lawyers and put you through the wringer?"

"Like what was happening with you?" Tina laughed. "It was the other way around with me. I decided to divorce him when I realized I'd just spent thirty consecutive nights out at his business functions—and it wasn't going to stop. I loved Andy, but only seeing him when he was surrounded by suits wasn't enough for me. So I told him I wasn't going to take anything. He was hard to persuade, though—which is how I ended up working at a trailer park he owns. I didn't know it was his when I took the job."

A couple of weeks earlier, that wouldn't have made any sense at all to me. I wasn't religious, exactly. I attended church, of course, going through the motions and enjoying the social aspect more than anything. But I had a sort of Calvinist faith that associated doing well with doing good. Living hand to mouth, with no luxuries at all because you had to was one thing. Choosing to live this way was something else.

I can't say that my eyes were opened to the virtues of poverty. If I'd been Tina, I would have asked for a few million dollars, at least—and my own trailer park rather than just a low-wage job in one. I would have preferred to drive a car I didn't have to worry about breaking down all the time. I would have preferred living in a place that had air conditioning and where I could fit into the shower.

Still, I had also begun see the merits of living the kind of life you chose to live rather than the life that other people expect you to live.

"We'll take those clothes to the thrift shop, then," I said. "Who knows, maybe I can help you find some new ratty t-shirts to replace them."

"Very funny. I have plenty of ratty t-shirts already."

"I'd sort of like this one." Lupe fingered a flirty little dress I'd thought would look perfect on Tina. But Tina was a grown woman who'd been married. Lupe was a junior high school girl.

"Are you sure—"

"Go ahead and try it on," Tina said. "We'll let you know if it looks right on you or if you'll need to wait a year or two."

Lupe practically skipped into my trailer to change her clothes.

"What can it hurt, Heather?" Tina was reacting to my open mouth.

"But it's sexy and she's thirteen. What kind of message is she—"

"Welcome to the new millennium," Tina said. "Girls are allowed to be sexy."

My response was cut off by Lupe's re-emergence.

She didn't really look sexy at all. She looked like a young girl getting to wear something really nice for the first time in her life. Her smile could have powered a small city and she bounced down the stairs like her next step might launch her into the stratosphere.

"I am *so* pretty."

"Looking good, sista," Tina announced. "The boys will be lining up."

"I'm a StrongGirl. I don't need boys."

"You keep that attitude, girlfriend," Tina said.

"Nancy Drew always looked nice," Lupe said. "So, now I figure we've got it all. We'll solve your case and we can get on with our lives. And once you're off the hook, Heather, they'll *have* to let you back into the StrongGirl program. They might even make me the President of the StrongGirls. I mean, who else has solved a murder."

"Speaking of murder, tell us about your lunch with Nick," Tina demanded. "Are you ready to clear him?"

I ran them through my morning without answering her question.

"I've got some Nutty Bars," Tina told me when I'd finished, concluding that I hadn't gotten anything to eat but the salad. "Hang on a second and you can eat them right now."

"My cousin owns the pawnshop on Jefferson and Tyler," Lupe said after Tina had come back with the chocolate-covered cookies and a bottled water. "He would have given you a better deal on your watch. You should take him your jewelry."

"Good idea, Lupe." Tina waited patiently until I'd finished stuffing the Nutty Bars into my face and had swallowed the last bite. "So, is Nick our man, or are we still up in the air?"

I thought about it. Nick was keeping secrets and, if my guesses about conflict with his father were right, he had plenty of motivation. I still didn't see him as the killer. "Maybe the cashier."

"Not," said Tina. "How's a cashier going to know the CEO is working late? And how's she going to know your gun's in your car? You didn't leave it out where everyone could see it, did you?"

"Of course not."

"Whoever killed Martin knew you and knew you had a gun in your car. He, or she, knew Martin would be working late, and they cared about Betty."

"You're right." A cold twist settled in my gut. The cashier hadn't been a realistic suspect. I wanted to find that a stranger was responsible because the alternative was unpleasant. But I couldn't afford to run away from unpleasantness. I wasn't in Frisco any more. "I need to talk to more people, find out what was really going on in those last days between Nick and Martin. But Gary told me that Nick was real clear on this. I'm not allowed back there."

"We could hang around the parking lot," Lupe suggested. "Grab people when they come out and put them to the question."

"The parking lot is private property. Gary's security guards would kick us out."

"That Joe Moses seemed to like us," Lupe reminded me. "Maybe he would sneak us in."

I considered, then shook my head. "First, I don't think he'd go against a direct order from Nick. He might blow off one from Gary, but that's about it. Second, if he did ignore an order and got caught, we'd be responsible for getting him fired. I don't want to risk that."

Then there was the possibility that he was the killer himself. I didn't dare put myself in his power.

Tina linked her fingers together and pushed them straight out from her chest, cracking all of her knuckles in what sounded like the kind of gunfire I'd heard too often since I'd moved into the trailer park. "Sounds like it's up to me, then. Considering how little money I've made from my shareware business lately, maybe it was time for me to get a real job, anyway."

"What are you talking about?"

"Montag is always hiring, and good coders are in demand again, now that the crash has, more or less, worked its way through the Dallas economy. What better excuse to hang around the building than having a job there?"

"I couldn't ask you to do that. There's a killer out there somewhere. And Lupe and I wouldn't be around to protect you."

Lupe grinned at me, obviously glad to be included in the protection idea. Actually, I figured she would be at least as effective in protecting Tina as I would be. Unless I sat on someone and squashed them, I wasn't equipped for a fight.

"You weren't asking," Tina reminded me. "I volunteered." She looked at the stack of Leah's clothes I'd brought for her. "Maybe I'll hang onto some of these outfits after all."

"But you'd never make it past security. Joe Moses and Gary French have both seen you."

"I'll use my maiden name. With a little makeup and these funky clothes of your daughter's, they'd have to have pretty sharp eyes to spot even a resemblance between Tina Anderson and Christina Thibodeaux."

"I really don't deserve friends like y'all," I said.

* * * *

Tina was right about software designers being in demand. Of course, I suspected her landing the job so quickly had something to do with the nice clothes I'd bought my daughter. The right clothing really does make the man, or woman.

A couple of days later, she was setting off for work at her new job for Montag Industries.

She'd also been right about changing her appearance. She wore her hair down instead of up in spikes, and had added some red highlights. Dressed in a pretty lavender suit that Leah had desperately needed and then never worn, Tina looked like a complete professional—except for her aging Geo Storm.

I caught her first thing in the morning as she rubbed sleep out of her eyes and trudged toward her car. I wasn't a morning person, either, but she was doing this for me. The least I could do was see her off. I handed her a cup of coffee through her open window (her air conditioning didn't work either).

I'd pawned my jewelry and gotten enough to pay off the electric bill, get myself a cellphone, and even repay Tina for the drinks she'd bought for Kayla. I'd spent a bit of what was left on some really excellent coffee, a coffee grinder, and a coffee machine that turned out a far better brew than I could get at the neighborhood food-mart.

"Don't worry," Tina told me when she saw my expression. "Nobody's been murdered for days."

That didn't make me feel better. "Promise me you'll be careful."

"I will. And don't forget to pick Lupe up after school. I told her mother we'd watch her for the next few days."

She'd reminded me of that six times the previous evening, as if I couldn't be trusted. Well, maybe I couldn't.

Tina took a hit of her coffee, smiled, waved, and turned out of the trailer parking lot.

Her car didn't smoke as badly as mine did, but it definitely sputtered as she headed toward the freeway.

I took a sip of my own coffee, then looked around the park.

I didn't have a thing to do.

Before Martin's murder, I'd filled up my life with politics. Since then, I'd been obsessed with the murder and with my assignment with StrongGirls. But Tina was doing everything we could do about the murder, and the StrongGirls didn't want me. Which left me with nothing to occupy myself. I couldn't even watch TV unless I wanted to sit in my trailer and swelter.

I'd been putting it off, but I decided it was time to actually look for a job. I had *some* money left from pawning my stuff, but it wouldn't last forever. Especially not if Leah was serious about charging me rent for using the trailer.

Besides, I wanted to do something with my life. It was more than a little sad to realize that while I had filled up my time with activities, but hadn't really done anything.

I put on a professional outfit I'd salvaged from my former life. After considering my car and the price of gasoline, I took the bus downtown.

I got a few looks when I climbed onto the big yellow Route 50 DART bus, but the experience wasn't as bad as I'd feared. Sure there were plenty of minorities aboard, but none of them seemed to think it was completely weird that a fat, middle-aged white woman took the ride.

Downtown Dallas is like most modern downtowns—a maze of banks, financial service organizations, law firms, and the lunch-only restaurants that cater to them.

A number of the old warehouses and factory buildings had scaffolding around them and workers inside gutting and transforming them into condos. I'd known Dallas was having something of a downtown renaissance, but I'd never understood why until I'd moved into the trailer. Living in the city, in a neighborhood where people could walk to shops and know their neighbors, was different from the walled-in suburban fortress-life I'd shared with Martin, but it had a real appeal.

I trotted around from bank to stockbroker, smiling at the perky receptionists who looked like they'd all been hired for their good looks, and handing filled out applications for anyone who would take one.

My face was getting sore from maintaining the pasted-on smile when I went into another of a string of stockbrokerage offices and got one more patronizing stare-down.

"Aren't you Mrs. Montag?"

I'd just filled out my twelfth application and handed it to the twelfth beautiful receptionist. I'd expected to hear the increasingly familiar sound of a paper shredder as I left rather than my own name.

I scanned my memories. Right, Larry Miller. I'd met him at some charity function a year or two previously.

"Well hi, Larry. I'd forgotten you worked here."

"It's great of you to stop by, Mrs. Montag. Rachel, this is Mrs. Montag, of Montag Industries."

Rachel didn't look impressed and tried to call her boss's attention to my application.

But Larry was on a roll, in full-sales mode. "How about I buy you lunch and we can talk about the full-service financial planning we offer here. I take it you're considering your options with your portfolio."

"Uh, Larry, hello. Mrs. Montag is looking for a job," the receptionist, whose nametag, I saw, read Stephanie, obviously decided she needed to step in before her boss made a serious mistake.

"A job?" He gave one of those little ha-ha-ha fake laughs.

This was the closest I'd gotten to an interview and I wasn't going to let it get away from me. "I think I'd be a real asset to your organization, Mr. Miller. I have a wide circle of acquaintances in the upper income brackets of Dallas, and I've always been interested in sound investments."

"Of course." He looked torn between being polite to a potential investor and blowing off a hopeful applicant. Blowing me off won. "The radio says the police are getting near charging you. Surely you don't expect us, or anyone else, to hire you with that cloud hanging over your head."

Chapter 14

"How was school, Lupe?"

I'd arrived half an hour early and joined the line of cars outside Nathan Forrest Middle School. My wheezing Toyota blended in with the other mostly-aging vehicles waiting.

Unlike the Frisco schools, though, where administrators would probably call the cops if a child announced plans to actually walk home, plenty of these students left on foot or climbed onto DART busses was well as the familiar orange school buses.

Lupe's smile widened when she saw me. Although it had to be over a hundred degrees, she'd worn her new leather coat.

"Leather breathes," she explained. "It helps you stay cool in the summer and warm in the winter."

From the way sweat ran down her face, it didn't seem to be working. But I didn't want to spoil her mood. "You hungry?"

"I'm a kid. Of course I'm hungry."

I took her to this ice cream place I'd spotted in Bishop Arts, a sort of urban redevelopment zone not too far from the school. I was getting to appreciate the funky feeling of urban life and this collection of one-story brick buildings reminded me of the new mall developers were creating in the suburbs—they hadn't quite gotten it yet. From what I picked up from the murals on the walls of many of the buildings, Bishop Arts had been exactly that—a mall, back in the days when trolleys provided the primary transportation within Dallas. Rather than serving a community that drove in for miles, it had served people mostly within walking distance.

There was a poetry reading going on inside the ice cream shop and when one reader started listing body parts, I hustled Lupe outside. There were also downsides to the whole urban thing.

Still, a few yards of distance was enough to protect us from having to hear a poet's diatribe against whatever she was protesting.

Safe from age-inappropriate literature, we sat on a concrete park bench, licking our cones and watching the bustle of pedestrian traffic.

Lupe didn't say anything until she'd finished her last bite. "I had a test in math," she said. "It wasn't too hard."

"Great." I tried to remember if I'd ever been blasé about a math test.

"What about you?"

"I applied for jobs."

She removed her jacket, folded it carefully over her lap, then leaned back into the cool concrete of the bench. "That's excellent, Heather. If you want to be a StrongGirl, you've got to make your own way."

"I didn't have any luck."

She nodded seriously. "Sometimes it takes a while. My aunt Gaby was out of work for weeks after the salon where she cut hair closed."

"Weeks actually sounds good. I couldn't even get out of these places before they were shredding my application." It felt weird to be sharing this with a thirteen-year-old, but I was living in a new world for me. I wasn't in the StrongGirl program any more, but I still needed a mentor to help me figure out how to navigate the realities of urban life.

"Maybe you should apply somewhere else, then."

I took a breath. It went against everything I'd believed in when I'd been Chair of the League, but I was increasingly desperate. "What about welfare, Lupe. Do you know how to apply?"

"For what? You don't have young kids, do you?"

"No. Does that matter? I thought you could get welfare when you were out of work." Or just plain too lazy to work. That had been the prevailing philosophy among my old crowd.

"You can get AFDC if you have little kids, but that's it."

I guessed I shouldn't be surprised. It felt as if I hadn't changed neighborhoods, I'd changed worlds. The thirty miles between Dallas and Frisco might as well have been thirty light years.

"If you had a job and lost it, you might be able to get unemployment."

"I haven't worked since college."

"I think that's too long to qualify."

I thought so too.

I ate the last bite of my own ice cream and tossed my napkin into a waste paper basket.

"Some of my cousins work in shops around here," she said. "I can talk to them about you, see if anyone needs help. It's too bad you haven't learned Spanish yet. They're looking mostly for bilingual people."

She was right. This part of Dallas was a colorful mix of blacks, Latinos, and whites, but while the children seemed to use English as much as anything, the older Latinos spoke primarily Spanish. I'd been amused the first time I'd seen a family using a little five-year-old kid as their translator, but it was so common, I'd gotten used to it.

"I guess I'll have to work on my Spanish, then."

"I have some other ideas, though."

When Lupe pulled out that familiar yellow hardback book, I suspected the other ideas didn't have anything to do with getting a job, although, as Larry had pointed out, getting a job while the police were telling the newspapers they were preparing charges against me wouldn't be easy.

"I was studying some more."

I tried not to sigh. Nancy Drew was back, and I was afraid she hadn't brought good news.

"Maybe you should have studied more for your math test," I suggested.

"What Nancy does a lot is set a trap for the bad guys." Lupe ignored my comment.

I had a vague memory of Nancy Drew's traps. "Is this where she gets knocked on the head and put into a cellar to die?"

Lupe nodded seriously. "She's always okay, though."

"That kind of head-knocking can result in a long term reduction in brain functioning. Did you know that soccer players who do a lot of headers can permanently injure themselves?"

"I'm not suggesting we get hit on the head. I'm talking about setting a trap that works, not one that backfires. Nancy is smart, but she's sometimes a little careless about her own safety, and that of her friends. For a modern StrongGirl, it's safety first."

"That sounds smart," I agreed. "Except we don't know who to trap, and we don't know how to make it safe."

Lupe looked at me seriously. "You really think things through, don't you, Heather?"

"Part of my problem is, I didn't used to. I used to go with the flow. Since Martin was murdered, I've had to change a lot of things."

She nodded. After a few moments of silence, her hand stole across the few inches of bench that separated us. She clutched my hand and squeezed it. "We'll figure out a way to keep you safe."

There was something wrong with this picture. Lupe was a thirteen-year-old girl. She shouldn't have to feel responsible for a fifty-year-old woman like me. Still, her words, and her small hand in my own, comforted me.

"Maybe people were more impressed by your application than they let on," Lupe said. "There will be some nibbles."

"I came close to being a nibble. One guy sicced a pit-bull on me. But I outran it."

"That was a very bad pun. I hope you don't intend to apply for jobs in stand-up comedy."

"The only job I ever held was lifeguarding during summer break in college. That isn't the kind of experience most employers are looking for."

"We need to get started with your Spanish. Then you'd be able to get a job in a restaurant or something."

* * * *

"What a bunch of perverts."

Tina's first day at Montag Industries hadn't gone well but we were celebrating anyway.

Lupe and I had stopped at Norma's for take-out chicken-fried steak, mashed potatoes, green beans, sweet iced tea and pie. They'd thrown in some rolls, and we'd decided to use the rolls to feed the ducks at Kidd Springs Park.

Tina had suggested we feed the chickens scratching around the parking lot at the trailer park, but Lupe had her heart set on ducks.

"Maybe things have gotten worse since Martin died," I checked and made sure Lupe was busy with the birds. Thirteen-year-olds might not be as innocent now as I'd been, but they still didn't need to hear about office perverts.

Tina shrugged. "I don't think it could get this bad, this quickly, without a good head start."

"What was bad?" Lupe dragged her attention from a scrawny teenaged boy

129

who made an art out of his casting for fish in the small lake in the middle of the park. He hadn't caught anything, but I noticed Lupe wasn't the only girl checking him out. He looked like an underaged and undernourished hoodlum-in-the-making to me, but apparently he was something of a babe for the younger set.

I fished half a roll from the bag of rolls and cornbread we'd gotten at Norma's and gave it to Lupe for the birds.

"I got propositioned twice before lunch," Tina complained when Lupe took her roll and started tossing bits of bread to the ducks within a few feet from the fishing boy. "Everyone seems to be sleeping with somebody. And did you ever see so many bimbo secretaries?"

"They're called administrative assistants." I think it was Tina who'd reminded me of that a few days earlier.

"Is that what you'd call my friend Angie? Because these women were hired for, and are getting paid for, exactly what she sells. Any administrative work they do is strictly on the side."

I shot a quick look at Lupe, but the teenager was using every ounce of her energy pretending not to notice the cute boy—who was pretending to be cool and not notice her at the same time. Tina's description of the soap opera at Montag Industries didn't have a chance against the combined appeal of ducks and boys.

"Martin wasn't a saint," I admitted, "but his big interest was making money, not in getting laid. Surely he wouldn't have stood for unprofessional behavior."

"Considering what we know 'bout his relationship with Betty, I don't think Martin was in any position to throw stones."

"That was different. Betty might have been putting out, but she was a good administrator. She kept Martin organized, helped him figure out which problems he needed to be involved in personally, and smoothed out a lot of the political problems in the company." I'd gotten to like Betty in the early days of the company, back when Martin used to confide in me and look to me for advice.

"I'm not sure everyone else would have seen it that way. Once you give permission to start sleeping with the help, you've opened a door that you can't shut. But Betty isn't really the point. You're forgetting about Kayla. She got to take over the legal work because of what she did in Martin's bed. And don't even try to tell me he couldn't have hired a more experienced and capable law firm."

I'd lied to Larry Miller about being interested in investments. But I did seem to remember that Montag Industries stock had been down over the past year or so. Could Martin's distraction with women have made a difference in how the company was doing? Maybe he'd been killed because some investor got pissed over losing his, or her, money. "Hey, that—"

"I have to say that your son Nick's little ditz would do better if she'd take a leaf out of Betty's book," Tina interrupted.

I'd forgotten about Desiree and her motives. "She wasn't wearing any fancy diamond jewelry, was she?"

"As a matter of fact she had on a necklace so heavy she had to lean over all the time. Or maybe her inflated chest was what made her top heavy. White diamonds all around, and a huge blue one that nestled between her boobs. Believe me, there was a lineup to see it. Most of the guys were more interested in the padding than the rocks, though."

That sounded like the necklace Martin had given me a decade earlier to celebrate him making it onto the Forbes Richest 500 in America list.

For the first couple of years, we'd tracked Martin's progress up the list, as he'd moved from five hundred into the low four hundreds. I couldn't remember the last time we'd had that celebration. Could it be that Martin had quietly dropped out of the list?

And now Nick was carrying on his father's worst traditions. I hoped he'd carry on some of the good ones, too. Before he'd gotten caught up in whatever midlife crisis he'd been going through before his unexpected end-of-life-crisis, Martin had been a great businessman. I wasn't sure Nick had the same intensity or drive to make the company succeed. Giving in to Desiree's demand for jewelry when he knew that doing so could complicate his inheritance showed a side of Nick that indicated he might not be ready to be CEO of a major corporation.

"I guess Desiree didn't take Gary's message seriously," I admitted. "He said there could be problems with the probate if the safe contents were tampered with."

"Why should she?" Lupe was still pretending not to notice the boy. "Nick is the boss, not Gary. If she could get the boss to say it's okay, what's Gary going to do? Call the police?"

He'd called the police on me, but Lupe was right. He wasn't going to call the cops on Nick. He depended on Nick like a pilot fish depends on a shark.

"Maybe he was lying to you about the whole probate thing," Tina pointed out. She took a hunk of cornbread, broke off an edge to eat, then crumbled the rest and fed it to a flock of grackles that migrated around the table like gypsies.

"Who cares about jewelry or who's sleeping with what?" Lupe shook her head when Tina offered her another piece of bread. "What did you learn about the murder?"

Tina shrugged. "Funny. Nobody came up to me and confessed. I was surprised too."

"That wasn't what I meant," Lupe insisted.

"I'm not exactly a prude, but if I'd known the business was so much about sex, I would have suggested we send Angie instead of me," Tina admitted. "She couldn't program her way out of an if-then statement for a lifetime supply of flavored condoms, but she sure could give some of those administrative assistants a run for their money."

I tried gesturing in Lupe's direction without the teenager noticing. It didn't work.

"I know about sex, Heather."

"Well don't do anything about it. You're too young."

"StrongGirls are in control of their own bodies and don't let anyone pressure them to give up that control."

Some days it seemed like an eternity since I'd been a teenager and my hormones had run so strong I could hardly keep myself from jumping every guy I saw. Other days, it seemed like only a few moments had passed, that the girl I'd been was still there, just buried under a hundred pounds of fat.

"Stay strong," I urged.

"If nobody is going to talk to you about the murder, what are you doing there in the first place?" Lupe seemed bored by the sex talk and got back to murder. Lupe's hormones were still those of a girl rather than those of a budding woman. Nancy Drew still had more appeal than whatever sex-stud-star was currently setting adolescent female hearts on fire.

"I *am* keeping my ears to the floor, trying to pick up on the office politics," Tina answered. "But the real cool thing is, the IS department doesn't have good data segmentation. Although my job is in data warehousing, it took me all of fifteen minutes to hack into the HR system."

"What's that?" Lupe asked.

"It's what big companies call their hiring and firing office. Where they keep all their employment records."

"Be careful with that, Tina." I had sudden memories of what had happened when Tina had hacked into Martin's e-mail. Sure she'd discovered Martin's list of girlfriends, something that had been critical to everything we'd done since then in finding the real killer, but corporate security had been all over us in no time at all.

Tina showed her teeth in a truly evil grin. "I'm on the inside this time. If they want to catch me, they'll need to be a lot better than I think they are."

Lupe bounced herself against the table. "So? What did you find?"

"What I found is that Montag uses something called a *three-sixty review* for promotions and bonuses."

"What's that mean?" Lupe beat me to the question.

"Rather than just have managers report on their subordinates for annual salary discussions and promotions and stuff, they interview peers, managers, and subordinates. Three-sixty, as in degrees, like a circle, you know."

I thought that made a lot of sense and said so.

"Sure it makes sense. Suppose you've got an employee who sucks up all the time and his boss thinks he hung the moon but everyone else knows he's dumping his work on other people and not contributing. Three-sixty will pick that up and anyone with have a lick of sense will be able to see it."

"So, what's the problem with this three-sixty thing? And how does it help us?"

"No problem for us. But if you read between the lines, you can see the knives come out. Superficially, everyone is oh-so-polite, at least at the senior level. But they didn't make it to corporate VP by playing fair. When someone comes around and asks them what they think about the guy who just might be fighting it out with them for their next promotion, they're going for their zings —it's part of their personality."

"Sort of like when you set someone up to get caught passing notes in class, so they can't take a test and mess up the curve," Lupe guessed.

"Exactly. And equally unethical." Tina took a couple of bites of pie. "Here's the thing. The knives were out and these guys were playing for keeps."

I wondered what a three-sixty would have looked like if someone had done one for the League. With all of the catty members, *tooth and claw* would have been a better description than knives.

"Since Martin had no intention of retiring, the top executives couldn't have gotten much out of that." For Martin, and for guys like him, money was just keeping score. The game wasn't about wealth, it was about power. And there was almost nothing more powerless than an ex-CEO.

"The guys were getting in their digs everywhere they could, but you'll never guess who the primary target was."

"Desiree?" Lupe guessed.

"Kayla," I hazarded.

"Close. It was your son, Nick."

A part of me wanted to run back up to Frisco and give those mean executives a piece of my mind. How dare they attack my son? Couldn't they see how hard he worked? Didn't they realize he was doing the best he could, that it was hard to work for your father?

I fought down the urge. If I went back into Montag Industries, Joe or Gary would call the cops on me—again. And the son I wanted to protect would tell them to throw away the key.

"I guess going after Nick makes sense," I said. "He's in his twenties and he was already in Martin's cabinet, in charge of sales, which is one of the most critical elements in the company's performance. That would have to create some jealousy."

Tina shook her head. "It's more than that. Remember, Martin was in charge. They would have had to be pretty brave to insult the boss's son if the boss didn't want them to."

"Unless the boss made it clear that it was okay to go after Nick," Lupe observed.

I could understand Tina's cynicism, but I wondered how Lupe had gotten so insightful into business life. She was a junior high school kid. How would she know about the way the corporate world works? Still, the idea that Martin might have okayed attacks on Nick was absurd.

"There's no way Martin would—"

Tina ignored me, patting Lupe on the head. "Bingo. They didn't know Martin was going to be, uh, retired, but they were going after Nick like he was a cockroach in a clean room. So, they must have picked up on something else— which could only be the conflict between father and son. Nick might *believe* that any argument stayed between him and Martin, but the other senior managers figured it out."

I looked around the park trying to get my thoughts in order. It was after eight, but the sun was still well above the horizon. Vendors drove three-wheeled bicycles along asphalt paths selling popsicles and what looked like fried pork rinds with hot sauce. Gross.

Screaming children jumped from jungle gyms and played soccer in the fields. I remembered what I'd told Lupe about soccer players and their heads. I felt like I'd been smacking my own head against something a lot more solid than a ball working on this case. But thanks to Lupe and Tina, We were finally getting somewhere.

"If all those executives hated each other and had their knives out for Nick, they wouldn't have wanted Martin dead. At least not yet. They would have waited for Martin to take care of Nick for them. This has got to cut down on the suspects."

Both Lupe and Tina stared at me and I realized I was missing the most obvious thing.

"This makes it look even worse for Nick, doesn't it?"

Chapter 15

My lawyer, Barry Levitz, called me after I got home from feeding ducks. I was off the hook for community service. As he'd promised he would, Gary French had notified the judge that Montag was withdrawing any complaints they had against me and explained that the whole thing was a misunderstanding.

I'd been mad at Gary when he'd sent me off to jail, but he seemed to be the only person at Montag who'd actually kept a promise.

With no community service to worry about, I got up early the following morning and set out with a thick stack of resumes I'd had Tina produce for me on her computer.

I lowered my standards a bit from the previous day, applying at law firms, dental offices, and architectural design companies in the trailer park's neighborhood rather than taking the bus downtown.

I didn't hear anyone shredding my resume before I'd even got out the door, but my lack of Spanish was a bigger obstacle than I'd imagined. If I wanted to stay in the neighborhood, I'd just have to take Lupe up on her offer to help me learn the language.

Even when I'd been in high school back in the early seventies, it had been obvious that the Hispanic community would play an ever-larger role in the Texas economy. Still, my mother had advised me that sophisticated women spoke French. I'd taken that language through high school and college and never bothered with Spanish.

It was September, but in Dallas, September is still a long way from fall. By the time I'd visited the first couple of places, sweat soaked through my suit. I could justify abandoning the job search, since I knew I didn't look my best. After checking what I had left from pawning my jewelry, I made a deal with myself. I'd keep going until I'd given out twenty resumes or filled out that many applications.

I finished around noon and then battled with myself between going to one of the little taquerias in the neighborhood or heading back to the trailer where I had some cold cuts in the refrigerator.

A few more seconds with my rapidly thinning wallet persuaded me to head for home.

Tina's friend Angie poked her head out of her trailer door when I got off the bus and headed back into the park. She gave me a semi-friendly smile. "What's going on?"

"Getting lunch."

"Really? Feed me and I'll let you eat at my place. My A.C. works."

"What makes you think my air conditioner is broken?"

She snickered. "Because Ralph used to rent your trailer."

I wished I hadn't asked. I didn't want to think about somebody named Ralph doing it with Angie on the bed where I slept.

My conservative friends would have been horrified at the idea of lunch with a hooker. I figured that Jesus hadn't been too good to eat with and talk to prostitutes and I was definitely not a better person than he was. So I made a couple of ham sandwiches, layered on the mayo the way I liked it, and headed over to Angie's place.

I don't know what I was expecting inside. Maybe red velvet wallpaper and whips. Unlike Tina's constantly messy trailer, though, Angie's was spotless. As she'd promised, her air conditioner blasted chilled air.

I melted down at her dining room table and let cool air spill around my body like water over a surfer.

"Wine, coffee, or fruit juice?" Angie asked.

I considered the wine. I was tired and frustrated with my job search. Taking the edge off just a little with a couple of glasses of wine would give me sounded wonderful. But I needed all of my brainpower intact. Thanks to the warnings I'd gotten from Barry and Tina, I had a sneaking suspicion that the police weren't going to let me wander around free forever. They were looking for more evidence that I'd killed Martin and Betty. Eventually they'd decide they had all they needed. That's when they'd come and arrest me.

At that point, they'd have to give me a lawyer and cough up some money for investigators, but I'd be in jail. The chances of me making bond in a murder case were somewhere around those of a caterpillar surviving on a chicken farm.

Coffee would be good for my brain, but even with Angie's AC blowing full blast, I didn't want the heat.

"I know it's a lot to ask, but do you think I could have iced coffee?"

"No problem." She disappeared into her kitchen for a few seconds and came out with two large glass mugs filled with coffee and big chunks of ice. Each had a small mountain of whipped cream floating on top. It looked divine.

Angie inspected the sandwich I'd brought for her approvingly. "Tina always gets that whole wheat bread. I figure, if we'd been meant to eat whole wheat, we wouldn't like white bread so much."

I didn't tell her I'd only bought it because it had been on sale at a Mrs. Baird's thrift shop I'd discovered on Davis Street.

She took a sip of her own iced coffee, then looked at me. "So, are you interested in Chris Blanchard?"

I considered, but I drew a blank. "I just lost my husband so I'm not interested in anyone right now. But I don't even know who Chris Blanchard is."

"He's the guy who helped push your car the other day. Nice guy. Chews tobacco and drives a pickup truck. He's got a few extra pounds on him but he's not bad. Sweats some, but what man doesn't? Didn't you even ask his name when you got him to help you?"

I looked down at Angie's table so I wouldn't have to meet her eyes. It was nice, and obviously an antique since it had ivory inlays and ivory hadn't been legal in years. But it didn't have anything to say to make me feel better about myself.

"I guess I didn't think of asking his name."

"Well, it's Chris Blanchard. He runs a yard service. Makes a decent living.

Like I said, he's not a bad guy."

"Why are you telling me this, Angie?"

"Because he likes you. He asked me to find out whether you'd be interested in maybe seeing him."

I considered, but only for a moment. I knew I was being elitist, but Chris smelled and chewed so the idea grossed me out. I could understand the sweat. I mean, if he ran a lawn service in Texas, he'd get hot and sweaty—even a powerful deodorant can only do so much. But the tobacco thing was just not my cup of tea.

"I'm sorry I got him to help me and didn't even ask his name, but I'm still not interested in dating."

"You know what they say about getting back onto the horse when you're bucked off."

"My husband just got killed, Angie."

"Yeah, but he was dumping you first. That has to lessen the pain a bit, doesn't it?"

I took a bite of my sandwich and considered Angie's question. I *had* mourned Martin. But the more I thought about it, the more I realized that my mourning had been more for me than for him. And it had been more about his abandoning me, something he'd done before he'd been murdered, than about his death.

I hadn't dated anyone but Martin since high school. I wasn't ready to change that any time soon, but I realized I would have to consider my possibilities if I didn't want to spend the rest of my life alone. And a fifty-year-old murder suspect who carries an extra hundred pounds wouldn't exactly be getting lines outside her door.

"I'm still not ready to date."

"Oh, well. I told him I'd ask. But I mostly wanted to talk to you about the murder and Tina. I mean, it can't be coincidence that Martin gets killed the day he tells you he's getting a divorce, can it? It's got to be someone connected with you. Like your son, maybe."

I knew the police had glommed onto that coincidence early since it supplied their motive for me killing Martin. But that didn't make Nick, or me, responsible.

"I think there was something weird going on at the company."

Angie shrugged her shoulders. "Sex or money. It's always one of those two. If it's money, who had the motive? Other than you, of course."

"Why are you asking me this? I know you're Tina's friend, but why do you care whether the cops arrest me or someone else?"

Angie took a sip from her coffee and another bite of her sandwich, chewing daintily. When she shrugged her shoulders, her whole body got caught up in the wiggle and I wondered how it was that Martin hadn't added Angie to his list of conquests. He seemed to have combed through the rest of Dallas.

Then again, maybe he had.

"We women have to stick together," Angie said.

I almost fell out of my chair. A prostitute was the last person I would have expected to feel any kind of solidarity with other women. I mean, Angie made her living out of breaking up marriages.

"That's not what I do at all," she told me when I'd explained my reaction to her. "I don't do anyone who doesn't come looking for me. Don't you think that guys have a responsibility to keep their pants zipped?"

I'd had a similar realization a few days earlier so I could only nod.

"Good. Because I was thinking about joining Tina and getting a job at Montag Industries. I thought I'd get you to tell me which of the VPs was most likely to hire a woman with my skill set."

"You want to help me? Why?"

"If you want to know the truth, I'm worried about Tina. I figure, if I'm around, I can watch over her and make sure she doesn't get into too much trouble."

Angie didn't look like much of a fighter, but she seemed determined. So, I went over the list of VPs and other cabinet members with her.

Besides Nick, there was the VP of operations, who had to be pushing the corporate retirement age of sixty-five, the marketing VP, who was a woman and probably immune to Angie's charms, the H.R. Director, and the Chief Financial Officer. I wondered about the marketing VP for the first time. Tina hadn't turned up her name in the mistress list, but that didn't mean she wasn't one of them. Could *she* have a motive? Certainly there was always a love/hate relationship between sales and marketing, with each trying to claim dominance over the other. Perhaps she was at the bottom of any conflict between Nick and his father.

Angie instantly focused on the CFO. "Tell me more about the bean counter."

I wasn't surprised Angie narrowed in on the Chief Financial Officer. She'd already guessed that murder was about either sex or money. Who better to explore the money motive than the man in charge of watching the company's finances?

Lupe, Tina and I hadn't completely ignored the money angle, of course. After all, money was a big part of any motive Nick might have to murder his father. Martin and Nick might have disagreed over the women in their lives, but that wouldn't have led to violence. I really didn't think either had cared that much. Money, thought, was a big deal to both of them. And even the few bad quarters the company had suffered lately was enough to raise all kinds of questions, create all sorts of conflict within the company as executives came up with schemes to end the bleeding and bring the company back to the high-growth track. The CFO would know about these schemes, would know who was fighting with whom, and would know whether Nick and Martin had reached a deadlock.

Or, given the spate of corporate plundering cases, who better to actually do the dirty work than the man who'd been hired to make sure all of the numbers added up? If CFO Howard Bale had been stealing from the company, he would have the best motive of all to murder Martin. Because Martin loved his company and would have obsessively tracked down whatever was causing its financial downturn.

I told Angie what I knew about Bale. He'd been with Montag for about five years after a longer stint with a defense construction company. During that five years, he'd risen quickly become Martin's right-hand-man.

"Car?"

"A Jaguar, I think."

Angie nodded. "Perfect."

I bristled. "A lot of people drive Jaguars. That doesn't make them criminals or murderers."

"A guy who drives a jag is a guy who wants female attention."

"Oh. Well, Howard divorced a couple of years ago, but I haven't heard anything about him sleeping with the help."

"Had you heard about *anyone* sleeping with the help before all this started?"

She had me there. I'd lived in blissful ignorance. In some ways, I wished I could go back. But really, would I want to go back to a life where I was kept happy only because people surrounded me with lies?

* * * *

I didn't recognize Chris Blanchard when he stopped by my trailer a few hours later. He'd showered, his hair was slicked down, and his shirt was clean. While his jeans were permanently marked with the shape of a dip can in his back pocket, both that pocket and his mouth now seemed free of tobacco.

He must have noticed my look. "Angie told me it was a disgusting habit. I decided to quit."

"I'm flattered that you'd be interested in me," I said, realizing I really was flattered. Angie might think Chris had a few extra pounds on him, but her standard must be perfection. I certainly didn't see where he was carrying anything he didn't need. Without the sweat and the tobacco, he had a definite earthy appeal.

I wondered, just for a moment, what the women in the League would think if I showed up with Blanchard on my arm. If everything else that had happened hadn't gotten me banned for life, that would.

"I hope you understand," I said, "that I just lost my husband. I'm really not up to dating."

"Angie told me that, too. So I figure, great. The pressure's off for both of us. We can get to know each other, find out if we like each other, and we won't have to worry about the whole sex and physical side of things for a while."

"Huh?" That certainly hadn't been the reaction I'd been expecting.

He winked at me and all of a sudden I was a girl again, hormones running wild through my body and thoughts of dressing up running through my brain.

"Don't know if you noticed, but I'm a guy. And most of us guys are afraid to get sucked into the whole relationship thing before we're ready. So, I figure if you aren't ready to date, we won't date. We can take the whole getting to know each other slow. No pressure on you, no pressure on me."

If I'd been the honest, good person I wished I was, I would have told him to move on, to approach some other woman who'd appreciate him. But I couldn't make myself do that. After hearing about Martin's jokes, after the humiliation of being the last to learn I'd been dumped, I craved male attention.

I was sure Chris wasn't my type. He probably hadn't even gone to college and he worked with his hands rather than with his brains.

Still, I was a different person than I had been. Since Martin's death, I'd given myself a chance to be open to friendship. Every time I had, I'd been grateful. Besides, Chris was a guy and, now that he was clean and wasn't chewing tobacco, he did things to my libido.

I tried to remember the last time my libido had gotten involved. I couldn't.

I told him about my afternoon plans and Chris suggested we take his pickup truck to fetch Lupe from school. After some consideration, I went along with the idea. I'd meant what I'd said about not wanting to date, but we'd be picking up a thirteen-year-old chaperone. Which meant neither of us would be tempted to try anything we'd both regret.

While he went to pick up his truck, I ducked back into my trailer to change.

Between the iced coffee and Angie's air conditioning, I'd stopped sweating, but that didn't last long. Although I'd showered and changed right before lunch, I was a sweaty mess again. I didn't have time for another shower, but I needed to change. I flipped through the clothes I'd taken when Gary had let me into my own house, looking for just the right thing. It took me a couple of minutes of rejecting everything before I realized what I was doing. Despite what Chris and I had agreed on, I was trying to find something attractive to wear. The high-school-girl part of me still wanted to dress up for a guy.

Considering the fat I carried, dressing sexy was out of the question. I gritted my teeth and settled for comfortable—putting on another muumuu-style dress I'd bought at the thrift shop.

Chris grinned when I stepped out of my trailer, then got out of his car, walked around it, and opened the passenger-side door for me.

The truck smelled like pine needles—not exactly wonderful, but better than male sweat. Although the vehicle was far from new, its air conditioner worked and the engine purred like a contented kitten. I was pretty sure the truck's exterior had been faded when he'd pushed my car after it had died, but now it gleamed like it had been newly painted.

"Washed and waxed it," he commented when he caught the direction of my gaze. "Truck gets dusty on the job. It's fun to shine it up once in a while."

Chris had been making changes in his life—for me, and I didn't know how I felt about it. I couldn't remember Martin *ever* going out of his way for me. He'd made the decisions and expected me to go along—and I always had.

Lupe was just coming out of the school as we pulled up.

I deducted a couple of points from Chris when he beeped his horn for her and it played the opening notes to Dixie. Not that a lot of League members weren't caught up in the whole States Rights thing. Still, in an ethnically diverse neighborhood like this, the hint of racism seemed somehow worse.

Chris must have caught my frown, though.

"Don't like the horn?"

I explained my problem but he didn't have a chance to answer before Lupe walked up and peered in my open window. "What's *he* doing here?"

"Lupe, do you know Chris Blanchard?"

She shook her head.

"Then let me introduce you. Lupe, this is Chris Blanchard. Chris, Lupe Gonzaga."

"Nice to meet you, Lupe," Chris said.

Lupe stared at him for a good three seconds before finally speaking. "I'm Heather's mentor. That means I watch out for her, make sure people don't give her trouble."

Martin would have laughed in her face if he'd heard a teenage girl make that kind of announcement.

I was surprised when Chris simply nodded. "Taking care of your friends is a good thing. *Muy importante.*"

"You making fun of my Spanish?"

"Don't know why I would. I grew up speaking French, mostly. Never liked it when people poked fun at us Cajuns. Don't figure I'd start making fun of people who also want to hold onto their old language."

"Oh." Lupe waited for me to get out of the truck before sliding between us on the bench seat.

"So, Chris," she said, when she was satisfied with the way we were all situated. "Do you know much about murder?"

* * * *

Tina, Angie, and Lupe went shopping that evening. I went along, but I wasn't shopping. I still had some money from the pawnshop, but it wouldn't last long if I wasn't careful.

Tina hadn't learned anything new at her job. The entire programming team had been dragged offsite for an all-day training session in the latest version of the Oracle database system. She'd probed for gossip, but none of the programmers knew anything about the sexual habits of upper management. Still, she was not pleased when Angie announced that she'd submitted an application and would be interviewing with the CFO the following morning.

"There've already been two people murdered, Angie."

"It's okay for you to put yourself in danger but not okay for me? Don't you think I know something about protecting myself? I deal with people, some of them really scummy people, on a daily basis while you sit in your trailer and deal with electrons."

"Tina knows a lot about people," Lupe objected. "Did you know that she wrote *StrongGirl Roundup*?"

"Hello! That's a video game, remember? I think you made my point."

We'd squeezed into Tina's Storm and driven up to Jefferson where small dress shops sold discounted brands that never made it into the top-tier department stores.

We'd stopped in at a couple of shops, but it had taken a while before we'd found one that excited Lupe, Angie, and Tina. As for me, I figured I'd stick with the thrift stores for a while. The neighborhood shops seemed to cater more to the younger and thinner crowd.

Angie was flipping through racks of size-two pants, trying to find a pair that would show off her perfectly toned rear and still be easy to take off for her night job.

It had taken me less than a minute after we'd arrived to see that there was nothing in the shop for me. I hadn't been able to fit in a size two since I'd rocketed through it on my way from children's to adult's sizes back when I'd been about half of Lupe's age.

Lupe held a tiny halter thing with fake gold coins dangling from it up to her chest. "Isn't this cool?"

"Hot," Angie agreed.

At the exact time I blurted out, "Oh, no."

Lupe looked hurt and Tina put her hand on the teenage girl's shoulder. "She's concerned that boys would objectify you if you dressed like that. That isn't a positive StrongGirl message."

"Angie dresses like that."

"Guys objectify Angie all the time. That's how she makes her living."

"Oh." Lupe put back the top, but she did so reluctantly.

Well, I could understand. I had considered dressing up for Chris and I didn't even know that I wanted Chris's attention. How much harder would it have been for me if I'd been a teenager and desperate for any guy's admiration?

"Hey, I've got an idea." Lupe pulled a purple dress from a rack. The thing looked like something Honey West would have worn. *Honey West* being one of my favorite TV shows back in the sixties when I'd been a little kid. Honey West wore super-tight dresses and kicked bad-guy butt.

She held the dress up to her and grinned when she saw that the hemline was so high it would barely cover her butt. "How about if *I* get a job at Montag. School is boring and I look old for my age."

"No!" The three of us answered simultaneously.

Her lips trembled as she clung to the purple dress. "You guys get to do it and I just have to go to school. It isn't fair."

"School is important," I reminded her. "Isn't that what the StrongGirls teach you?"

"StrongGirls teach us to take care of ourselves and our friends. You're my friend, Heather, but I'm not doing anything to help you. I'm afraid you'll end up going to jail and it'll be my fault for not stopping it."

"You're our backup," Angie said. "If anything goes wrong, you're the one who knows where we were, who can bring in the police to save us. If you put yourself in danger, we wouldn't have that backup and we'd be in more danger as a result."

Lupe's eyes glistened and she blinked a couple of times before clearing her throat. "You know what? I think you're making that up because you think I'm dumb because I'm just a kid and a sucker who'd fall for any line you give her. You never let me know where you are."

"That's because Tina was off-site and I haven't started yet. And besides, I hadn't thought of it, but it's still a good idea." Angie picked up a black suit with a skirt that looked more like a belt than anything designed to provide coverage. "This should be perfect for my interview. I'll get a job for sure."

"Don't you think it's a little obvious?" I asked.

She looked at me as if I'd sprouted bunny ears. "I'm interviewing with *men*, Heather. You have to be obvious with men. Subtlety is for women."

"You're changing the subject," Lupe said. "If you want me to be your backup, you have to promise stay in touch. I want reports every hour. If I don't get them, I'll know you're lying. And then I'm just have to get a job there too."

"But you're in school," I reasoned. "How can they get you hourly reports?"

She wrinkled her nose at me. "Duh. By phone. I set it to vibrate when I'm in class but I can check it between periods."

I'd finished school before cell phones and couldn't even imagine how they had changed things.

"Do we have a deal?" she demanded.

Neither Tina nor Angie looked thrilled, but they reluctantly agreed. Calling in once an hour, even if it was obvious make-work to let Lupe feel involved, was better than letting her drop out of school and pretend to be old enough to work.

Chapter 16

With Tina working, Angie at her interview, and Lupe at school, I counted on another day of job hunting.

I should have figured things had been too quiet lately.

At nine in the morning, just after I finished cleaning up after breakfast, the cops arrived.

Again.

Detective Luscombe, from the Plano group investigating Betty's murder, caught me coming out of my trailer, a stack of resumes in hand, on my way to the bus stop.

"Mrs. Montag. Looks like you're going somewhere."

For a moment, I thought my heart had stopped. I'd known the cops thought I had killed Martin, but some part of me had managed to stay in denial. Surely they would realize that I wouldn't have done it, couldn't have done it. Surely they would find the real killer and tell me this was all a big mistake. Surely no one who knew me could really believe I had killed anyone, let alone my husband of almost thirty years.

Yeah, right.

"I…"

"Mrs. Montag. Are you all right?"

I swallowed hard, then cleared my throat. Lupe and Tina had been right all along. I felt guilty for wishing Lupe were with me, but I definitely could have used some StrongGirl reminders. "Of course I'd be happy to talk to you. I want to do anything I can to help you identify the killer—and put all of this behind me." The word *happy* was a lie, but everything else was dead-on true.

Luscombe and his partner, a pretty redhead named Detective Julie O'Conner, walked me back to my trailer, took one step inside, and instantly noticed the lack of air conditioning. It had barely cooled down the previous night and already my trailer felt like a sauna.

I opened my mouth to make excuses for it, then shut it. This wasn't the life I'd chosen, but that one hadn't worked out so well, either.

Luscombe and O'Conner took a long look at each other, then O'Conner suggested that they take me to the Nodding Dog coffee shop in Bishop Arts.

I clutched my sheaf of resumes and considered. My finances didn't extend to five-dollar cups of coffee.

"I'll buy," Luscombe must have read my mind.

"Okay, then." I'd already had a morning cup, but I figured I'd get one of those really fancy coffees as a treat. Possibly my last before a nice long prison stay.

Nobody said anything as we drove the two miles from the trailer to the coffee bar.

There were plenty of parking spots near the café, but Luscombe pulled into a loading zone.

"Aren't you worried about getting towed? The Dallas Police didn't seem to like you guys much last time you came down."

He practically growled. "Come on in. Let's talk."

I shrugged. It wasn't my car.

At nine in the morning, the sun was already high in the sky, beating down with the intensity all too common in Texas. Outside, cicadas droned and grackles and pigeons hopped from tree to ground, gobbling invisible scraps left by coffee drinkers who'd sat at the tables outside the café. Those tables were deserted now, the heat driving everyone inside, or to their cars.

It hadn't reached a hundred degrees yet, but the weatherman promised it would, for at least the twentieth day in a row. Despite the company, the coffee shop's air conditioner was highly welcome.

The Nodding Dog is like Starbucks, but it's privately owned and funkier than the more corporate coffee shops. I had my mouth set on a frozen coffee drink, but Luscombe didn't take orders. O'Conner hustled me toward the back while Luscombe bought three black coffees from the barista at the coffee bar. I noticed he didn't even leave a tip. He carried a small pitcher of half and half and several packets of sugar over to the dark spot O'Conner had picked.

Luscombe looked around to make sure no one was nearby, then pulled a small recorder from his suit jacket, set it on the table, and read in the time and date, my name, his own name, and that of Detective O'Conner.

"You don't mind if I tape this conversation, Mrs. Montag?"

I wondered what would happen if I'd said I minded a lot, but I shook my head. "Can you give me a minute, though?"

Luscombe shrugged.

"Great." I walked over to the large coffee bar and handed the teenager working there my resume. "I'm looking for a job."

She looked up from the manga book she was reading, something Lupe had explained to me, and gave me a good look at her pierced eyebrows. "Don't you think you should fix things with the cops before you go applying?"

I was frustrated enough to scream, but I took a deep breath and tried to look chipper. "They're just asking questions. I'm helping them with an investigation."

She nodded as if I'd given her an answer that made sense and put my resume under the counter. She didn't shred it, but I suspected that might be because the shop didn't have a shredder.

One thing I'd learned from my years with the League was, the more you try to explain things, the worse they sound. I gave the girl a smile, thanked her, and headed back to Luscombe and O'Conner.

The two had been watching me carefully, as if afraid I would make a run for it.

The idea of all two hundred pounds of me trying to flee from young, fit, and armed cops struck me as humorous in a pathetic sort of way, but somehow I didn't find it difficult to control my laughter. I realized I'd had no trouble controlling my laughter for a long time—a long time beginning well before

145

Martin's fatal decision to divorce me.

Back in my seat, I took a sip of my coffee and waited as Luscombe went through his introductory routine with the tape recorder again.

I felt as if I'd been put in one of those woodworking clamps Nick had used when he'd taken shop for a semester in junior high school and built a model boat. No matter how I squirmed, the cops twisted it tighter and tighter, until I couldn't move, couldn't breathe, couldn't think.

A part of me wanted to start babbling, telling them something, anything, to persuade them to leave me alone. I had to physically grit my teeth together to keep quiet, to let them ask their questions before I tried to anticipate them and dug myself into a hole I'd never escape.

They'd let me know why they'd come back when they were ready. Whatever that reason, I felt certain it would be bad news.

I'd expected Luscombe to take me through the day Betty had been killed again, trying to confuse me on my schedule, to find some inconsistency with what I'd said the first time they'd questioned me. Instead of taking me through that timeline again, though, Luscombe asked me about my car.

"Huh?"

"I believe you drive a Cadillac Escalade," he consulted his notes as if uncertain. "Is that correct?"

My earlier life seemed impossibly long ago, although it had less than two weeks since Martin had cut me off from my home and money, and then been killed.

"I did. But it turned out that the corporation owned that vehicle so when Martin decided to divorce me, the company took it back."

O'Conner nodded, her eyes filled with sympathy. "That must have been a blow for you."

"I wasn't pleased." For a moment, I believed her sympathy. I wanted someone important to be on my side. But she was a cop and any sympathy she pretended could vanish as quickly as a Texas snowstorm. Luscombe and O'Conner had divied up the good-cop/bad-cop responsibilities. Today, O'Conner was my good cop.

"Isn't it true that your car had coded electronic entry?" Luscombe made it sound like this was something I'd want to deny.

"The company's car. But yes, it did."

"Besides yourself, who had access to this code?" O'Conner's voice was still sympathetic, but she was leaning forward as if ready to catch me if I made a break for it.

"I don't really know. I gave it to the kids, but who knows if they still remembered it. Martin knew it for sure. He drove whenever we went someplace together." I thought for a moment. "And Maria, of course, my housekeeper. That's everyone I can remember giving the code to, but if it was a company car, I imagine that a lot of people at the company would have known it. Maybe Howard Bale, the CFO; Vincent Dodge, the facilities guy; Joe Moses in security, Gary French, the director of security."

When I ran out of steam, Luscombe waited, daring me to come up with more possibilities.

Then I remembered Tina's job. "I wouldn't be surprised if it was stored on a computer somewhere, too. Which would make it available to just about anyone who wanted to hack around a little."

Luscombe made a note in his palmtop computer and Julie smiled at me as if I'd walked into some trap. Her good-cop act wasn't so good after all.

"And of those people, how many knew you carried a weapon in your car?"

I shrugged, trying to figure out where they were going with this. The Frisco police had already asked me about my gun.

"My kids and husband knew about the weapon for sure. I didn't tell anyone at the company, but Martin probably did. He was proud of himself for buying me a gun. Thought it made him some sort of stud—guy whose wife packs a weapon. Now that I think about it, I wonder if that's why he announced his divorce that way."

Then I caught myself. This was exactly the kind of musing that Tina and Angie had warned me against. I kept talking to the cops even though I'd been warned because I thought it was the right thing to do. Once again, my suburban instincts were leading me in exactly the wrong direction.

"So Mr. Montag had reason to be frightened of you?" Luscombe demanded.

"I didn't say that."

"It sounds like you were angry with your husband, Mrs. Montag. Is that accurate?"

I did my best to duck that question. "I wasn't angry with him until he divorced me, and then I was more surprised than angry."

"What about now?"

"Martin was having simultaneous affairs with three women. He let me know he was divorcing me by having me locked out of my home. He did his best to make sure I couldn't touch a penny of the money that Texas law says is community property but that he considered his own. So, yes, I guess I am angry with him."

Both cops scribbled notes about that. I wondered if a jury would see anger at a philandering husband as proof of murder. Not, I decided, if I got a jury with married, or better yet, divorced women on it. I might not be able to persuade them I hadn't killed Martin, but I couldn't believe they'd blame me for being angry.

I also wondered why *Plano* cops were asking me about this. Martin had been killed in Frisco. So, why weren't they asking me about Betty? There was something going on that I still didn't understand. I'd learned that what I didn't know was going to bite me.

"Let's consider that a bit more fully, Mrs. Montag," Luscombe barked. "When, exactly, did you learn that your husband was having an affair with Ms. Rope?"

"When I visited Martin's office after his death. His e-mail included his correspondence with Betty as well as with Kayla Switzer and Caitlin Leitmol."

"Ms. Leitmol and Ms. Switzer have informed us that you harassed them about these alleged relationships."

It wasn't a question so I didn't answer it.

"Do you have anything to say about that, Mrs. Montag?" Luscombe raised his voice just a bit.

"Someone killed my husband. Since it wasn't me, it seemed possible that one of his mistresses might know something. As far as I could tell, the police weren't following up on that angle. Or any angle other their suspicions about me."

Detective O'Conner must have forgotten she was supposed to be playing good cop. She jabbed her pencil toward my face. "So you decided to interfere in an ongoing police investigation and confront each of Mr. Montag's lovers. That seems a strange choice, considering that you were angry with him and wished him dead."

Despite the café's air-conditioned chill, sweat beaded on my face and between the rolls of fat on my stomach and thighs. "I never said I wished him dead, just that I was angry with him."

"From what Ms. Leitmol and Ms. Switzer told us," Luscombe continued, "tempers flared when you met with them. I imagine the same could be said for your meeting with Ms. Rope."

I nodded. Considering that she'd assaulted me, 'flared tempers' was a mild way of putting it. But then, I'd already told Luscombe that.

"Can you speak to the recorder please?"

"There was some anger. Betty didn't want to hear it when I suggested that Kayla might be a better candidate for Martin's next wife than she. Not that it really should have mattered at that point, since Martin was dead."

"In fact, there was not just anger but violence, wasn't there? A fight. Blood."

"I'm sure I already explained this to you. The blood you found was my blood. Betty popped me in the nose. When I left her place, Betty was alive. I was the one who was injured."

"It would be understandable if you defended yourself when Ms. Rope attacked you. Perhaps it was self-defense."

Another non-question. I remained silent.

Luscombe took a deep breath. "Okay, Mrs. Montag. You want to play tough with us, that's your choice. But don't think you can get away with it. We've found the murder weapon."

This was another non-question, but it didn't take a genius to figure out what that meant. It also didn't take a genius to figure why they'd been asking about the Escalade's entry code. I should have seen it coming.

Since I hadn't, I tried for a delay to give myself a chance to think. "Really?"

"Yes, really. Someone had slid a semi-automatic pistol into the storm drain near Ms. Rope's home and covered it with grass clippings."

I nodded. That made sense.

"Aren't you curious about that weapon, Mrs. Montag?" O'Conner demanded.

"Oh, yes. Very curious."

"Maybe you'll be more than curious when I tell you that it was *your* gun," Luscombe shouted. "The Glock your husband gave you. The same one you used to kill your husband. Did you figure that it was too dangerous for you to keep it after you'd shot two people with it? Did you really think we wouldn't find it?"

Luscombe and O'Conner tag-teamed me for another hour, demanding answers to impossible questions like "did you plan to kill your husband and her lovers, or did you initially intend to kill only him?" I wasn't happy with either of those either-ors, but Luscombe wouldn't accept a none-of-the-above answer.

They only let me go when Lupe called and reminded me that I was being an idiot and that I didn't have to answer any of their questions without a lawyer. Another of her cousins had spotted me in the Nodding Dog and phoned her at school.

I didn't know whether Lupe was keeping up with Angie and Tina, but she certainly was doing better keeping track of me than I was myself.

If I hadn't felt as if I'd spent hours being beaten with rubber hoses, I would have laughed when we walked out of the café and Luscombe's car was missing.

"There's a police substation just half a block down Bishop," I said. "You can report your stolen car there. I suspect they'll tell you it's been towed."

"You think that's pretty funny, don't you?"

"Not hysterical. Perhaps slightly ironic."

Luscombe's normally pale face went bright pink. "Well let me tell you something ironic, Mrs. Montag. If you have anything you need to get done, any pressing business that you need to do in person, you'll want to get it done this week. Because I have this ironic suspicion that next week will be too late."

I didn't tell Luscombe that he misunderstood the meaning of the term irony. Tina probably would have explained things to him, but she was better at the sass thing than I was. Instead, I could only think that it was already Tuesday afternoon. Which gave me exactly five days to solve the mystery.

* * * *

Lupe was at the picnic table at the trailer park, playing checkers with Chris, when I got off the bus and dragged myself toward home.

I'd only handed out the one resume at the Nodding Dog and I didn't have a lot of hope about that one, considering the report that would go with it. But passing out the resumes had dropped in my priority list. If I got convicted of murder, prison officials would find me a job.

I looked at the construction worker patiently playing a game with Lupe, then blurted out my reaction without thinking. "Don't you ever have to work?"

Chris frowned. "But sure." I heard a hint of his French/Cajun accent in that answer.

"As it turns out," he continued, "I finished a job early today. When Miss Lupe called, I realized there must be something wrong. So I came home."

"I told him that the police had picked you up," Lupe said, beaming as if she'd done something wonderfully clever. "And that you were talking to them without a lawyer. How could you have done that after everything we told you?"

Okay, I wasn't interested in dating. But that still didn't mean I wanted Chris's nose rubbed in the fact that the police believed I was the only possible suspect in two murders.

"What did they want?" Chris asked.

"They found the murder weapon. They'd been pretty sure it was my Glock the whole time, but now they have it and they're not guessing any more, the lab confirms it."

"Both Martin and Betty got killed by the same gun?" Lupe asked.

"That's what the police say."

Chris brushed a knuckle across my arm, leaving a tingle behind that had nothing to do with the summer heat. "Who else had access to the weapon?"

"That's what the police wanted to know. It could have been just about anybody at Montag. I don't think the cops cared for that answer, though. Detective Luscombe said they that they're going to arrest me on Monday."

"Good thing Angie starts at Montag Industries tomorrow, then," Lupe said. "Did I tell you she got the job? Tina is smarter, but Angie can get any man to talk."

"The Angie, she is something," Chris admitted.

I wondered if anyone would find me interesting.

* * * *

Tina and Angie didn't get back until near dark that night. Apparently she hadn't just gotten the new job, Angie also rounded up a number of Montag clients for her other profession. One of them had required immediate service and she'd been happy to oblige.

"We're all going to Gloria's," Angie announced when Lupe told her about my run-in with the law.

Everyone else looked happy so I dug around until I found a smile. "What's Gloria's?"

"A Salvadoran restaurant on Davis," Lupe told me. "Good food. Let's go."

I remembered that one bunch of cops had planned on going there after they finished with me.

Chris offered his truck. Tina and Lupe got into the back and Angie, me and Chris squeezed into the cab. Angie got the middle seat.

Even as I told myself that I didn't care, I watched to see how Chris responded to having a sexy young woman sitting next to him instead of a fat middle-aged ex-housewife.

He didn't seem to notice, which struck me as either good acting or weird. Martin sure would have perked up if a sexpot insisted on squeezing up against him in a tight vehicle. I'd noticed that about him even when I'd thought he was faithful to me.

Lupe had called home so her parents weren't expecting her, and we ordered Honduran beer for the adults, milk for Lupe, and several of the Gloria

Superspecial meals to share.

Neither Lupe nor I admitted that Chris had grilled us hot dogs earlier that evening. She was a growing girl, and I just liked to eat.

Which made me think of Martin again. He hadn't been mean, exactly, but I knew he'd make fun of me if he'd caught me having a second dinner. Chris didn't seem to mind. Which was a little beyond strange. I'd had my nose rubbed in it enough to be past denial any more. I was fat. It's okay if a guy is fat, but for a woman, it's like a mortal sin.

"Howard Bale didn't know what hit him," Angie bragged, talking about her interview with the CFO. "I walked into his office and he fell off his chair. Literally. Turns out that he was jealous all the other executives had sexy admins and he was stuck with a guy. So, he's going to promote the guy and have me do the dirty work." She winked at me. "If you know what I mean."

"Did you ask him about Martin?"

"Wouldn't that have been suspicious?" Lupe interjected. "I mean, you're interviewing for a job."

"Actually I did," Angie said. "Bale liked it—said it showed I'd done my homework. He claimed Martin was a heroic figure and his death a tragedy, but that Martin had taken his eye off the ball lately, that maybe it would be better for the company that he is gone."

"Jeez, and he was Martin's best friend," I said.

Angie nodded. "I told you that guys were different, Heather. Martin *was* Howard's best friend. Howard said how they played golf every Wednesday, and he even told me how they'd used the company to try to screw *you* out of your community property. But Martin is gone now and Howard is afraid he's going to take the heat for the company's problems."

"I'm surprised they didn't pick me as the fall guy in the corporate problems. I've been set up to take the blame for everything else." I described my visit from the Plano police and how they'd as good as told me I was going to be arrested on Monday.

"That only gives us five days," I concluded.

"And two of them are weekend," Tina added. "We won't be allowed in the Montag offices then."

"Nancy Drew would set a trap." Lupe circled back to the suggestion she'd made earlier. "We've got to let them believe we know something, and trick them into coming after us."

"But who are they?" Chris wanted to know.

That was a heck of a good question. Unfortunately, none of us had a good answer.

Chapter 17

I had a brainstorm that night.

I hadn't completely eliminated the possibility of Martin getting murdered by one of his girlfriends, but I'd talked to all three of them. It wasn't Betty, unless she'd somehow managed to get murdered with the same weapon she'd used to kill her lover. Kayla's excessive drinking might have been caused by guilt, but she was a lawyer and I doubted if she knew the meaning of the word. As for Caitlin, I just didn't see it.

If it wasn't one of the lovers, I realized that the murder had to involve Nick. Either Nick *was* the killer, or someone wanted to set him up. Not set up as the *killer*—they could have done a lot better job at that, but as the fall guy for what had gone wrong with the company. Martin would have been too aggressive, too protective of his company. Anyone who'd been looting Montag had to get Martin out of the way. But Nick wasn't experienced in corporate politics or finance. He'd be the perfect chump.

I woke up sweating, nervous, but happy, certain I was onto something now.

The pieces were coming together.

Too many people knew about the conflict between Nick and Martin. How had they learned it when Nick had been certain it was a secret?

If only one or two people had known about the family problems, I would have written it up to loose lips somewhere—probably Desiree's lips. But what Tina had learned from the 360 program meant that every single one of the executives knew. Gossip didn't work like that. Not about the kind of secrets that could tear a company apart. Anyone who learned would have kept it secret.

The only possible answer was, someone wanted everyone to know. Someone wanted to accentuate the father-and-son conflicts. Someone wanted everyone to know that the two had problems so, when it became clear that the corporation had been looted, they would guess that Nick had been responsible.

If that was right, Martin had been killed as part of a cold-blooded plan to loot the company and walk away clean.

I got a pad of paper and wrote everything down to make sure I wasn't forgetting anything important, then looked at the time. It was already nine in the morning. I called Tina on her cell so nobody at Montag could listen in through the corporate phone system and gave her my theory.

"If you're right, the man we discussed last night is the one behind it."

"What man? You mean Bale?"

"He's the one."

I wasn't the only person worried about eavesdropping, I realized. I might have been paranoid, but Tina was just being logical, considering that she worked in one of those open-space cubicles. A hundred people worked within hearing distance of her.

"Why him?" I asked.

"Because of his job." She was still being vague.

"You mean finance?"

"Right. The, uh, janitors are either responsible for the problems, or they're responsible for the cleanup." She lowered her voice. "You put in a sales guy as CEO if the company is growing and you want that to continue. If the company has problems, you want to bring in someone to sharpen pencils and make sure everything is by the book. And our guy is just the kind of person who'd play that role."

"I wonder if Angie can find out anything about him."

"I'll talk to her. If you're right about the motives, we now know who we want to target for Lupe's trap. I should be able to find out a lot more about the, uh, janitors. We have more than one person here who work for him, if you know what I mean."

"You mean you?"

"Right."

"Really?"

"Finance is responsible for Information Systems in a lot of companies. Goes back to the days when computers sat in big raised-floor rooms and ran mostly accounting programs."

I was going to have to take her word for it. I'd used a computer to handle the mailings for the League, but I didn't really understand how they worked or why some people found them fascinating.

"Okay. You two work on turning up dirt on Bale. I'll get with Lupe and Chris and try to think of how a trap would work."

"Think about what you just said, Heather. You're talking about a Nancy Drew trap for a janitor who's already, uh, cleaned two houses. Don't you see the head-clunking opportunities here?"

That confused me for a moment, but then I remembered that she was speaking in code to confuse anyone listening. Cleaning two houses meant killing two people. And she was right.

"He doesn't have the gun any more."

"We're in Texas. There are unregulated gun shows just about every weekend within a two-hour drive. He could have an arsenal."

"Yeah, but—"

"But nothing, girlfriend. You said yourself that Nancy Drew always gets konked on the head. I may not have the most beautiful head in the world, but it's the only one I've got. I don't want it knocked in—and I don't want to get shot."

Tina had a point. I realized I'd better stop talking to her because she was forgetting to talk in code and might be spilling information that would better be kept secret. Still, as I sipped my third cup of coffee and considered that I was down to four days before my arrest, I couldn't think of anything else we could do to catch the real killer.

At least we had someone in mind now—Howard Bale, the Chief Financial Officer. The next step was to find a safe way to trap him and get him to admit something.

The more I thought about a trap and about getting knocked on the head, the more I wished we had someone reliable to help us. Someone male and not afraid of violence. Someone who could help us figure out how to bait the trap, someone who would make sure Bale didn't hurt us, and someone reliable enough that when we went to the cops with what we'd found, they would believe us and not think we'd made up some desperate story just to keep me out of jail.

I thought about Nick, but only for a minute. Nick was too involved. As the man who'd staked a claim to the CEO's office, anything he did would be seen as tinged with political motivation. Not to mention, he'd hardly seem unbiased if he tried to get his mother off the hook for a murder charge.

Chris might be willing, but he was a working guy. I needed someone with business savvy who could help us bait the trap, and someone with political clout so the cops would believe him.

I felt like an idiot when I called Lupe and left a message on her phone telling her my situation and asking for her advice. I mean, she was a thirteen-year-old girl. I was the supposed adult in the bunch.

But I needed someone to bounce ideas off of, and Tina and Angie couldn't exactly talk freely from their cubicles at Montag.

Lupe called me back in her next break between classes and told me to hold tight—that we'd brainstorm after school.

Which left me four hours to sit and steam.

Instead, I took the bus to the library, signed up for a library card, and logged into one of their computers.

Angie and Tina might be the experts at finding information about men, but I'd known Bale for years. Surely something I knew about him could help me figure out how to trap him.

The librarian gave me a few pointers on how to use the major search engines and before long, I was clicking away.

Who knew you could find old newspaper articles going way back to the eighties? Even barely circulated ones like those from Universities.

But you could and I did.

I was surprised to see that Howard had been expelled from Stanford University when he'd been treasurer of the student association and had been caught dipping his fingers into the treasury. That tidbit hadn't been on his resume.

Had he learned his lesson back then? Or might that have been just the start of his life of crime? If he'd been stealing from the company and Martin had found out, killing Martin might have been his only way of staying out of jail. Martin would never put friendship ahead of the company.

* * * *

"We'll call him and tell him we know about his stealing," Lupe said when I showed her the printout I'd made from that old article.

I'd walked over to Nathan Forrest Middle School, carefully staying outside the school property because I didn't want Deb Solomen, the StrongGirls instructor, coming down on me.

I felt guilty when Lupe came out of one of the classrooms chattering away to a cluster of friends who surrounded her like bees attracted to a flower. If she'd frowned, made any sign she'd really rather hang with her girlfriends than spend time with a fat middle-aged woman with whom she had little in common, I would have understood and insisted that I could take care of myself.

Instead she waved and grinned when she spotted me, then brought over her flock, introducing me to an assortment of Marias and Juanitas, a Kate, and a Phoebe.

I catalogued the names as carefully as if I'd been in a League meeting.

"I gotta go, you guys," Lupe announced. "See you tomorrow."

Obedient if not anxious, the gaggle dispersed, leaving the two of us alone so I could show her what I'd found.

After re-reading it, she handed me back the article. "So, are we going to do it or not?"

"It isn't that simple."

She nodded. "You're worried about getting me involved, aren't you?"

I hadn't been that smart when I'd been thirteen. Or maybe it wasn't just a matter of intelligence. When I'd been thirteen, I'd been the center of my own universe. I'd never had to be perceptive to other people's needs. Which wasn't unusual for a thirteen-year-old, I realized. What made it bad was that I hadn't changed until a few weeks ago. Spending time with Tina and Lupe had broadened my outlook on life.

"I'd rather go to jail than get you guys hurt."

"Then we'll need to figure out a way to stay safe, huh?" Lupe dragged a sneaker-clad foot through the dirt at what should have been a grassy strip but had been beaten down by Texas heat and too many schoolchildren walking on it. "Want to stop at my place and get a glass of iced tea?"

I nodded. That was a good idea. I was responsible for Lupe being absent from her home for far more time than her parents could have dreamed possible. I owed it to them to explain what was happening, and to make sure they knew the kind of person their daughter was spending her time with.

Lupe entertained me with 'Aggie' jokes as we walked the three blocks to her apartment. Unfortunately, the jokes hadn't changed since I'd told them back when I was Lupe's age.

Lupe's mother must have seen us coming down the street. She met us outside the main door to the apartment. "Heather. How nice that you're visiting."

"We came for iced tea," Lupe said.

"That, and I was hoping we could spend a few minutes together," I added.

"Great. We'll have our iced tea and talk."

She shooed a couple of kids into the apartment, told someone to turn down the music because it was giving her a headache, and gestured to a plastic table on the porch. "Join me here."

"What can I do to help?" I asked.

"I already set up a pitcher on the porch. Sit, sit."

I started by telling her how I'd been kicked out of StrongGirls. I wasn't sure she'd want Lupe to spend any more time with me if she learned what a criminal the police thought I was.

It turned out, though, that Lupe had kept her mother up to date on my status and on her role in helping—which made me feel a lot better.

Lupe's mother nodded firmly when I ignored Lupe's scowl and promised to keep the girl out of danger.

"There are many bad men in this country," she said. "In every country, I suppose. Mexico is no different."

I couldn't argue with that.

I waffled for a moment on how much to share with her, then decided that I might as well trust her. So, I told her everything, including our suspicions of Howard Bale and how we thought that there might be a connection between Martin's death and the financial problems the company had been going through.

I was glad I did, because Lupe's mother had a good question.

"So you think it is a coincidence that it happened right when your husband decided to divorce you? This seems unlikely."

I hadn't thought about that, but it did seem a stretch.

"Financial issues come out during a divorce," Lupe explained to both of us. "Lawyers would snoop everywhere trying to make sure Martin wasn't hiding anything. If someone else was hiding things, they would spot that too."

"That's right."

"So your Martin's divorce plans would have forced this Mr. Bale's hand," Lupe's mom said. "If not for the divorce, he could have kept stealing and no one would have been the wiser. What is the saying, 'who watches the watchman?'"

"Right," I agreed.

"Obviously," Lupe said. "What we need now is a plan to get him to confess. We've got to trap him somehow."

Lupe's mother nodded seriously. "I've seen this on television, so I know what you do. First you call him, carefully dialing that special code so your phone doesn't show up on his calling line ID. Then you disguise your voice," she demonstrated by lowering her voice half an octave—I would still have recognized it instantly, "and tell him you know *the secrets*. When he asks which secrets, you say 'if you want to learn what I know, you must meet me,' and name a hideaway spot where he thinks he'll be able to kill you."

That did sound like the plot from a lot of movies I'd seen. Unfortunately, movies use extras to handle anything dangerous. We didn't have any extras around. I definitely didn't do my own stunts.

"What if he doesn't come?" I asked.

"They *always* come," Lupe's mother assured me.

"Unless he's *seen* those same movies," Lupe said, pointing out a huge hole in the plan.

156

Lupe's mother waved her hand in dismissal. "Men never remember what happens in the movies. They only pay attention to breasts and explosions."

Okay, I *had* noticed that about both Martin and Nick. Still, was I really prepared to bet the rest of my life in jail on one woman's guess at a universal law of male pattern blindness?

"I think we need to be a little more specific than just a 'we know what you did last summer,' sort of thing."

Lupe's mother shrugged her shoulders. "The more you say, the more likely he'll sense that you're lying. Since you don't know anything for sure, you can't say anything definite."

She had me there.

Two glasses of iced tea later, Lupe and I headed toward the bus stop. My stomach sloshed with every step and I had to ask Lupe to slow down twice as she tended to skip ahead with the energy of youth.

"It's okay to be scared," she told me when she came back the second time.

More churches crowded Tenth Street than I'd known existed. Cars drove by, some screaming down the narrow street, others making that shrieking fan-belt noise and looking like they might not make it to the next block before falling off their wheels and retiring in place. The engines might have been a mixed bag, but the sound systems were uniformly operational. The brass beat of Mexican mariachi bands alternated with the low rumble of rap.

I waited for a brief break in the traffic and caught Lupe's arm. "What makes you think I'm scared?"

"Your voice gets squeaky. Anyone can tell."

"Oh." No one had ever pointed that out to me before. I wondered if that was how Nick and Martin had always known when I was going to cave. It hardly seemed fair.

I plunked down on the concrete bench at the bus stop and told my vocal chords to relax.

"If we can prove Bale robbed from the company, the cops will have to look at him as the murderer as well."

"With Angie and Tina at Montag, we might be able to figure out how much money he stole," Lupe admitted, "but how could we prove he was the one who did it?"

"Martin wouldn't steal from his own company. Besides, he was rich."

"Lots of people steal from their companies. And being rich has never stopped anyone from stealing."

She was right. *I* knew Martin loved his company more than he loved anything else, including his wife. I doubted that the police would believe me, or even care if I explained. Still, learning how much money Bale had stolen would let us be more specific when we lured him into our trap. The more I thought about it, the more I suspected that the movies Lupe's mom and I watched might contain certain shortcuts to make sure they fit into a ninety minute made-for-TV spot. They might not contain the complete guideline for risking my life.

I explained that to Lupe.

"Could be," she admitted. "You'd making yourself safer, but you're assuming that Angie and Tina won't get caught when they go snooping."

There was that.

The good news was, both Tina and Angie worked for Howard, which meant they were likely to be on the inside of many mechanisms that the company would have set up to protect its financial status. But a crooked accountant would have other ways of keeping track. The more dishonest he was, the more likely he would suspect everyone else of being bent, too.

"We've better call them and tell them to be careful."

"We've *been* telling them that," Lupe reminded me. "Telling them one more time isn't going to help."

I wasn't sure what would help, but something had better. The day was getting away for us, which left me only four days before I'd be arrested for murder.

* * * *

Lupe surprised me by insisting that we have dinner ready for Tina and Angie when they got home from work. This time, she said, take-out wouldn't do the job.

So, I remembered a pork chop recipe I'd used back when Martin used to come home for dinner with me and the kids. I suggested that.

Lupe must have been thinking of something on the stovetop. She looked at me like I was crazy to want to run the oven when it was a hundred degrees outside, but I only knew so many recipes—and what cooking I'd done, I'd always done in an air conditioned kitchen.

I seared the chops, then put them on some rice, added orange juice and chicken-rice soup, then put the mix into the oven to bake.

Once we got the oven going, the trailer heated up in excess of a hundred degrees, so Lupe and I went outside, just in time to see Chris get home from his job.

He got out of his truck all dusty, with sweat streaks cutting through the dirt on his face, and with a smear of blood where he'd scratched his muscular arm on something. His hair was matted down from the straw cowboy hat he'd worn, and his work boots didn't look like they'd seen polish in years.

Two months before, I would have tuned him into invisibility. Men like Chris were not a part of what had been my universe, except when the house had needed repairs or when I decided to landscape the lawn.

I wondered how I'd become so narrow minded. Chris wasn't rich, but his sweat and dust came from honest hard work. The contrast with the political animals who ran Montag, and who might have killed Martin, definitely added to his appeal.

Ten minutes in the shower had Chris sparkling and clean, his dark hair slicked down with water and his eyes, dark as semisweet chocolate, flashing with humor. No amount of time in the shower could have done the same for Martin's killer, because he, whoever, he was, wore his filth on the inside.

Chris tousled Lupe's hair, brushed a scarred knuckle softly against my palm, and poured all three of us glasses of lemonade from a pitcher he'd brought from his trailer.

The tang of real lemons and the sweetness of sugar reminded me of my childhood when my mother had made lemonade and brought it out to me when I played my summers away in the back yard.

After a few minutes Chris went back to his trailer and emerged with chips, guacamole, and salsa.

By the time Tina and Angie arrived home, the chops were almost done, we were on our second bag of chips, and Chris was completely up to date on my theory.

"He'll want to run things," Tina said when she caught me explaining things to him. "Men always—"

"Speaking of men," Angie interrupted, "there's one man who could really help us out. Know who I mean?"

I shook my head but she wasn't talking to me.

"I'm not going to ask Andy." Tina's face turned a bright pink and she grabbed a lemonade from Chris and took a deep drink in what could be nothing other than an attempt to regain her composure.

"You know programming, but I don't remember you ever being any great shakes at accounting," Angie argued. "Do *you* know how to look at a ledger and see where money is being siphoned off? I don't think so. Andy writes software that does that kind of thing. He's the expert."

"He's my ex-husband. I can't go running to him every time I need help."

"Should Heather have to rot in prison, *chere?*" Chris asked. "Because you are to full of pride to ask for help?"

"That isn't fair." Tina held up a hand when Angie opened her mouth. "Yeah, I know, lots of things aren't fair. But Andy's a rescuer. Calling him in isn't good for either of us."

I didn't say anything. I could use all the help I could get, but Tina and the others were already doing more than I could ever repay. If this was a line she couldn't cross, I was prepared to live with it. Or maybe, considering Texas leads the nation on executions, die with it.

"Oh, hell. I'll do it." Tina punched two keys, an obvious speed dial, and spoke.

Her face drooped as she listened. When she put down the phone, it made a picture of depression.

"He can't make it?" Lupe guessed.

"No such luck. He's on his way."

* * * *

Andy Anderson pulled in as Lupe and I were serving the pork chops. I was used to big appetites from feeding Martin, Nick, and, uh, me, so I'd made a mountain of chops—enough that adding an extra dinner guest didn't matter.

Andy drove a perfectly restored classic Mercedes sportscar that would have put every car in the Montag Industries lot to shame.

When I saw him, I realized that Tina had to be crazy to walk away from this. Andy was a babe, with a great body and hair that any woman, even me, would want to run her fingers through. He wore his white shirt rolled up past muscular wrists, affecting a casual look. I recognized that shirt as custom-tailored.

"You always end up in the middle of things, don't you?" he said to his ex-wife.

Tina bristled, obviously taking Andy's comment as condescending, although it seemed wry to me. Anyone with half an eyeball could see that Andy still loved his ex-wife, that he wanted to be helpful not because he had any sort of martyr complex, but because he wanted to do nice things for the woman he'd married.

That Tina couldn't see that meant that she was closing her eyes as hard as she could to justify walking away from a guy who had it all—looks, money, and affection.

"It's Heather here who's in the middle," Tina snapped. "The cops are planning on arresting her come Monday. Unless we can give them a better suspect."

"And you think it's Howard Bale?" He paused a moment, then nodded his head. "Possible."

"What do you know?"

She probably didn't notice, but Tina moved closer to him, letting her fingertips touch his well-muscled forearm.

Andy noticed. He might hide his smile from Tina, but I saw it clearly.

"When Bale hired on at Montag, the company had just gone through a growth spurt. Sales were up, but margins were down and their cash flow was in horrible shape. Bale developed a reputation as a whiz, straightening things out, making sure the bills got paid as late as possible and micromanaging the cash flow to the point where a salesman had to get his permission to upgrade his car rental."

"But that's good, isn't it?" Lupe demanded. "I mean, people shouldn't just spend money because they have it."

Andy grinned at the teen. "Sure it's good—in some ways. If you're actually managing costs. Not so good if you're one of the companies that isn't getting paid on time because Bale has decided to hang onto money you're owed a bit longer. But there were rumors that he was playing games, setting up off-books subsidiaries, that kind of thing. Obviously nothing solid. I've never heard that the SEC was investigating. Just hints of something below-board that don't have substance behind them but that might mean something."

"How did you hear this?" I asked.

Andy shrugged. "Dallas isn't that big a city, Heather. Not at the corporate level, anyway. Just as I've run into you and Martin at events like Dallas Museum of Art fundraisers, major corporate managers bump into each other all over the place. At the Admiral's Club in the airport, the golf course, and when the politicians try to knock us up for money. When businessmen get together, we talk shop.

"The thing is," he concluded, "a reputation as a hard-nosed numbers guy is the perfect cover for Bale to plunder the company later. He saved the company, so nobody would suspect he was raping it."

"This is just rumor and speculation," I said. "Together with a fifteen-year-old college incident. Can we *prove* anything's going on at Montag?"

"Let me finish this dinner and I'll run the numbers Tina stole through the battery of tests I developed to help with corporate auditing. There is one problem, though."

"Only one?"

He grinned. "Okay, a lot of problems, but one big one that's worrying me right now. Since Tina stole the information, it won't be admissible. If you take it to the cops, they'll arrest you rather than Bale. Even if my tests prove he's robbing the company blind. Even if they prove he killed half a dozen people."

Lupe couldn't hold herself back a moment longer. "That's why *we're* going to trap him. We'll get legally admissible evidence that way."

Andy looked at Lupe for a good thirty seconds before turning his attention back to his ex-wife. "*You* are *not* going to put yourself in danger. Not again."

I wish he'd asked me for advice before he opened his mouth. Lecturing his ex-wife as if she were an irresponsible child would not create future harmony.

"You're not the boss of me." His father act brought out Tina's inner child.

Andy looked smug. "If you don't want my help—"

"Oh, no. The more help you can give us on that accounting stuff the more we'll know and the less danger we'll be in. You get to decide if your pride can stand helping us or if you're going to take your ball and go home. You don't get any say into how I help my friends."

I froze. The few times I'd disagreed with Martin, I'd lived in fear that he'd lose his temper and explode. I'd never have confronted him in front of other people. Like most guys, Martin hated being contradicted, hated the notion that he didn't control everything and everyone around him. If attacked in front of an audience, he would fight back with everything in his power. Which, now that I thought about it, was probably what *had* happened between him and Nick. Nick had probably disagreed with him at a staff meeting. Martin would have gone ballistic.

Andy didn't explode, though. He simply shrugged. "If you set a trap, I'm going to be part of it."

"Moi too," Chris put in. "You women may be smarter than me, but smart doesn't help so much when someone is throwing a punch."

I'd gotten a college degree, but he was defusing a situation I was ready to run from. So, which of us was the smart one?

"Do we have a deal?" Andy kept his eyes on his ex-wife, but I knew I'd better answer him, though. Tina was so caught up in her independence that she'd turn him down just to make a point.

I didn't have anything to prove—except my innocence. I'd been praying that someone would come along and help rescue us. Andy looked like the answer to that prayer.

"Deal," I said and held out my hand.

After that, we turned our attention back to eating. The men talked about the Dallas Cowboy football season, and their grim certainty that the 'Boys would, once again, find a way to fall short of their abilities. Angie entertained the female side of the table with what I assumed were cleaned-up PG-13 versions of how different guys would walk into Bale's office, see her sitting at the desk, and go into vapor lock, completely forgetting why they'd come into Bale's office in the first place.

"Unless they were just coming to get a look at you," Lupe guessed.

"*Looking* might not be the best description of what they want," Angie snickered. "One guy offered me twenty dollars to go off with him after work. Can you believe anyone is that cheap?"

"I'm surprised you came home with me," Tina observed.

I resisted the urge to cover Lupe's ears but changed the topic as quickly as I could.

Everyone thanked Lupe and me for the work we'd done on dinner, but I noticed they seemed even more enthusiastic about the big tub of Blue Bell Rocky Road ice cream Angie brought from her trailer. She also carried an extension cord and plugged Andy's laptop into it, ignoring his assurance that his battery was topped off. She wasn't subtle about letting him know that it was time for him to pay for his supper. Then again, I'd noticed Angie wasn't the subtle type.

"Run the numbers, then we'll get Bale on the phone and hit him before work tomorrow. One day in an office like that is enough of an eternity. I'm ready to retire."

Chapter 18

Angie's thinking we could trap Bale that quickly was a dream.

Tina had put the company's entire accounting system on a couple of memory sticks with numbers going back to before Bale had come on board. Even on Andy's really hot machine, crunching that amount of data through all the tests took hours.

Tina lit citronella lanterns and Andy muttered to himself, tousled his pretty hair, and made noises along the lines of "hum," and "oh-baby," and "gotcha," but refused to explain what he meant.

Finally, Lupe, Tina, Angie and I decided that we'd assume Andy would find what we needed and got together to talk about the trap, leaving Andy to his computer and Chris to, incomprehensibly, take one of Tina's chickens for a walk.

"It's too late to trap Bale tonight," Lupe said. "I've got to get home so I'll be ready for school tomorrow. We'll have to do it tomorrow night. So, let's just agree on the basic plan now."

"You're going to have to be our backup again," Angie said.

Lupe shook her head. "You think I don't know what you're doing, trying to keep me safe and away from the action? My mom has a phone so *she* can be backup. I'm going to be there. I'm still Heather's mentor and if anything happens to her, I'm responsible."

"This is my deal," I said. "If I'm going to be a StrongGirl, I need to do it myself. *All* of you guys, including Chris and Andy, are backup. What we need to do is figure out where I can talk to him, how I'm going to record what he says, and how I'm going to make sure he doesn't kill me, too."

Everyone agreed those were good goals.

Angie suggested the Admirals Club at DFW Airport as a meeting place. The airport would make sure Bale wouldn't bring a gun or knife.

I reminded her that I'd need an airline ticket and boarding pass, as well as Admirals Club membership for them to let me in. I didn't have the money.

"Andy would lend it to you," Angie said.

I shook my head. I was tired of owing people. Besides, while being at the airport might keep me from getting murdered, it wasn't a great spot for the others to be able to watch from. I wanted witnesses ready to testify that I hadn't messed with whatever recording I got.

"How about at Kidd Springs Park," Lupe suggested. "There are lots of good hiding places in the trees and stuff. And we could plant microphones to pick up whatever he was saying."

"He'll be suspicious of something so close to your home," Tina said. "Not to mention that people from up north think that Oak Cliff is a dangerous free-fire zone. It's got to be more his territory."

"The Country Club," I said, careful not to mention that I'd been one of those who'd thought of my new neighborhood as a free-fire zone until a week or so earlier.

I wasn't sure I was legally still a member of the club, since the membership was in Martin's name, but I'd reserved private meeting rooms for the League so often that I was sure the staff would go along with whatever I asked. "Howard is a member, so he should be comfortable with the club. And I can smuggle you guys in, maybe even have you dress up like the wait staff."

"I could do that." Lupe's eyes were bright. "Angie and Tina will have to hide because Bale would recognize them from work, and Andy wouldn't work, but nobody looks at the Mexican waitresses and, even if they did, he's never seen me. Chris could dress up, too. He's not Mexican, but he's got a tan. He could pass."

"Too dangerous," Tina argued.

"Maybe," Angie said, disagreeing. "Just as backup, though."

"We'll see," I temporized. I was inclined to agree with Tina on this one. Adults are supposed to protect kids. StrongGirl or not, Lupe was a kid. I was supposed to be looking out for her, not the other way around.

* * * *

After a couple of hours of planning, we took Lupe home. Andy was still crunching numbers when we got back, but it was getting late.

Angie complained about her day job messing up her regular evening work hours as she, Tina, and Chris yawned, then finally headed back to their trailers at about midnight leaving Andy, me, and a couple of chickens alone in the darkness.

After half an hour of silence, broken only by Andy's occasional mouse clicks, he pressed a couple of keys on his computer and looked up at me. "If Bale killed your husband and Betty Rope, he won't be afraid to kill again."

"I'm already plenty scared without your help."

"You should be. There's a runaway train roaring down at you and you're stuck on the tracks and can't move."

It did feel like that, although how Andy would recognize the feeling, I hadn't a clue. Certainly the person I'd been a month earlier wouldn't have been able to identify.

"Can you tell me if you're finding anything that points the finger?"

"Even if Tina had gotten this info legally, I'm not getting anything you could use in court, but I'm pretty sure he's robbing the company blind. A decent auditor would nail him to the wall, at least if we pointed her in the right direction. But auditing firms still only rock the boat if they have to."

I'd been so sure we were on the right track. "So it's hopeless?"

"Not hopeless. I *can* give you enough to persuade Bale that you're on to him. Suppose I did that, though. How would you use it?"

"I'll offer him a deal. I'll tell him that I'll expose his robbery unless he signs a confession about the murders. If he signs the confession, I'll let him skip the country or something."

Andy shook his head. "He'd never agree to that."

"He doesn't have to agree, just as long as he says something the police can use into the little recorder Tina found for me."

"Won't work. He'd sniff out a trap if you went to him with a rotten bargain like that. He'd know you wouldn't believe he'd take it."

I'd thought it was a pretty good idea, but I could see Andy's point. If I offered Bale a deal like that, he wouldn't bother sitting down to talk about it, but he might kill me. "How about if I offer to vanish if he gives me a couple of million dollars. Everyone will assume I killed Martin and ran. He'll get to keep looting Montag Industries and will have his money back in no time."

Andy wrinkled his forehead. "He's got to be smart enough to know he couldn't actually make that deal, because he couldn't be certain you'd keep your mouth shut once he paid you off. But he might not think *you'd* figure that out. If you have to go with one of them, go with the second plan. He's likely to meet with you, if only to kill you."

My laugh was a little shrill and I remembered Lupe had told me my voice got funny when I got nervous. "I don't expect him to agree to any sort of bargain. He's already killed twice to protect his secret, so I wouldn't think he'd have any moral scruples about killing again. But surely he wouldn't kill me at the country club." I took out the tiny digital recorder Tina had given me. "With this, I should be able to catch him saying something. And if I can get that to the cops before he kills me, they'll have to look into it."

"If you're dead, having that digital recording won't be as useful as you might—" he broke off when his computer beeped at him.

"Got it."

"What?"

"Okay, if Tina had gotten her info legally, we really could prosecute. Bale has set up about thirty layers of holding companies, with supposed offices in places like Aruba where it's hard to get corporate ownership information. But I've been doing this kind of research for years now and I've got ways of looking beneath the surface. It's sort of technical but here's the bottom line. Since Bale came on board, Montag Industries has shifted almost all of its purchasing into companies controlled by Bale. He passes the orders to the real companies who make the stuff, but keeps about ten percent of the cost as pure profit."

"Is that illegal?"

"If it's being done by someone with fiduciary duty to the company, and if it's undisclosed, then yes—it's criminal. Montag's SEC statements explicitly deny that kind of self-dealing, and Bale has to approve those statements. He's made it complicated, but he definitely hasn't made it legal."

Despite my fatigue, relief flowed over me like cool air down from Canada. I hadn't even admitted to myself that I'd harbored a horrible fear that we might be on the wrong track, that Nick, rather than Howard, could be behind the murders. But Montag was a multibillion-dollar company. A few percent added to the price of everything they bought could generate tens of millions of dollars a year. That kind of money would be worth killing for. Certainly a better motive than who was sleeping with whom.

"This is exactly what I need," I said. "Give me the names of the holding companies and I'll take it from there."

"You promised to include me on the trap."

"So you can look after Tina? I know."

"You're right I want to look after her. She has a tendency to rush into things without thinking, and to put herself in dangerous spots. That isn't all, though. I also hate to see executives use companies like their personal piggybanks. Guys like Martin shouldn't break their backs to build something special just to let losers like Bale rip them off."

He clicked another couple of keys on his computer, then shut it down. He hadn't given me the front-company names.

"I need those names if Howard's going to believe I know anything."

His teeth gleamed in the moonlit night. "Tina's got wireless. I just sent them to her printer. I sent her an e-mail as well with instructions. She'll drop them off in the morning on her way to work."

"Oh." I stood, stumbled because my legs had gone to sleep, then recovered as gracefully as I could considering my situation. "Well, thanks again, Andy."

"I know you didn't ask for my advice, but you're going to get it anyway. Don't do this, Heather. Bring in the police and let them handle things from here. Even if this evidence is inadmissible, it'll convince them that you didn't commit the murders."

"If I use this information to bring them, it'll be 'forbidden fruit.' Howard might get off completely, both from embezzlement and from murder."

He sighed. "So what? At least you'd be safe."

I knew he meant *at least Tina would be safe*. I let myself consider his suggestion. Martin was dead. Betty Rope was dead. Nothing could bring them back. Putting Tina, Angie and Lupe at risk wouldn't help anyone.

Was it selfish to want my name cleared rather than just having the police drop any charges? And the only way my old friends would really believe I was innocent was if someone else were convicted and sent to jail for the murders, but what did I care about them. They'd been friends with a different me and I couldn't see myself going back to that world.

The insurance companies and the lawyers handling probate for Martin's will would probably cut me off from any inheritance unless the police at least officially charged someone else. But could my whole idea of a trap really be about getting hold of Martin's money?

I shook my head. Howard was doing his best to destroy the company Martin had devoted his life to. Without the courts getting involved, Montag Industries would never get back all those tens of millions of dollars that Howard had stolen. Thousands of people had invested in the company because they believed in Martin and in Martin's dream—and they shouldn't be sold down the river. So, this wasn't just about avenging people already dead. And then there was Nick. He'd be blamed for Montag's failure. Nick hadn't been very nice to me lately, but he was my son.

Most of all, it was about making sure Howard Bale didn't pillage more companies, destroy more dreams, murder more people. Because without an indictment, Howard would be free to walk into another company, set up another scheme, and rake himself off a few million more dollars—and kill anyone who got in his way.

"I've got to do this, Andy."

He stared into my eyes for a moment, then nodded. "I'll do what I can to keep you safe."

* * * *

I knew I was awake because I could hear myself breathing, but my eyes seemed to be glued shut.

For a moment, I worried that I'd been struck blind during the night. Then I remembered that Andy hadn't finished his work until nearly three in the morning. He'd still looked perfect, but I knew I was a mess. I'd been running short on my eight hours of sleep a night for a long time.

I didn't think I'd get anything close to eight hours sleep if I got sent to jail. The prison population just might be unfriendly to a fat middle-aged white woman. Especially a fat middle-aged white woman who'd been quoted on television as saying that judges were too lax and that they should lock criminals up and throw away the keys.

I considered staying in bed all day, but my trailer was already too hot to stand.

If I stayed here, I would definitely plant some trees to give my trailer some shade. That sort of long-range planning, though, was out of line with my circumstances, considering that it was Friday. I had three days before I got arrested for murder.

I actually managed to turn around in the trailer's tiny shower stall without having to step outside first, so I figured I was getting the hang of my new way of life.

No amount of getting used to things created enough room for me to bend over and shave my legs, though. For a radical moment, I considered wearing pants and leaving my legs hairy. I discarded that idea when I remembered what my rear had looked like the last time I'd worn pants.

I put on another thrift store muumuu, then checked my mailbox. Sure enough, Tina had left a stack of computer printouts for me.

I flipped through them. Andy's programs had worked. Better yet, he topped the report with a nice graphical layout. Arrows connected each of the companies Howard Bale controlled, showing how money had trickled through them, leaking out at each step of the journey. Even someone who couldn't balance her checkbook, like me, could see the way Howard had charged the company for things he hadn't delivered, and overcharged them for things he simply hired someone else to supply.

Should I call him now, or wait?

I called Lupe instead.

"Don't give him too long to plan his reaction," she said. "Pick me up after school, we'll go up there, and you can call him when we're set up in the country club."

It sounded like good advice, so I took it.

Then I left "I love you" messages for my children and zapped myself a bowl of oatmeal in the microwave.

One bite persuaded me that this was healthier than I really wanted to be. I found a bag of sugar and loaded up the cereal.

My phone rang when I was in mid-pour, and I jerked, sending sugar all over my table and floor. Great. Now I'd have ants in addition to all of the other problems.

I caught the phone about half a ring before it sent the call into voice mail. "Hello."

"I got caught."

"Tina?"

"Yep. They're firing my butt for messing with corporate records. Nick wants to call in the cops, but Bale is arguing to just toss me out. At least Gary French is on Bale's side on this one."

"Where are you now?"

"Sitting outside French's office while they argue. They've got Joe Moses watching me, making sure I don't go anywhere."

"Keep me posted. If they call the cops, get me on the phone. I'll track Andy down and have him hire you a lawyer. If they don't, stay up in Frisco. Don't go anywhere with just Howard, though. We know he's already killed at least two people. Lupe and I will be up there as soon as she gets out of school."

"Not sure we can wait that long. Something is happening and I think they're just using me as an excuse. Bale said he's calling an emergency board meeting. Maybe he's using me as justification to take over the company."

"Okay, I'm moving now."

I called Lupe's mother and got her permission to take Lupe out of school. I felt horrible about that, but I'd promised Lupe I wouldn't do this without her and hey, this figured to be a lot more educational than anything I'd ever done at school.

Once I'd picked Lupe up, I handed her the phone and had her call Chris, Angie, and Andy, letting them know that I was heading up north.

While waiting at a red light to turn onto Interstate 30, I called the country club.

They weren't happy about a last-minute request, but finally agreed to arrange a private lunch for two. I figured I could surprise them with the free wait staff once I got there.

The light changed and I lead-footed my car north. My car did the best it could although its temperature gauge kept creeping further into the red zone.

We were nearing the end of the Tollway when my phone rang again.

I passed it to Lupe. I'm not such a great driver that I can talk and keep control of the car at the same time.

"Heather Montag's line, Lupe speaking." She paused. "Oh. Okay. I'll see you at the country club."

"It was Tina," she reported as she slid my phone back into my purse.

168

"They've decided against the police but they're escorting her off the property."

No police was good. But since Howard had argued for that and Nick had wanted to bring the cops in, that could also mean Nick was losing the power struggle. Even Gary French, who I'd been certain would take a bullet for Nick after everything Nick had done for him, seemed to be deserting him.

I pulled into the tollbooth, dug around in my purse until I found enough change to pay for using the highway and then turned into a parking lot.

It was time to confront the demon.

"Try not to squeak" Lupe reminded me when I reached for my phone. "If you can convince other people that you're brave, you'll convince yourself, too."

"Should I whistle a happy tune also?"

"Huh?"

Evidently *The King and I* was no longer a part of the universal consciousness. "Never mind."

One advantage to having Angie working as Howard's admin was that she'd given me his direct number. I dialed it.

"Howard Bale speaking."

"This is Heather Montag." We'd decided that the disguised voice thing was something better left to those made-for-TV movies.

"I'm pretty busy, Heather."

"I'm pretty busy, too, Howard. Busy getting ready to go to jail if I don't do something about it."

"Obviously I'm sorry about your problems, assuming that you are innocent and didn't kill my best friend."

Yeah, right. The best friend he'd ripped off for something like eighty million dollars over the past three years.

"That's the thing, Howard. The cops are so sure I did it that they aren't really looking at anyone else. It almost makes me want to run."

"That would be a bad idea."

"You're right. Without any money, it would be horrible. So, I figured, how about my friend Howard. With all the money he's stolen from Montag Industries, he could help me out. Eighty million bucks, more or less, right? Ten percent of that would set me up fine."

His breath hissed for a moment and I imagined him fighting for control of himself. "I don't know what you're talking about."

"Really. What about H and M Supply Company? Or Grand Banks Holding?" I named just two of the companies he'd used in his chain of interlocked holding companies.

He was quiet so long I worried he'd hung up on me. "That woman wasn't a corporate spy, was she? She was working for you. I should have listened to Nick and sent her to jail."

"You didn't do that because you knew the police would ask questions—questions you didn't want to answer. So, think about it, Howard. You've got enough money to set both of us up for life. Give me enough to get away and I'll vanish. No police, no talk, no arrests. And my vanishing will make it easy for you to get away with your thefts."

"I don't—"

"Shut up, Howard, and listen." I'd never talked like this to a man before. I'd been brought up to be a proper southern woman. Well, hey, being a StrongGirl was sort of cool.

"Here's how it's going to be," I said. "I'll meet you at the country club in two hours. Come alone and bring the money—in cash. I want eight million dollars. Just ten percent of what you've stolen."

"I don't have that kind of cash lying around."

"I think you're lying, Howard. I think you're the kind of guy who plans ahead, realizes he just might need some money for an emergency. Guess what, I'm making this an emergency. Meet me at noon or I'll be meeting with SEC investigators at two."

Another long silence, but I could hear him breathing this time. He hadn't gone anywhere.

"I might be able to come up with a hundred thousand."

I faked a pretty convincing laugh. "I don't want to run out for a shopping trip, Howard. I'm talking about changing identities, moving to Costa Rica and setting myself up in a villa there. Two million bucks, minimum. Either pay in cash, or figure out how you're going to spend your money when you're sitting in jail bringing cold drinks to your new boyfriend."

Despite everything, I was having so much fun I almost giggled at my tough words. I'd laughed when Lupe had told me she was going to be my mentor, turn me into a StrongGirl, and I had a ways to go before I was as strong as someone like Tina. But I'd come farther than I would have thought possible. The truly bizarre thing was, only a few weeks earlier, I hadn't even known I needed to travel that road.

"I'll bring the money." He kept his voice low. He might have a private office, but the walls were still thin. "But don't even think about backstabbing me. If you do—"

"See you in two." I hung up the phone before he could get creative on what he'd do to me.

Lupe gave me a high five. "You were awesome."

"I think I'm going to be sick."

Chapter 19

We had an hour to spare when we pulled into the country club parking lot.

The lot attendant sniffed when I parked and headed toward me, a lecture already forming on his lips. This was the members' lot, and members drove new BMWs, Mercedes and Cadillacs. There wasn't another beater in sight.

In the years I'd been going to the club, I'd never noticed that, never wondered where the employees parked since country club wages probably didn't afford too many of the waiters and cooks the chance to buy luxury cars or SUVs.

"You can't—Oh, Mrs. Montag."

I put my nose up in the air, grabbed Lupe by the arm, and breezed in.

The nose-in-the-air act felt familiar. When I thought about it, I realized it was a look I'd cultivated for years.

I liked the new me a lot better than the old.

"Mrs. Montag. It's so nice to see you again," Maitre 'd Fernando gushed when I sailed into the main dining room. "I'm glad to see that all of the stories we've heard are unfounded rumors."

I glared down my nose at the obsequious maitre 'd. "Thank you, Fernando. I brought Ms. Gonzaga with me because I'll be in an important business meeting and don't want to be disturbed by your wait staff. *She* will serve me."

"But Mrs. Montag—"

"Are you arguing with me, Fernando?"

"No, Mrs. Montag. But—"

"I trust your staff, of course. But I'm afraid Mr. Bale is the suspicious type. He doesn't know them as well as I do."

"Ah." His eyes darted from Lupe to me and then to the door. "Of course. Mr. Howard Bale."

* * * *

Angie phoned us when Howard left the office at eleven.

By that time, Chris and Andy had already arrived at the club. Andy wore tennis whites and buried himself behind a wall of margarita glasses, putting on an early-drunk look.

Andy had brought a tiny digital recorder, which I duct taped to the table I intended to use.

Chris had found the white uniform of a bus boy. With his dark Cajun looks, he didn't exactly fit in, but he wasn't out of place, either. I didn't tell him, but he filled that uniform out a lot more attractively than any of the other bus boys the country club hired.

Tina watched the parking lot, hidden in her ex-husband's car. I didn't think that Howard would come in shooting, but I wanted a warning either way.

At noon, Lupe looked at me and shrugged her shoulders. "He's late."

Had I overplayed my hand? Could Howard have run rather than face me?

Considering that he'd already killed two people to hang onto his position, that didn't seem likely. Still, I was relieved when my cell rang at ten after.

"He's getting out of his car. He's carrying a briefcase that's really dragging on his arm. Maybe it's full of money."

Or maybe it was full of guns.

I forced myself to breathe. "Thanks, Tina. And stay out of sight. He guessed that you're with me so if he sees you, he'll suspect a trap. Oh, and call Angie and get her out of Montag before she gets in trouble too. Howard will be suspicious of all the new hires once his brain starts working."

"Got it. And Heather—"

"Hmm?"

"Good luck."

I sat at the table, took a sip from my water glass, and wished I'd gone to the bathroom again.

"Ah, Mr. Bale. So nice to see you. Mrs. Montag is waiting for you in the back room," Fernando, the Maitre 'd said.

Howard walked in.

He was scary.

He'd always seemed like a nice guy. He laughed at Martin's jokes, picked up the check when the three of us went out to dinner, and entertained us with self-deprecating stories about the twists and turns of his love-life with an ever-changing variety of young actresses and dancers.

That easy-going and fun person was gone now, exposed as the superficial mask it had always been.

"The other room." His voice rasped like a file on a rough burl.

"I beg your pardon."

"You've got this room bugged, don't you? You think you're going to make me spill something. I'm not that stupid."

If we moved, our concrete evidence would be gone. If I insisted on staying, Howard wouldn't say anything.

"If it's that important to you." I waved to Lupe where she was refilling a water glass outside the door just behind Howard. "Miss, we're going to be moving to the next room. Could you bring me my lunch in there?"

Lupe wrinkled her nose, shook her head firmly, and pasted on her fake no-speaking English act. "Senor Danton—"

"I'll work things out with your boss."

"You'll have to get used to the *manana* attitude if you go to Costa Rica, Heather." Howard smirked at Lupe.

Howard ran his hand down my back as I passed him on my way to the second small meeting room—my skin practically crawling to get away from his touch.

He wasn't being affectionate. He was patting me down, looking for any evidence that I was wired. Which, unfortunately, I wasn't since I'd counted on Andy's recorder, taped to what turned out to be the wrong table.

Chris bustled in with silverware and presentation plates, setting up the table before fading into the background.

Howard watched him like a hawk, making sure he didn't wire anything.

After Lupe brought us both water, she stepped out and Howard shut the door. I was alone with the man I was morally certain had killed my husband and one of his lovers.

"You had something you wanted to say to me."

"I—" my voice squeaked, again, so I made myself stop and clear my throat. "Did you bring the money?"

He stared at me, his eyes unflinching, as if he expected me to shrivel up like one of the flies Nick used to catch and zap with a magnifying glass—before I'd caught him at it and sent him to his room without dessert. "We'll talk about money once you've convinced me you have something to sell."

"You wouldn't be here if you weren't convinced. Come on, Howard. The cops aren't standing still. Neither one of use can stand much investigation."

"I understand why *you* need money. I just don't understand why you think *I* should give it to you."

"Let me spell it out for you, Howard. If I'm arrested, I'm not going to sit quiet. I'm going to sing my guts out. And the song I'll be singing is called, 'Howard Bale is the one with a motive. Howard Bale robbed the company blind. When Howard Bale thought he was going to get caught, he killed Martin. When that turned out not to be enough, he killed Betty Rope to make sure no one spilled his secret.'"

"Killed?" He sounded shocked. "No one will believe that."

"Come on, Howard. It's just us chickens here. You made us switch rooms to be sure I wasn't recording you. You didn't check me out because you like fat girls, you were looking for a wire. But you didn't find one, did you? I've got a lot more need for money than the truth. So, let's put our cards on the table. You stole from Martin and when he found out, you killed him."

He stepped forward, closing the distance between us until his hard chest banged against my chin. "If that were true, Heather, which it isn't, why would I pay you off? Why wouldn't I just kill you, too?"

I backed off and made sure I cleared my throat first, before talking.

"That's why we're meeting in a public place, a place where I'm known. You don't think I was dumb enough to come here without telling anyone, do you? Mr. Daton, the manager; Fernando, the Maitre 'd; the waitress; what's his name, the bus boy; they all know you're here with me. Plus, I told my lawyer I'd be seeing you. If I turn up dead, you'll be suspect number one."

"But if I was going to vanish anyway—"

"Why would *you* vanish? Pay me off and you can loot a lot more from Montag. Martin is gone and you've got Nick set up to take the blame for the losses at Montag. If you kill me, you'd have to leave all that behind. If you pay me off, you'll be able to replace your lousy two million a hundred times over."

"Very convincing, Heather. If I really were the criminal you think I am."

I laughed. "I don't *think* you're a criminal, I know you're a criminal. I can prove you looted the company. What I can't prove is that you killed Martin. You were right about my spy, you know. But you didn't catch her in time. If the police got serious, they'd find that Montag is just one more victim on your list, wouldn't they? Considering that you started thieving back when you were at Stanford. If not before."

I stuck a finger in his chest. "Look, Howard. Tens of millions of dollars give you a better motive than I had. So, how's your alibi for that Friday night?"

This time Howard stepped back. He reached for one of the water glasses Lupe had filled, took a deep swallow, then jerked off the tablecloth and pulled the table off the ground.

My water glass, silverware, and the display china smashed into the floor.

"No wires, see?" I swallowed hard. "No games. You killed Martin and Betty. Well, guess what? Neither one of them is a great loss to the world. I know you did it, but the cops don't seem interested in looking. They like me for the murders and they're going to arrest me on Monday. I'm not interested in spending a year or so in jail waiting for the trial, even though I know I can throw so much dirt your way I'll cause reasonable doubt. A couple of million dollars and I keep my mouth shut and you walk away rich and free. Sounds like one hell of a deal to me."

Howard leaned back in his chair and shoved his cowboy-booted feet into the country club's deep carpeting. "Let's agree, hypothetically, that I was stealing from the company."

"Oh, yes. Let's do that, Howard."

"Assuming I was, why would I kill Martin? He was an idiot who thought with his dick. I was helping him figure out how to divorce you without having to give up any of his money. I was supplying him with girls. Who do you think he went to when he wanted to add Caitlin to his string? I found her the condo, bought her the car. Martin trusted me and wouldn't listen to what anyone said against me.

"Martin was going to fire his own son because he believed me rather than Nick. Losing Martin put my whole operation at risk. Why should I kill him? And as for Betty, she thought I hung the moon. I'd persuaded her to vote for me as the new Chairman of Montag Industries. Her death, like Martin's, made things worse for me, much worse."

"Easy for you to say considering they're dead and can't contradict you. We both know a good divorce lawyer would have gone through the accounts, found what you'd looted."

"Not a chance. But even if I'm willing to buy into your insane motive for killing Martin, what possible motive would I have to kill Betty?"

"Betty knew about Martin's appointment book. She must have known—"

"Martin didn't make appointments to see me. We just got together."

"Again, easy for you to say, now."

Despite the air conditioning blasting through the country club's restaurant building, sweat beaded on Howard's forehead. "You really do think it was me, don't you. I figured it was you. So, we were both wrong. Who else could it have been?"

* * * *

174

Somewhere outside our little room, a door slammed, someone shouted.

The solid door to our private meeting room muffled the words but someone sounded angry.

"Is this your trap?" Howard asked. His hand snaked toward his briefcase.

He was going to shoot me now. "I don't know what you're—"

The door burst open.

"Mother. So you're involved with Bale on this. I wouldn't have believed it if I didn't see it." Nick shoved his way past Chris, reaching for Howard. He had a gun in his hand.

Howard backed away, straight into the arms of my nemesis, Kayla Switzer, who yanked the briefcase away from Howard.

Howard hung on grimly while Nick waved his pistol. "Drop it or I'll shoot."

Neither appeared to hear him, but the combined yanking on the case triggered a latch. The large briefcase exploded open and bound packs of hundred-dollar bills splashed everywhere, some exploding like confetti eggs in a parade.

So, this is what two million dollars looked like. I was impressed.

What I didn't see was a gun in the case. Sure Howard might have one under his jacket. But Nick was patting him down and didn't seem to be finding anything.

Howard let go of his half of the empty brief case, his gaze probing my own. "Heather, I swear I didn't kill your husband."

So help me, I believed him.

But if he hadn't, who had?

"Damned right you didn't kill him. You had Dad right where you wanted him, didn't you?" Nick's face turned bright red and spit flew as he screamed into Howard's face. "You persuaded him that *my* sales team wasn't bringing in quality contracts. You liar."

"Calm down, Nick," Kayla said.

"I'll give this thief some calm all right. It's bad enough stealing from the company he's supposed to protect, but stealing a father's love from his son is purely evil."

"Nick—"

"Don't Nick me, Mom. Do you know what this jerk did? When I told Dad what Bale was doing, my own father just laughed at me. He said I was jealous. Jealous of Howard? Not hardly."

Kayla set the case on the table. "Nick, you're saying too—"

"I'm not saying anything that doesn't need to be said. Your little partnership got busted when someone nailed dear-ole-Dad, didn't it, Howard? I'll bet you didn't know that Kayla here has been running the numbers, checking the accounts, tracking down the missing dollars for months now. Just like everyone else, you assumed that my future wife was a bimbo who'd slept her way to her position at Montag."

"Didn't she?" Despite the gun pointing at his face, Howard had gone calm.

I wondered if he was acting, if his voice wanted to squeak up the register as mine had. "She was hopping in and out of bed with both you and your Dad. Maybe she was doing—"

Nick slapped the gun across Howard's head, hard.

The accountant moved with the gun, but not fast enough. The impact made an ugly sound, like a fist smacking into jelly.

Blood spurted down Howard's face and over his white shirt. He slowly collapsed to the floor.

Nick grinned as he watched his enemy fall. Just like he'd grinned as a boy, when I'd caught him with bugs and the magnifying glass.

A chill ran down my spine.

Martin had trusted Howard over Nick. Martin had seduced Nick's fiancée, probably with Howard's pimping. Of course Nick would be hurt and angry. He'd want to strike back.

Tina and Lupe had tried to persuade me that Nick was the killer, but I hadn't believed them. I'd told myself that I knew my son, that he was incapable of murder, doubly incapable of killing his father.

Looking at his face now, I knew he was capable of anything.

Howard was in horrible danger, but I didn't have a lot of sympathy to waste on the thief. From what he'd said when he'd entered the room, though, Nick thought *I* had something to do with Howard, believed that Howard was somehow buying me off with the millions of dollars in his briefcase.

Which meant, I might be next on his list.

If I didn't get out of that room in a hurry, I was a dead woman.

"Calm down, Nick," Gary French, Nick's longtime flunkie, grasped his arm. "The cops will be here any minute. Let *them* take care of Howard."

Nick yanked his arm away, brandishing his gun.

I watched with sick fascination as Howard's blood dripped off the end of that weapon.

Nick shook himself like a Labrador jumping out of a swimming pool. "Yeah, you're right. Let the cops do it. But what about my mother? She was part of this."

"Stay calm, Nick."

"We've got them where we want them." Kayla raised her voice to be heard over Howard's gasping breaths. "You don't have to do it all, babe."

Gary looked at Nick, then at me. "Back away slowly," he whispered, his voice largely covered by Kayla's outburst. "There's an emergency exit behind you. I can't control Nick and his gun is loaded."

I'd never dreamed I would some day run from my own son. But his knuckles were white and his finger twitched on the trigger. From the gun safety class I'd taken, I was pretty sure that bullets would be flying if Nick hadn't left the safety in place. It wouldn't take before he figured that out.

I couldn't believe it, but the evidence was beyond question. Nick had killed his father and framed me for it. It wouldn't take him long to stage something in the club if he could get Kayla and Gary to help. A couple of Gary's men had pushed back Lupe and Chris before they'd closed the door so they couldn't witness anything.

Nick could make it look like Howard and I had a falling out and that we'd ended up killing each other. That would neatly do away with his enemy, Howard, and with the woman he suspected of being involved in his betrayal—me.

I nodded to Gary and edged toward the emergency exit.

Howard groaned even more loudly and flopped over on the floor, distracting everyone's attention for just long enough.

I thanked my lucky stars for smokers when the back door opened silently, making a lie out of the sign promising an alarm would sound.

Gary popped out a moment later. "Get in the car. Hurry."

My car, or rather, the Escalade I'd driven back in my earlier life, was parked directly outside the exit.

That was weird. But I didn't have time to think that through. Not if I wanted to stay alive.

Gary screeched out of the parking lot and onto the highway. A string of cop cars swirled by, sirens blaring and lights flashing and I breathed a sigh of relief when they passed. They'd take care of Howard Bale and they'd stop Nick from hurting anyone else.

"I guess it's safe now. Thanks for your help, Gary. You can let me out anywhere. My friends will come and get me."

I reached for my phone.

He plucked my phone from my hands and dropped it into the central console.

"What the heck—"

"You know that I'd do anything to help Nick," he answered. "Anything."

"You're a loyal guy all right. If you turn around and drop me off in the Country Club parking lot, you can go back and help him clean up the mess he's getting himself into."

"No, Mrs. Montag. I don't think we should do that." He reached into his jacket and pulled out several stacks of hundred dollar bills. I hadn't seen him grabbing them after the briefcase exploded, but I supposed that was possible. I just couldn't figure out why he'd take them and why he was showing them to me. I mean, it was a few thousand dollars. Big deal. If he got caught stealing them, he'd lose his six-figures position. I didn't think he was that much of an idiot.

"What the heck are you doing, Gary?"

"Didn't you say that you were going to Costa Rica, Mrs. Montag?"

"Yeah, but—" I caught my breath. "How'd you know that?"

"How do you think we knew about your meeting with Howard? I'm the Montag Industries security director. When Nick told me Bale was stealing money from the company, I bugged his phone. It's easy, really. Just a couple of lines of code in the company PBX and all of his calls are copied into voice mail and beamed to my iPod."

"Oh. Well, you must know that I was just trying to trap Howard, to get him to admit that he'd killed Martin."

"But now you know that isn't true, don't you?"

He kept driving, heading west, away from the country club, away from Dallas, away from the more populated parts of North Texas, away from my friends.

"I don't get what you're doing, Gary."

"I thought you were more on the ball than that, Mrs. Montag. I'm protecting Nick, just as I've always protected him."

"But—"

"Nick was right. Mr. Montag had one heck of a mid-life crisis going. Bale wove a spell over your husband. He'd wave sluts like Caitlin Leitmol in Mr. Montag's face and all Mr. Montag could think of was getting rid of you and chasing after younger babes. Lots of younger babes. When Bale figured out how to keep you from getting any of his money in a divorce, Mr. Montag thought he was a miracle-worker. He decided to make Bale Company President—and name him in his succession plan. Nick was out."

"So Nick—"

Gary laughed. "Nick whined and worried, but that was about it. Do you think Nick could kill his own father? He didn't have it in him. Not even if it meant losing his job and everything else."

I almost hated to ask the next question but my mouth moved before my brain could turn it off. "If Nick didn't, who did?"

My voice squeaked. I was perversely glad Lupe hadn't heard it.

The road ahead was dead straight all the way to the horizon. Which was lucky considering that we were bombing along at better than sixty miles an hour and Gary took his eyes off the road for a long time, just looking at me.

"Come on, Mrs. Montag. Your dumb act may have persuaded a lot of people, but it doesn't persuade me. I've been watching you for a long time."

And then I knew. I should have guessed from the minute Tina had mentioned the possibility that Nick was involved. I'd been right to doubt that Nick would kill his father, or kill anything larger than a bee. Without Nick in charge, though, Gary would be nothing. His job depended on his keeping Nick's favor, and on Nick maintaining his position in the company. To make sure that happened, Gary had managed everything, and kept Nick in the dark.

Gary had killed Martin because he'd picked Bale rather than Nick as successor and Bale would be certain to fire Nick. He'd killed Betty because she, as Howard had said, was going to vote her shares for Howard rather than for Nick. They had gotten in Nick's way—and they'd died.

And now *I* was in Nick's way because I knew too much.

So, what had I done about it? I'd gotten in the car with him, abandoning my friends back at the country club.

"Oh, shit."

* * * *

"You'll never get away with this, Gary." He'd been quiet for a good half-hour as he speeded deeper into the country, letting me mull over my mistakes and my options. I hadn't come up with any *good* options and we'd passed Denton and were heading into more desolate parts of Texas. "I have friends back at the country club. They knew I was there. They'll know you took me. And Nick won't thank you for killing his parents—he'll know now. You could keep the knowledge of killing his father from him, but he saw you taking me."

He laughed. "Really? Did your friends even notice me when Nick burst in with his gun out and his entourage of guards? I doubt they counted corporate security people. As for Nick, he'll see what I tell him to see. Half of Martin's money is gone, you're gone, and your car was stolen from the Montag lot. We have your recorded voice telling Howard that you intend to head for Costa Rica as soon as you get enough money to flee your arrest. Nick will believe what you said. The cops may come looking, but they'll be looking south of the border and they'll be looking for you. Only you won't be there, will you? Somehow, in your attempt to escape from the cops, you took a turn off the road and smashed up. Maybe it was guilt over what you'd done, or maybe you were just tired. So sad.

"With any luck, it'll be weeks or months before your car is found. West Texas is pretty desolate, isn't it? And since your window was down, predators will almost certainly disturb the remains making it difficult for the crime scene people to learn anything. Even if they determine you were murdered rather than killed in an accident, who would be surprised? You've been living in Oak Cliff, for God's sake. You've been surrounded by criminals and minorities. So, you picked up the wrong accomplice down there? How sad for you that the person you chose decided he'd rather take a hundred percent of the money than whatever split you'd offered him."

"You're a sick man, Gary."

He gave me the innocent look that had always made him a favorite of mine —until then. "This isn't easy for me, Mrs. Montag. You've always been nice to me and I appreciate that. But I have no choice. I've got to do this for Nick. Can't you see that he needs me? With Bale out of the way and with Kayla and me there to help him, he should have no problem being elected Chairman. He'll do a good job. You should be proud of him."

Yeah, right. Proud that my son's friend had murdered enough people to put Nick in charge.

After we'd passed Denton, Gary turned off the main highway and drove along smaller state roads—roads with so little traffic I couldn't try to signal my distress to anyone—not that I'd had much luck back when we'd been on traveled roads. The Escalade's dark tinting meant nobody passing had seen my signals and Gary had turned off my window so I couldn't roll it down. He'd kept moving so fast that, even if I could get my door open, I would certainly fall to my death.

"You could have brought in the police in the first place, Gary. They would have arrested Bale. You didn't need to kill Martin and Betty. What was Nick thinking?"

He giggled. "Police involvement could damage the company reputation. Do you think I'd let Nick know about any of this, Mrs. Montag? I told you weeks ago that the first law of security is 'need to know,' remember? Nick still believes that *you* killed his father. He won't be surprised that you've run to Costa Rica. I'm sure he'll be heartbroken when your body is found short of that target, but he'll get over it."

The clues had been there all along, but I'd never seen them. I'd known Gary would do anything for Nick. I'd known that his friendship with Nick and his job as security director gave his life the purpose it was otherwise lacking. And I knew Nick, knew that he could never kill his father. Gary was a natural follower, but that didn't mean he wasn't also a schemer.

Considering the circumstances, learning the killer's identity didn't provide me much satisfaction. I wished I'd kept Tina's recorder on my body rather than taping it to the table. Still, even if I could have recorded Gary's confession, hoping that coyotes didn't chew up the recorder wasn't the revenge I wanted. All of a sudden, even jail didn't sound so horrible. I'd existed for fifty years and had only discovered living in the weeks I'd been with Tina and Lupe—and Chris. Despite everything, I found I liked it. I wanted to stay alive.

"Suppose you and I do the same deal I offered Howard, but this time for real?" I said. "I'll take what money you have and my car and head for Costa Rica. You'll never hear from me again and you won't turn your best friend into an orphan."

He shook his head sadly. "Sorry, Mrs. Montag. I knew you'd try that scam on me, but you're forgetting that I already heard you run it past Bale. You put on a good act, but even if you mean it now, how could I trust you once you were out of reach? Bale was an idiot. He thought the world really did revolve around money. Because *he* could be bought off, he thought anyone could be. Unfortunately for you, I'm not that stupid."

He slowed as we crossed an intersection, then speeded back up as he went through it, ignoring the stop sign. "Oh, and don't bother trying to open that door. It'll only open from the outside. Part of the advanced childproofing available on this model."

The sound of *In the Hall of the Mountain King* ripped through the car. It took me a moment to realize that the phone I'd borrowed from Angie.

He'd taken my phone but it was sitting there in the console. If I could just get to it—"

"Don't."

"I beg your pardon."

"I don't want to make this painful for you, Mrs. Montag. But I've gone too far to stop. If you reach for the phone, I'll have to hurt you and you still won't be able to answer it. So let it ring. After all, a fugitive on her way to Costa Rica is hardly going to be picking up her phone when the cops call her, is she?"

I'd done the full Nancy Drew. I'd set the trap, caught the killer, heard him confess. Unfortunately, just like Nancy Drew so often found herself, now I was stuck with the consequences of my plan. So far, at least, I hadn't been conked on the head.

It was almost time, I decided, to be a StrongGirl.

I waited for my phone to roll over to voice mail, then watched carefully for my chance as the Cadillac ticked away the miles.

"It'll be more realistic if you veer off the highway during the night," Gary wasn't reading my mind but he did answer the one question I had.

"Good thinking, Gary. You certainly have got everything figured out, don't you?"

"I had to, Mrs. Montag." His voice was earnest, still looking for the approval he so desperately needed. "Nick is a great guy, but you have to admit that he's too emotional. That's part of what makes him a good salesman and a good friend. But if he's going to be emotional, then someone else has to handle the logical side for him. That's my job."

I wasn't much for prayer, but I closed my eyes for a couple of seconds and asked for any help the boss upstairs wanted to send my way. Then I grabbed for the steering wheel and jerked.

Chapter 20

We roared off the road, smashed into crater-sized holes, and slammed through underbrush. The tree I aimed at, an increasingly rare artifact as we went farther west in Texas, loomed closer.

Gary grabbed the wheel back from me, smacking the back of his fist into my nose at the same time, but I was certain we could crash. In the confusion, I'd have a chance to escape. At worst, maybe we'd both die. That wasn't a great solution, but I wouldn't have to worry any more about Gary trying to solve more of Nick's problems by murder.

Somehow, though, Gary managed to straighten the wheel. The passenger side of the SUV clipped the tree, and the safety glass in my window bowed in, cracking into a mosaic of shards but not actually losing its integrity.

For a couple of seconds, we rumbled over rocks and dirt, spewing a huge cloud of dust behind us. Then it was over. Gary fought the SUV back onto the road.

He swerved from side to side, but it wasn't as if there was any traffic coming at us to worry about.

"You really shouldn't have done that, Mrs. Montag."

I checked my door just to be sure he wasn't bluffing about the childproof thing. He wasn't.

"I meant to wait until dark, but you just aren't going to make this easy, are you?"

I said nothing. I had nothing more to say.

A pop sounded and the SUV lurched again.

The car only had ten thousand miles on it, so the tires shouldn't go, but maybe our brief cross-country trip had damaged the sidewalls. At any rate, we'd suffered a blowout.

My head was still ringing from the clout Gary had given me, but I grabbed for the wheel again.

A second bang signaled a second blowout as we veered back off the road. Unfortunately it was all dirt and brush here, nothing that would stop a two-ton SUV.

Gary punched me in the temple and laughed as I leaned back in my seat, woozy from the blow. When I'd joked with Lupe about Nancy Drew getting hit in the head, I hadn't really thought it would happen to me. I decided I'd have to tell her about it—and then I realized I must be more disoriented than I'd thought. I wasn't going to be telling Lupe anything.

"I was going to take you further, but you're making me make things rough for you," Gary said.

Rather than pull back onto the highway, he let my SUV trundle off into the brush that lined the road.

He wasn't going faster than five miles an hour when he smacked the car into another tree, disturbing a couple of cows that were taking advantage of its shade to catch a little cud-chewing.

Right before we hit, he reached over and flipped my seatbelt loose.

We hit hard enough to deploy the airbags.

Gary was better prepared than I'd been. His seatbelt was fastened and he'd known the crash was coming.

I flew forward, meeting the airbag halfway. The exploding plastic smashed me back into the leather upholstery.

Half a second later, Gary had the car door open.

He squeezed strong fingers around my neck and dragged me across the center console.

This was it. I was going to die out in the middle of some god-forsaken bit of Texas ranchland. The only witnesses were a couple of cows who probably didn't care that I'd had dreams, friends, and a new life that I'd just started.

"I'll take—" Gary grunted with the effort of trying to drag two hundred pounds of woman across an SUV the size of my Escalade. "I'll take good care of your son, Mrs. Montag. Don't worry about that."

My neck hurt. My body hurt from where the airbag had hit me. There also had to be something wrong with my hearing thanks to Gary's punch to my temple because a throbbing buzz almost obscured his words.

A part of me wanted to give up. I was a middle-aged woman and he was a strong young man. I was fat and out of shape, and he worked out every day. The only fighting I'd ever done had been backstabbing other women in League meetings. And Gary was a killer.

But what would Lupe think if she knew I hadn't done my best? I wasn't much of a StrongGirl, despite the coaching she and Tina had given me, but I wasn't a quitter. Not any more.

I straightened my arm, poking a battered fingernail that desperately needed filling at Gary's face.

To my surprise, I hit something soft and he backed away cursing up a storm.

"You complete bitch."

Yeah, right. I was the bitch because I didn't go along with his killing me. If that was an example of male logic, I'd stick with the female variety.

He'd dragged me most of the way into the passenger driver's seat.

So I scrambled and stumbled the rest of the way out of the car.

Gary pulled what looked like a piece of leather from his pocket. "This is going to hurt a lot worse, Mrs. Montag. Sorry."

He didn't look sorry at all. I'd been concerned about Nick and his magnifying glass thing, but he'd been ten at the time and I hadn't seen anything like that from him again—at least not until he assaulted Howard. Gary had the adult version of psychopathology down pat. He was going to savor every moment of my pain.

He slapped the leather thing on his palm and let me hear the solid chunk. Memories of old-time detective movies popped up—this was a sap. One clunk with that and I'd be unconscious. Even worse, the injury would probably look like something that had happened in the accident that had deployed the airbags.

A real StrongGirl would have suddenly remembered studying martial arts and disarmed him. Not me.

I turned and ran toward the road hoping I could flag down one of the rare vehicles. It was a long shot. I mean, it wasn't as if I could outrun Gary. Still, standing up and fighting wasn't going to work.

I zagged when his hands clutched at my dress and he misjudged my motion and ran past me.

It was good that he hadn't caught me, but he was now between me and the road.

I bent, picked up a stone, and threw it at him as he faced me.

"Why don't women ever learn how to throw?" He caught the rock easily, then threw it back at me—*hard*.

The rock hit me in the stomach, knocking out my breath. I needed to keep moving but I couldn't. Instead, I bent over and retched.

The leather-slapping sound told me Gary was getting closer and ready to use his sap.

I fought down my barf reflex. I wasn't going to win this fight, but for the first time in my life, I felt like a StrongGirl. I'd never have a chance to tell Lupe and Tina how they'd transformed me, but I straightened myself and got as ready as I could.

Gary stepped up to me. He looked like a doctor, checking me for just the right spot to smack me with his sap.

I beat him to the punch, headbutting him in the nose.

I think that headbutt hurt me more than it did him. I'd already taken a couple of clouts to the head and this was just one too many. Pain and nausea ripped through my body. I bent over and puked just as a whirl of displaced air passed over my head. He'd missed with his first swing of the sap.

I didn't think I'd be so lucky on the second.

* * * *

I tried to right my body—this time I failed. Instead, I fell over, landing in my own barf. This was not the way I wanted to go.

Gary had lost his smile and his nose was bleeding where I'd popped him with my forehead, but he didn't look angry. He looked like a man doing a dirty job that he'd been forced to take.

All of my StrongGirl intentions fled. I shut my eyes and braced myself for the crunch of leather and lead against my all-too-soft skull.

I heard the oof I'd expected, but didn't feel the surge of pain.

Cautiously, I opened my eyes.

Chris held onto Gary sap with one hand. With his other hand, he twisted the killer's arm behind his back.

Tina pointed a rifle at the man who'd tried to kill me and Lupe waved a shotgun around.

I suspected that Gary was in less danger from Lupe's weapon than the rest of us were. It would be beyond ironic if she blew us all away at the exact time when it looked like I might actually have a future that could be measured beyond seconds.

"You! I should have had Nick lock you up." Gary's voice cracked as he shouted at Tina.

"Are you okay, Heather?" Lupe dropped the shotgun and rushed to me. "We got here as quickly as we could."

Gary's eyes flickered to the fallen shotgun, to Tina, and then back to the shotgun.

"Careful, he's going to—"

My warning came too late.

Gary twisted his hips and Chris flew through the air, landed on his head, and sprawled, unmoving.

The security manager did a summersault across the dusty red earth of west Texas and came up the shotgun and a triumphal gleam in his eyes.

He pointed the gun at me and Lupe, but kept his eyes on Tina. "Drop your rifle or I'll blow them away."

Tina shouldered her rifle and stared at him through the iron sights. "Not going to happen, dickface. You drop the shotgun and lay down on the ground."

"As if you could hit the broad side of a barn."

It was a standoff. Even if Tina shot Gary, his reflexive jerk would pull his trigger. With a shotgun, he wouldn't have to aim too carefully and he was close enough that the shot would turn us into shredded meat.

"We've got to split up," I whispered to Lupe. There was no point in letting him kill both of us with one shot.

She nodded almost imperceptibly, then inched away from me.

"Don't move." With his loss of control, Gary had lost his calm as well.

"Or what, you'll kill me?" Lupe demanded.

"You think I care that you're a kid. I'll kill all of you if I have to."

Lupe laughed. "Don't give me this 'have to' stuff. You enjoy killing, don't you. I'll bet you used to kill neighborhood cats when you were a kid." She was playing another Nancy Drew trick, trying to make Gary mad enough that all of his attention would be on her. This would have been a good time for Chris to sneak up on Gary, but Chris still wasn't moving.

I hoped he was unconscious, not dead. I wasn't ready to date, and I wasn't sure he would ever be boyfriend material, but he had helped us a lot, had risked his life for me, and had asked for nothing in return but my friendship.

If it had just been me, I would have given up. My head throbbed, my stomach still rebelled from getting hit by that rock, and my legs didn't want to support my weight.

I crawled.

My knees complained. A dress is hardly a practical garment for crawling and two hundred pounds was a lot of weight for them to carry. I told them I'd do something for them later. Right now, I needed to get away from Lupe.

"Hey Gary," Lupe said. "I heard Nick say that he was going to give Joe Moses your job. That his Dad was a racist and that's why you got the job in the first place."

"That isn't true. Nick would never do that."

"Why not? You took care of his problems, so he doesn't need you any more."

"He's my friend. Of course he needs me."

"Afraid not, Gary. You need him, but he doesn't need you."

"You know what, little Mexican slut? You just persuaded me that you're going to be the first to die. Right now."

My searching hand found another rock. If I survived today, I was going to make Chris take me out back and teach me how to throw like a boy. Lacking that skill, I launched myself at Gary, the rock in my hand like a club.

He must have caught a glimpse of my movement in his peripheral vision, because Gary swiveled to meet me.

I ignored the gun and swung my arm at his head.

I missed his head but the rock smacked into his collarbone and the shotgun slipped from his numbed fingers.

His gave a high-pitched shriek.

Fortunately, Gary was right handed and I'd broken his right collarbone. His arm twitched as he tried to use it, but the broken collarbone meant it was effectively out of the action. By the time he realized this and brought his left hand up for a punch, I had swung the rock a second time and smacked it into his groin.

He gave a squawk like a baby mockingbird and collapsed, grabbing his package as if losing it was the worst thing that could happen to him.

I reached for the shotgun, but Lupe beat me to it.

"Maybe I should hold that," I suggested. "It didn't work too well last time you had it."

"It isn't actually loaded," she said. "Chris told me I wasn't trained in weapons and he'd need my parents' written permission before he'd let me hold a loaded gun anyway."

Chris! He lay on the ground in the same broken position he'd fallen in.

I ran to him. "Chris, can you hear me? Are you all right?"

Nothing. He was unconscious—or dead.

I pressed my finger to the side of his neck and felt a steady strong beat.

"He's alive." I was even more relieved than I'd imagined I would be. How horrible it would have been to have my own life be saved only at the cost of the life of a friend.

"Don't try to move him," Tina said when I reached for him to do just that. "If he has a neck or back injury, you could aggravate it. I'm calling for help right now."

While she talked to the police, I went and sat on Gary's back to keep him from getting up. Being fat and old was a disadvantage in fighting and running. When it came to making sure the man wasn't going anywhere, it was just the thing.

Chapter 21

"Here's to our own StrongGirls." Chris held his champagne glass. His arm was in a cast, but that impediment didn't stop him from raising it high in a toast.

"I think you've been through enough with us to become an honorary StrongGirl," Tina said.

We were standing in the living room of my new home celebrating the official engagement between Nick and Kayla. I savored having the people I loved around me—the children I'd given birth to, the three women who had become my new family, and Chris.

It had taken a while to work out the apologies and explanations. Gary had persuaded Nick I was working with Bale and responsible for his father's murder. He felt like an idiot when he realized his best friend had been lying, and worse when he saw that Gary thought he was doing it for Nick's own good. As for Leah, I'm afraid she was still self-absorbed, but I had hopes she'd changed. At least she hadn't brought Richard.

After a few more toasts to the happy couple, Nick and Leah cornered me.

"Are you sure you don't want to move back to Frisco?" Nick urged. "Even if you don't want to live in your old place, you could get something a lot nicer than this."

I looked around my home. I had beautiful wood floors in the living room, a bathroom with a huge shower and a bathtub big enough for me to wallow in without touching either side, and a kitchen I was still beginning to explore. Chilled air swirled out from the AC ducts. "But I love this."

"It's a trailer, Mother." Leah's nose wrinkled at the idea that her mother could live in the trailer park where she'd sent me in disgrace not too many weeks before.

"This is the newest thing in manufactured housing," I corrected her. "And I'm close to my friends."

"What about us, Mom?"

I looked at my son. "First, you're getting married, which means you're going to be very busy. Second, it isn't like Oak Cliff is in another universe. It wouldn't kill you to drive down and visit me once in a while. Especially once you and Kayla start delivering grandchildren."

"I don't see that happening any time soon," Nick said. "Kayla is intent on building her law practice."

"There is one other possibility." Leah pressed her hand to her stomach.

"You mean I'm going to be an aunt?" Lupe grabbed Leah and hugged her. "This is so cool."

"*You're* not going to be an aunt." Leah looked so uncomfortable as she wiggled free, any thought I'd had about moving back up north of Dallas vanished. "You may be my mother's friend, but you're not my sister."

Still, I was going to be a grandmother. "So that's why you're drinking apple cider." I should have known there was a reason Leah wasn't drinking. "Does this mean you and Richard are getting married?"

"That loser. When I told him I was pregnant, he got on his motorcycle and drove off."

"But—"

"Don't worry, Mother. If I need help, maybe I'll come down and live in my trailer."

"Get the air conditioning fixed first," I suggested.

"I can't imagine needing *that* much help."

Chris came over and took my hand, a public display of affection that surprised me. "Heather, the police are here."

My heart dropped into my stomach. Police? Gary had denied everything, of course, but Lupe and Tina and Chris had seen him trying to kill me. The life insurance company had even coughed up the money for Martin's death, letting me build a new manufactured home in Tina's park. Surely after all this, the police didn't still think I had anything to do with Martin's death. Or did they?

* * * *

I didn't recognize the uniforms at first. Then I saw that it was a Dallas Constable.

"Are you Mrs. Heather Montag?" The cop, a Latino about my own age, leaned against his police cruiser.

"Uh, yes."

"You've been served." He handed me a large envelope and made me sign for it.

This seemed like a strange way to arrest me, especially when he got back in his car and drove away.

I took the envelope into my kitchen and slit it open… and nearly fell over.

It was money. A check for half a million dollars along with a letter from the Collin County Court saying that it was just the first payment as part of the recovery of the money that Howard had stolen from Martin—money that should have been community property.

Tina joined me in front of the sink. "Bad news?"

I showed her the check.

"Good news, right?"

"I guess."

She sat down at the kitchen table. "It's just money. It's up to you to let it know who's the boss, to take control of it rather than let it take control of you."

"But I don't—"

"Of course you do. You're a StrongGirl, right?"

I grinned. "Yeah."

"All right then. After spending a couple of months with no money at all, you should be in better shape to take control of your life."

"I'll still be fat."

"Yeah? And I'll still be scrawny. That doesn't mean we're not StrongGirls, right?"

I nodded. It had been up to me the whole time, but it had taken Martin's death, the police believing I'd killed him, and everything that had happened since to prove that to me.

"Thanks, Tina. You and Lupe are the best."

"We're your friends, Heather. And everyone needs friends."

"Not just friends." Lupe put her arms around both of us, then gathered Angie in as well. "We're StrongGirls. I've officially graduated you so I'm not your mentor any more."

Tears filled my eyes. "I think being a StrongGirl is about the best thing I can imagine."

"Not better than being a grandmother, I hope," Leah said.

"If you're lucky," I said, "maybe Lupe will mentor her, too."

If you enjoyed MIDLIFE MURDER, please check out Amy Eastlake's other novels in the TEXAS TRAILER PARK series—available from Amazon and multiple eBook distributors.

www.ingramcontent.com/pod-product-compliance
Lightning Source LLC
Chambersburg PA
CBHW072137170626
46813CB00004BA/1598